Purely Sexual

Purely Sexual

Delta Dupree

APHRODISIA
KENSINGTON BOOKS
http://www.kensingtonbooks.com

APHRODISIA BOOKS are published by

Kensington Publishing Corp.
119 West 40th Street
New York, NY 10018

All Kensington Titles, Imprints, and Distributed Lines are available at special quantity discounts for bulk purchases for sales promotions, premiums, fund-raising, and educational or institutional use.

Special book excerpts or customized printings can also be created to fit specific needs. For details, write or phone the office of the Kensington special sales manager: Kensington Publishing Corp., 119 West 40th Street, New York, NY 10018, attn: Special Sales Department, Phone: 1-800-221-2647.

Aphrodisia and the A logo Reg. U.S. Pat. & TM Off.

ISBN-13: 978-0-7582-2703-4
ISBN-10: 0-7582-2703-5

First Kensington Trade Paperback Printing: September 2010

10 9 8 7 6 5 4 3 2 1

Printed in the United States of America

Purely Sexual

1

"Marriage?" Donnie shouted. What the devil would he do with a damn wife? In his current state of sexual affairs, a wife would be nothing but a frigging hindrance.

"Fontana, listen, goddamn it." Paul Tedesco settled his elbow on the desk, propped his cheek against his fist. "Spouses can't be forced to testify against significant others. You need to think about the issues. Think about the future. Survival. A number of people saw you with Susannah, and Challie saw you upstairs together."

Fists clenched at his sides, Donnie said, "I don't give a damn what the maid saw. I didn't beat the hell out of Suze." No way could anybody claim he'd hurt Pearson. Any woman. And why had every time he'd heard the maid's name or he'd caught sight of her, his dick jerked? "Suze was fine when I left her. Angry, but fine."

He marched over to the window and stared through the sheer curtains, then snatched a length of fabric back. Across the expansive courtyard, Paul's Silver Cloud was parked along the circular driveway. The driver/bodyguard, a humongous Samoan dude named Tupa, polished smudges off the Rolls-Royce. Bright sun rays enhanced July's blue skies, but thunderheads rolled in from the southwest. Dark. Ominous. Threatening as this damn situation.

Donnie spun around as the curtains fell back into place. "This is bullshit."

"Look," Paul said, holding his hands up. "Calm down. We'll get to the bottom of it. Soon, I hope. The police want to interview everyone who attended the party last night. I've got a list to turn over soon. Meanwhile, you have to keep Challie from testifying if things escalate to a trial."

Earlier this morning, the new maid had found Susannah. What idiot would attack a woman? The only thing Donnie attacked on the female species was the hot snatch between her legs.

"I don't have anything to hide." Damn it, why wasn't Paul listening or understanding? Abuse was not Donnie's game. He'd never laid a hand on a woman. Well, not maliciously. Maybe a good swat or two when she misbehaved. Or to get her undivided attention. All in fun and foreplay.

"Okay, okay," Paul said flatly. "The problem is Challie can point the finger at you, make your life miserable. Unlivable. If she tells the cops about the argument, you're in for some real problems. Mayhem I don't need."

"Exactly, an argument. Suze was pissed because she caught me with Ellie Brewsters. But I didn't fuck Brewsters, Paul," he said before his boss spit out his next belittling words. "Too many buddies are talking about her. She just has a mouth that—" Obviously he'd said the wrong shit again.

Paul's eyes narrowed. "Is sex all you ever think about? Jesus Christ." He was married, had two kids and an imaginary white picket fence surrounding this huge mansion, living ideally in loving matrimony.

Donnie's two-bedroom condo was pretty damn sharp, but it

was no comparison to Paul's modern-day castle. Pool, spa, pricey artwork, a library that gave the Phoenix metro area's bookstores a run for their money. Donnie would give anything to live high and mighty on unlimited resources.

"Your dick's gonna get you into a lot of trouble one day . . . correction . . . it already has. Where did you go after leaving here?"

"I didn't take off right away. Um." Paul was sure to jump pissed.

"I don't think I want to hear this." Perceptive, Paul gazed back, his dark eyes filled with annoyance. "As long as you keep your damn hands off *my* wife."

"I'd never touch Tina." He'd thought about it a few times. She flaunted dangerous swaying hips. Silky blond hair, one tiny dimple piercing her left cheek, vivid blue eyes, she was hot, boasting honkin' knockers. Sure as shit, her sexpot was . . .

Hostility gathered in Paul's dark eyes. He snapped the chair forward with a loud bang, as if he'd seen the burning lust in Donnie's gaze. "Picture this. Your balls stuffed, lacquered and rolling across my pool table before you get the chance to apologize."

Smarter than the average guy, Donnie's growing erection deflated. Clearly, Paul Tedesco had ways to control people. "I'm cool. No way would I mess with your old lady."

"Good damn thing. Saves your gonads for now." He leaned back again, rocking. "Did any guests see you to the door, wave good-bye as you left?"

He shook his head. "I took the back stairs, went out the gate. Vanessa's old man was coming up the main staircase."

"Vanessa? She's only been married to Bradley for three damn months."

"Guess he's not giving her what she wants or needs."

Sighing noisily, Paul adjusted his black horn-rimmed glasses. He lifted the half-smoked Cuban cigar from the ashtray, relit it in three big drags. The pungent aroma wafted toward air cleaners that his wife insisted they install. Outspoken Tina had iron nerves; she'd front him off, boldly defy her husband and come away unscathed.

"When I left here," Donnie continued. Why dwell on history? Think about the present, the future, his current problem becoming his biggest nightmare. "I went straight home for once, straight to bed. Alone." He never invited any hot snatch to his condo.

"Lousy alibi in my opinion. Anybody see you leave the premises or call your home phone later?"

Every bone in Donnie's body softened to rubber. Slumping, his brown-striped tie tightened around his neck like a noose. He pulled the choking polyester free, draped it over his shoulder then unfastened the top two buttons of his tan shirt as he moved across the room.

With the situation growing grimmer by the second, Donnie collapsed onto the visitor's wingchair and buried his face in both hands. "No. When I got there, I turned off the ringer as always. I needed sleep. Been out in the streets too much."

"Undoubtedly," Paul said. "The way I see it, you have two options."

Tensing, Donnie looked up. "Options? Why do I need any options? I haven't done anything wrong." He screwed up his face when Paul gave him a blank stare. "What are they, for God's sake? This nightmare has to end."

"Marry—"

"I don't want to hear that one, Paul." Donnie tunneled all ten fingers through his hair. Why the hell was he living in Scottsdale, Arizona? Of all the cities in the United States, he'd chosen one of the hottest sons of bitches. Now his ass was on the city's hotplate, ready to be fried to a fucking crisp for a crime he hadn't committed. "What if she doesn't want to marry me?"

"Not a problem. She will."

He shook his head. "Can't do it."

"Fine. Challie knows more than she's saying." Standing now, Paul adjusted his red silk tie. Combing his thinning brown hair, he moved across the room to the maple coat rack, lifted his navy jacket and thrust his arms into the sleeves. Tailor-made Italian suits were the only threads he wore, never the assembly-line creations from the business he owned. In essence, the clothes produced—part of PT Industries—was the main reason the district attorney had been sniffing after his ass. Sweatshop, as in illegal immigrants, some would say.

"Don't leave yet. What's my second choice? I'll take it, whatever it is. It has to beat marriage by a long shot."

Paul went back to the desk. He pulled the leather chair back and said, "Take Challie to the ranch. You can stay in the foreman's cabin next to Ray's place. Then—"

"Then what?"

The cabin was located in Bum-Fuck, Montana. Good pussy was scarce in an area of dazzling fields filled with cows, horses and manure. The great American countryside.

Paul pinned him with a level gaze. "I'll have Tina tell her you're vacationing and you need her to clean for arriving guests. I'll get a couple of my boys to join you. You've been there before, forty-odd miles away from Nowhere, USA. Closest neighbor is four miles downwind."

How could he forget? Other than fucking and fishing, the best part of Montana was horseback riding across 6,000 acres without a care in the world, the wind in his face, the smell of freshly cut hay filling his nostrils. "And?"

Paul yanked the desk's center drawer open. He withdrew his favorite .38-caliber S&W and set it on the gleaming wood. "Do whatever's necessary to take care of any problems."

Donnie straightened his back. *Do what's necessary? With a fucking gun?*

Was Paul really as cold and calculating as people had claimed? One particular detective had put his life under a high-powered microscope after his first wife's death. In the end, he'd pocketed millions of dollars from insurance and assets, not to mention old money Lana had brought into their marriage. When Donnie blatantly asked his boss about the incident, the answer was as chilling as an Arctic wind. *Ask me no questions, I'll tell you no lies.* Donnie's mouth had clamped shut like a trap door.

Sliding the weapon across the desktop, Paul said, "You don't have much choice. Pick one. If you have an aversion to marriage, you're looking at wearing the tears of a clown in jump-suit orange, day in and day out, if Susannah doesn't make it."

Ah, hell. He hadn't done anything wrong, hadn't laid an abusive hand on the secretary. Now, Paul was talking jail. Hell of a choice—marriage or prison. Either way he adjusted the picture, the old ball and chain action dominated the scene with one major problem: prison meant no female activity.

"What about our lawyers? What the hell do we pay them for?" he asked.

"Real estate and commercial business mainly. I don't want them handling this particular criminal case. I can't afford to have my name or any of my businesses associated with amoral activity, not with my current state of affairs. The district attorney's been harping on my ass enough already. If you're steadfast against marriage, take the gun," Paul said. "You lack an alibi and, remember, the police have already started the investigation."

Donnie slowly got to his feet, shaking his head wildly. "You're talking . . ." Hell, he couldn't get the word out.

Paul replaced the gun and shoved the drawer closed. "I've got a meeting with the symphony directors." Straightening his tie, he marched toward the double doors. "Lock the desk when you leave and put the key away as usual."

"I'm not doing it," Donnie snapped. He might as well take the pistol and blow his own frigging brains out. "Marriage or Montana. My ass'll be sealed up in prison two decades as some sloppy jailbird's goddamn girlfriend before—"

Paul swung around. His brown eyes narrowed thinner than paper. "It's not a request, Donnie. You will go to Montana and do whatever is necessary, be it marriage slash honeymoon or curbing all future problems while the perpetrator is still walking free."

Life was not going well.

Challie Baderleen had planned to go window-shopping this weekend with Aunt Hattie. Instead, Mrs. Tedesco was sending her to some out-of-the-way cabin alone with a man, leaving poor Jasmine to do *all* the mansion's cleaning.

Mr. Fontana was arrogant, a virtual stranger she had no respect for and had avoided. He chased any woman who wore a skirt. Almost any woman. He'd never pursued her because she wasn't shapely or leggy or big breasted. Her hair was blacker than obsidian, far from the blond women he shadowed. Curly, not straight, but it was long—sort of—if she pulled a lock straight out and held it there. Freed, the strands snapped back into unruly ringlets.

It didn't matter. Fontana had no use for her. He had no morals anyway. Without morals, a man was no good. Grandmama had always preached about bad men; although, this one was a handsome devil. He was tall and broad-shouldered. His thick hair was nearly as dark as her own, and it hung too long. Good businessmen kept theirs barbered like Mr. Tedesco's well-kept appearance.

No matter. Fontana didn't like her anyway. It showed on his face, his staring, frowning when they came in contact. With all the room inside this metal contraption, why was he sitting directly in front of her like a sentinel?

She didn't like him any more than the thought of riding in this giant bird. Was there such a thing as airplane sickness? God, she hoped not. She'd lost a hard-fought battle three weeks ago on the high seas. She might throw up all over this good-looking devil's baggy blue jeans. At least they weren't sagging britches hanging halfway down his backside. The young men she'd seen at the big shopping mall wore their pants hanging much too low on their hips.

But wouldn't that be a mess? Wouldn't vomiting knock Mr. Fontana off his cocky camel? Wouldn't she feel satisfied?

She settled back into the comfortable, soft-leather seat and gripped the armrests. Everything inside the plane was colored iron gray—carpeting, walls, the two-piece outfit the lady who'd shown them inside wore. When the bird rolled away from the building, Challie closed her eyes.

"We'll be on the runway shortly," Fontana said. "You have to buckle your seat belt."

She cracked open one eye. Seat belt? She didn't want to appear ignorant, but seat belt for what? She looked over at him, trying not to show bewilderment, and sucked in air. He'd pushed his sunglasses to the top of his head. Lord. She'd never been this close to him. His eyes were fierce. Light brown, no, hazel was what people called the color in this country.

When he leaned over to fasten her seat belt, she caught the scent of something delicious, something mouth-watering. But his hands . . . penetrating heat seeped through the only cotton skirt she owned.

"Too tight?" he asked.

She shook her head. She rarely spoke, but Challie knew English well, had studied the language all her life. Except, her confidence ran low around people like him. Staying quiet was easier than holding conversations with those people above her class, especially with men. She kept her eyes and ears open, absorbed everything she could, improving her knowledge.

Two nights ago, she'd seen Fontana arguing with the blond woman. Then he'd left. Later, when she went back to check the upstairs guest baths for cleanliness, she saw him again, his hand on the doorframe, leaning into the same room. There was something different about him this time. She couldn't put a finger on it, though. Dark suit, polished shoes . . . but something niggled at the back of her mind. Darn her noisy shoe soles. He must've heard her footsteps because he slipped inside the bedroom. The door stayed ajar. She heard the woman's voice again, except her tone didn't sound angry—calm, teasing. Aunt Hattie called Fontana a ladies' man, not a woman abuser.

But something terrible had happened. When Challie started her duties the next morning, she found the bloodied blonde in the same guest room.

She'd screamed. Hattie had flown up the stairs, guided her from the room and then called an ambulance. Shaken badly, Challie'd had difficulty breathing. Mrs. Tedesco had flitted around her like a worried hen.

On the other hand, Mr. Tedesco was more than worried or he wouldn't have asked all those questions. She'd played it smart and kept her answers short and sweet, knowing how close Tedesco was with his guests, especially Fontana. Saying the wrong thing might have put her at a disadvantage. Hattie would be angry if she lost the job.

"Are you afraid of flying?" Fontana asked.

She shook her head because the deafening roar inside the airplane stole her breath away. Everything shimmied. She was suddenly pressed back against the seat.

"Then why do you have a death grip on the armrests?"

Ignoring him, she risked a glance outside the small window. Buildings, trees and automobiles were moving farther and farther out of sight. The airplane pushed through low clouds. Were they leaving the galaxy? Challie swallowed several times. Of course not, but relaxing wasn't easy when her stomach cartwheeled. Without warning, the airplane leaned far right. She almost lost her cookies and she gripped the armrests tighter.

"Sipping soda will help," Donnie said, looking outside the window, checking the flight's ascent. "Once we reach cruising altitude, you'll be fine."

When the pilot announced a turbulence-free flight, Donnie ordered two glasses of ginger ale from the only flight attendant working the jet today.

He couldn't believe it. Of all the beautiful women whom he'd laid and left, he was on his way to Big Sky Country with a broad he hardly knew. A maid, no less. A woman who was too short, too quiet and too damned reserved. Dark-headed, with a body most men would call thick. With those penetrating storm gray eyes, though, she could wear a young buck down, bring a proud man to his knees if he didn't watch out.

She wasn't gorgeous in any sense of the word. Average. Okay, maybe better than average, but she had tits like a damn sparrow when he loved immersing his face into good wallowing material. And where the hell was she born? Bronzed complexion, steel gray eyes . . . she was biracial. He had no clue about her background.

Definitely not his type at all.

Once again his body gave rise to another hard-on. Staring at her unpainted lips, penetrating eyes, polished skin that had to feel like satin and even bird-sized breasts, all made him well aware of her, uncomfortably aware. He shifted in the seat, wondering why his cock sprung bone-hard every time he thought about this woman and every time he caught sight of her.

As Paul had climbed into his limousine, he'd said they had to consummate the union once they took the vows.

Fake wedded bliss until the courts cleared him. Shit.

An annulment was out of the question. Donnie was Catholic,

although not a practicing churchgoer. Should have been in the church pews every Sunday and maybe he wouldn't be here, flying to a frigging Montana utopia with a woman he didn't want as a damn wife.

Okay, so he'd marry her, fuck her and move into a Chandler three-bedroom condo far away from friends until the courts exonerated him. Then *boom*, divorce Molly Maid. He'd go on with his unencumbered sex life as usual. Best-laid plans ever.

Yeah, right. So much for bachelorhood for a while. Hell, so much for enjoying a prime piece of ass for the duration. Except his cock lurched, pulsed against his thigh when he looked at Challie again. She played with her fingers, didn't see the swelling entity throbbing between his legs.

Well, she woman. Me, jailbait.

"What's your real name, Challie?"

She looked up, huge eyes unblinking. "Like you said. Challie."

"No, I mean, you're talking shortened version. What's your birth name? Charlotte? Charlene?"

"Challie."

She sounded incensed. Tough. He'd need a variety of information for the marriage license. He had to ask a few surface questions about her background before they tied the knot and lived in Arizona, whether he wanted to know or not. "Oh. What's your last name?"

She hesitated, looked away. "Smith."

Smith. As in Jane Doe. Oh, this is just super. Just frigging dandy.

Did Paul know her full name? Did he even care? Why was he willing to see this union anyway?

Sure, Donnie's father had been friends with Paul for years. When Donnie's life shifted toward disgusting—running numbers and scamming were his best games—Pops contacted Tedesco. Paul started him out as the gofer of the year, but Donnie quickly worked his way up the corporate ladder. Paul treated him like a younger brother, giving praise for good work, berating the best of businessmen for substandard activity.

Donnie could sell himself to anybody. Anybody. Eventually, Paul promoted him to sales vice president in PT Industries. Donnie proved he could do the job. He showed loyalty to the company, would do almost anything for his boss. Except commit a felony. Unless the situation meant his life or one of his loved one's life was in danger, or even if Paul and his family were in jeopardy.

This request was completely out of the ordinary. Italian men never vaulted race lines. Well, some had. His best bud in high school had sniffed after the school's Jamaican prom queen. She was hot, her accent seductive. They'd later married and propagated a big litter of rug rats. More power to him. He was happy. Broke, but happy.

"Smith," Donnie said. Fat chance. She had an accent he didn't recognize for a Smith. "Where're you from?"

She looked away again. "Arizona."

Uh-huh. The Great Pretender. "Where were you born in Arizona?"

"Hospital."

Maybe he was too nosy for her taste. Tough. Given time, he'd find out all the particulars. Dames always spilled their guts. A little persuasion, she'd tell him everything he needed to know. He knew women like the back of his hand, or his cock did.

For the time being, he might as well get some sleep, dream about one of the wild, hot snatches he'd tamed. Donnie Junior, Duke, would be used, but totally unsatisfied for a while.

Like most men, his cock needed exercise to stay in shape.

2

The forty-five minute drive to the ranch cabin was far from silent at first. Fontana had tried without success to learn about her past. Challie figured he'd gotten tired of her one-word answers. The majority of those were fibs, as long as she hadn't stared into his eyes. He'd finally turned on the radio. She didn't like him or his loud, clanging music. By the time the oversized blue tank stopped, the blaring noise had intensified her headache. Compounding the beating, she'd needed a ladder to climb into the seat. Climbing out wouldn't be any easier. Fontana had said to use the "running" board. Not knowing what he meant, Challie said she hadn't packed one because she had no reason to run anywhere. The man's burst of raucous laughter had gotten on her nerves, the beginning of her headache.

"Do you like animals? Dogs?" Fontana asked. Several trotted across the gravel, barking incessantly.

"Yes." She feared few creatures. The bigger, the better. They were easier to see and hear.

"There's only one you'll have to watch out for. Hank, leader of the pack," he said, pointing to a big black hound. "He's mostly bark, but he lies in wait under the porches, growling to intimidate the fearful. Dogs smell fear."

Suddenly, five black-and-white balls of fur tottered toward the vehicle. Challie opened the door and slid from the tall seat, crooning. Every adult hound and cute puppy nuzzled her hand for pets. Even Hank, wagging his long tail, growled his way into the pack. The puppies parted for their sovereign leader. Dropping to his haunches, he rolled to his back for greedy attention. But the one animal that truly caught her eye was a brown and black mongrel. Timid, he was uglier than a monitor lizard but sweet, with smiling brown eyes.

"Ike the Swinger, the ugliest hound around, with his tongue constantly hanging out the side of his mouth," Fontana said.

Challie straightened. "Swinger?"

"He's always in trouble for chasing the horses, swinging by their tails. I'm surprised he's still here. Dogs come and go like ranch hands." He glanced around the premises. "Looks like no one's home. You'll meet the foreman, Charlie Lawson, but stay away from him. The man drinks like a fish, gets belligerent sometimes. He lives in a cabin down by Bloody Dick."

Huh? "Say again?" she asked, embarrassed.

His devilish chuckle rumbled through her body. "Local legend says Richard, an English trapper, lived up the creek back in the old days. He cursed a lot. Everything was 'Bloody this, bloody that.' So, people called him Bloody Dick. The creek was named after him."

"Oh." She looked down at the ground because he continued staring at her.

"Paul's son, Ray, should be somewhere nearby, or maybe he's out in the pasture. He's married. Got two little girls."

Knowing another woman lived close by lifted her sagging spirits.

"You won't meet the family this trip unless they come back from Washington early. Usually they stay until school starts."

And Challie's spirits settled back into darkness.

When Fontana pointed to the large house directly in front of them, Challie sighed. Another mansion to clean behind a man living alone. Ugh. Maybe his wife had taught him something about hygiene and filth before she left. Or maybe they had a maid of their own.

"Ray's place. Brand new, built last year. I'll have to ask him to give you a tour. It's sweet inside, but I miss the original farmhouse. In fact, I'll always see it standing here. Gave this place character. We're not staying there."

She looked over her shoulder. Grimaced. The little hut-style log building reminded her of the pictures she'd seen of the Old West. Was this where they would be staying? It was smaller than Hattie's apartment. Where was she supposed to sleep, on the floor? It still beat bedding down on dirt and rocks with the animals, even when she thought she'd never have to sleep on anything other than comfortable mattresses again.

"Bunkhouse," Fontana said. "Hired hands sleep there sometimes. We'll stay in the old foreman's cabin over there. Four bedrooms, kitchen, living room. Only one bathroom, though."

Thank God.

Not wanting or needing his help, she grabbed her tattered, brown suitcase from the backseat before he got hold of it. She went around the blue tank. Challie stopped dead. The buzzing sound was loud, all around the yard.

Shrieking, she backed away. "*Nyuki!*"

"What?"

"I mean, bees. Big bees."

Her aunt had warned her of these killers. Swarms had moved into many areas of Arizona. They were relentless stingers, according to Hattie. Removing colonies required expertise. The Tedescos had hired professionals. Challie was fast on her feet, but these easily angered creatures were said to chase intruders longer than she cared to run at top speed.

"Haven't you ever seen hummingbirds before? They're harmless."

Birds? "Oh. Oh," she said, panting, trying to slow her racing heart. She hurried toward the porch anyway.

Surprisingly, Fontana showed one gentleman's quality, probably the only one he had. He held the screen door open for her, but when Challie stepped inside the house, the sight brought her up short. The suitcase slipped from her hand, landing with a noisy thud.

"Kind of funky, huh?" Fontana said.

Funky? Dust and cobwebs were everywhere. Somebody had covered the furniture with bed sheets. She'd have to wash them twice to clean the dirt from the linens. Was there a clothes washer in this place? Or a stream nearby? A scrub board?

Filth and oily grime layered thick on windows. The linoleum floor needed scouring. The kitchen, which she could see from here, was worse than the oldest hut's nastiness. When a mouse scampered past, Challie gasped an air tank worth of stale oxygen. It hid under the refrigerator. She hated mice, hated anything creepy-crawly. Whoever had stayed here last hadn't cleaned at all with these tiny beasts making a home.

"We need a cat," she heard that man say from behind her.

What they *needed* was a new cabin. She picked up her suitcase, whirled around and started for the door.

"Where're you going?"

"Home."

"Home? You can't. We're forty-some miles from nowhere. The plane is headed back to Scottsdale."

"I'll walk. Hate mice."

"Challie," he said, grabbing her arm. A tug-o'-war for her suitcase resulted, but he finally gained possession and set it beside the couch. "I'll get a cat from somewhere. From town or a neighbor."

"Hate filth too."

"Then I'll help clean. You can't leave."

Help? He had gorgeous, begging eyes, the same look in them when he wanted to sleep with a woman. She'd seen the gigolo on the prowl before, only this time he needed a woman to clean for him. Servitude. When they wanted something, they always begged. Men.

Well, she'd promised Hattie, being how she supervised all household workers—maids, chef, Tupa, temporary employees—that she would do the job to perfection. Challie started back toward the couch. She picked up her suitcase when another rodent skittered by her feet. Screeching, she backed into the beggar, who held her a little too tightly. Blazing heat from his body penetrated every molecule she owned personally. She tried to wiggle free. Forget the mouse. Something really hard pressed against her bottom.

"Stop wiggling."

"Let me go and I will."

When he released her, Challie spun around, stared down at . . . surely not. The bulge strained against his jeans. She looked up into his eyes, witnessed . . . lust? Stepping back, she stared down at his jeans again. Goodness. Had she caused his man-thing to swell?

"Sorry," he said, grinning, pumping his eyebrows. "The wiggling."

Lordy. Biggest thingy she'd ever seen. Of course, she'd only seen one, long ago on her twenty-fifth birthday—four years in the past. Big mistake, too. If sex was supposed to be good, and her first encounter was good, well, she could do without, which was exactly what she'd done. She'd satisfied her curiosity. Man-things were like snakes, slithering and slick. She hated snakes as much as she hated mice. But this one . . . this python would rip her straight up the middle, tickle her tonsils, maybe strangle her if it got inside her body. Throbbing. Slick. Slithering.

Blood raced through her arteries, opening every pore in her

body. Breathing had become a real problem. Belly tingling, wetness dampening her panties caught her by surprise. She had the urge to pee, thought she had when her body caved in to a violent shudder.

"*Wapi* . . . I mean, where's the bathroom?" Good Lord. Every time her emotions turned topsy-turvy, she'd slip into her native tongue. She needed to think before she spoke.

"Through there," Fontana said, pointing down the hallway behind her. "On the right."

He wore an unsettling grin on his face. Could he tell what had happened to her? Thank God, she'd worn a skirt, except she hadn't felt wetness running down her legs.

Challie turned on her heels. She walked away stiffly, trying to keep her knees from buckling and her dignity intact.

Donnie chuckled. Her hips swayed gently. Women didn't bust a nut just staring at his cock, not when he hadn't touched her intimately. But a bizarre expression had etched across her face, followed by a tremor charging through her body. He'd scarcely heard her whimper. How did she manage to keep so quiet?

The body contact had affected him too. He ran his hand down the length of his erection. Aching after touching a woman's ass, Duke needed release. Bad. Thirty-three years old and he couldn't keep his libido under control. Hell, the man upstairs had given the rod to him for fucking. He'd put it to good use.

He pulled out several foil packages from his pocket. They stole away sensitivity, but confirmed bachelors had to keep the little DNA guys out of coed pools. Donnie stuffed the packages back into his pocket for safekeeping until Challie finished all her cleaning.

Once *they* finished all of the cleaning.

Duke went limp as a half-cooked noodle. Why the hell did

he volunteer? Cleaning was women's work, the very reason he'd hired a maid service to clean his condo, the same reason he ate in restaurants, except for grilling an occasional burger or two while in Montana.

A bloodcurdling scream broke the reverie. Donnie ran down the hall, banged on the bathroom door and jiggled the knob. "Unlock the door, Challie."

When it didn't open soon enough, he rammed his shoulder against it. Didn't take much effort. He moved in behind her. Absorbing a bit of her body heat jolted Duke. Damn. What was it about this woman? Moving closer, an arc of electricity shot between them. Did she feel it? Apparently not. She pointed to the tub. Dead mouse and dead insects, primarily spiders. He had to admit the bathroom was a filthy son of a bitch.

"I'm leaving." She shoved past him.

"Wait. I'll clean it. Sterilize it. First thing."

She came to a stop, kept her back to him. "Toilet, sink, counter, floor?"

"I'll clean it all. You can do an inspection when I'm finished. If it doesn't meet your standards, I'll clean until you approve. Stay. Please?"

He couldn't let her leave. They had to get married, consummate the union to keep him out of jail. He needed a piece of ass too. Hers, after watching those hips, perfect rounded hips attached to a plump ass.

Shoulders dropping, she turned and said, "I'll clean the kitchen while you deal with this mess. I hate cleaning bathrooms, especially after men."

It was the lengthiest set of words she'd ever spoken to him. She had a hell of a sexy voice. Deep. Throaty. With an accent from somewhere. She also had a familiar smile he couldn't quite place. In fact, this was the first time he'd really *looked* at her face. Her wide smile produced two eye-catching dimples. Why hadn't he noticed them before?

Duh. She'd never smiled at him, had avoided him like a nasty virus ever since the first time he'd seen her at the mansion; on her knees, scrubbing the marble floor, butt tooted straight up in the air. Instant hard-on.

"Paul said we'd need some supplies. As filthy as this place is, I can't imagine anybody wiped out all the cleansers."

"Maybe I can find something."

Donnie followed her to the kitchen. When she bent over, Duke rewarded her with a standing acknowledgment.

Oh, yeah. He could drive it home on this prime behind. Forget restraint. He was tempted to hike the flimsy skirt up to her waist. He'd have to go easy. He was big, long and thick. A woman's snatch had to be soaking wet before he plowed into her. Surely, this lady was ready for him after the first nut breaker, quiet as she was. Broads contained their lusty shouts better than he could; Donnie had a healthy set of lungs.

"What do you need?" Challie asked. She removed items from the lower cabinet.

You. He realized he'd stroked Duke into a fine frenzy. Swallowing, he said, "Everything. The works." Damn. He wanted to fuck her right here, bend her over the counter and work Ms. Smith with surefire finesse.

Hold up. Back off, bud. Get control of yourself.

He'd never let a woman get him so riled. Too much pressure. He knew his screwing days were cut short.

"Can you find a bucket somewhere?"

One big enough to hold his juice if he didn't get away from her. "I'll see." Donnie turned his back before she saw Duke flaring up.

Two hours later, Donnie came out of the bathroom madder than hell.

After unloading the Jeep Cherokee of supplies, he had to clean the funk some jackass had left behind. Goddamn hunters were nasty bastards. He'd remember this every time he used the commode. Seat up, aiming straighter.

He went around the corner into the kitchen. Challie stood on the counter, barefoot, wearing loose red shorts and a matching little top while wiping down cabinets.

Anger dissolving, he moved toward her. Duke went on the rise again seeing a pair of shapely, naked legs attached to her meaty ass. Metal detectors had nothing on his cock. Every time he laid his eyes on this woman's butt, his cock was lured forward.

She had small feet, slim ankles, well-developed calves. Muscled thighs looked strong enough to squeeze the breath from his body. All tempted him to run his fingers up her leg to the juncture waiting for his immediate thrust.

Bet she has a tight-assed sexpot as strong as her thighs.

He barely touched the back of her knee, but she shrieked. Spinning around, she lost her balance. Challie toppled right into his arms. Hell, she couldn't weigh more than a hundred and ten pounds, but the woman had two hundred decibels worth of outraged scream.

"Put me down!"

Donnie slid her down his body in major contact. No way would Duke's reaction go unnoticed. "What would you have done if I wasn't here to catch you?" he snapped, settling his hands at his waist.

She stepped back, bumped into the cabinet. "I'd still be standing on the counter," she shouted. She had both fists balled up tight, glued to her hips. "What were you doing sneaking up behind me? I hate sneaking."

Well, shit. Busted. "I wasn't sneaking."

"If you weren't, I would've heard you coming."

She shoved at his chest harder than he expected, but Donnie managed to hold his ground. "And?" he said, flattening his hands on the counter, boxing her in.

No way he'd let her sidestep him. She sucked in air when their bodies made connection, his throbbing cock in vibrant contact with her belly. Duke had reared up proud, vibrating.

Donnie dipped, rubbed his cock down to the tip of her heat and back up again. When Challie shivered, he caught her lips in a devouring kiss.

3

Everything tingled in her body; every atom multiplied. Challie was afraid to breathe, let alone think.

Amobi, the young man from the town near her village, had never kissed her this well. Never this thoroughly.

Fontana tasted like mint. The cool freshness danced over her taste buds. His tongue touched every crevice inside, almost went down her throat.

Goodness.

She matched his teasing, tasting every bit of him as his arms closed around her. As he lifted her off the floor, she wrapped her arms around his neck, pressing more firmly against his solid body, moving her hips to the exciting music playing inside her brain.

His man-thing pushed insistently against her pelvis, touching the tip of her most private possession, sending a devastating shimmer through her body. Automatically, she clamped her thighs around his waist, wanting to feel more, wanting something she didn't recognize.

She was wet again. Really wet. The harder his thrusts, the wetter her panties, the more her insides quivered in response. Gripping her bottom, he pulled her forward then eased her backward in a rhythm she remembered. Yet those memories weren't as sensuous as today's delicious event. Even the pain she remembered had nearly faded from her mind.

Until she thought about the python.

Challie broke away and turned her head. "No." Except she forgot to move her legs, or they forgot to move, or they didn't want to move.

Ignoring her protest, he smoothed his lips over her cheeks and nibbled a path down the sensitive column of her neck. Something free-flowing rushed through Challie's system. On fire, she clamped her lower lip between her teeth, nearly drew blood and gripped her legs tightly, thrusting her hips forward to meet his.

Donnie eased her back onto the counter. "Relax," he said.

Working free of the cumbersome jeans, he somehow got his zipper hung up. Damn. The more he fought the contraption, the harder his cock grew. If he didn't hurry, he'd ram into Challie like an unsophisticated teenager working his first piece of ass.

He fumbled, pulled and jerked, trying to free Duke with one hand, holding on to her waist with the other.

"I don't think I want to do this," she said, drawing her legs away.

Bullshit. He slid his fingers between the shorts and her leg, touched the source of her heat, stroking the lips of her opening, teasing. Her fingers tightened on his shirt. The sound of her seductive whimper urged him on. Donnie delved his middle finger into liquid fire. She was tight as hell, slick, sopping wet.

Finger two joined in. Challie squeaked. A good-sounding squeak, a lusty cry of pleasure. This pussy would open like a morning flower. Take him completely inside her. Consume him—if he was able to free his cock of these damn jeans.

When he twisted his fingers inside her, she let out a low groan and tried to wiggle away, still clutching his arms. Donnie forgot the pants. He gripped her hips, held her in place then smoothed his creamy fingers sensuously over her slick folds.

"I've only done it once," Challie said.

He stilled his fingers. It. *Oh shit.* Basically untouched. He'd never laid a virgin before, but there was always a first time. Except if he hurt her, made sex unbearable, she'd never marry him. They had to get married, but right now, he needed this fuck badly.

Leaning forward, nuzzling the soft tissue of her throat, he inhaled. She smelled cleaner than fresh mountain air. Donnie licked a path down her chest to her breasts. Through the thin shirt, he bit gently and sucked. Something hit the cabinet above him. Had to be her head.

Arching forward, she grabbed hold of his ears, held him in place.

He lifted the fabric. Large nipples budded, peaked. Donnie latched onto one and worked it with his teeth, gnawed, laving her breast with everything he had. He gave the second the same undivided attention.

Above him, Challie moaned, lacing her fingers through his hair.

Focusing on the object of her heat, he slid farther down. He circled his tongue over the button of her existence, then tore shorts and panties at the inseams, freeing all her glory. A triangular tuft of dark, springy hair. Inhaling deeply, nostrils flared, her scent aroused him. He loved the intoxicating fragrance of a woman in heat, a woman in every man's fantasy—in the take-me mode.

When he touched his tongue to the tip of her swollen nub, she tried to scramble away.

"No!"

"Oh, yes," he said. "Hell, yes."

Nothing could stop him, even when she'd nearly scalped him.

Donnie dove in with busy fingers and his tongue, tasting her sweet nectar. He took Challie to the brink of a powerful climax, had her writhing above him as she tightened her fingers in his hair, legs jerking. She was sure to explode at any moment, gushing.

He shoved her legs over his shoulders. Strong thighs clamped a viselike grip over his ears. He continued the assault, thrusting his tongue, retreating slowly, thrusting again. Latching onto her clit, Donnie sucked hard while his fingers kept busy.

She peaked, came apart bit by electric bit. Challie's high-pitched scream surely rocked the prairie, stampeding cattle, clearing every acre of the ranch. Trembling as the tumultuous climax subsided, her legs dropped limply to Donnie's shoulders. He eased her through the aftermath with gentle tongue licks.

So this is what was supposed to happen, Challie thought. Had Amobi started his seduction the same way, before plowing his giant man-thing inside her, she would've happily continued having sex with him. Maybe the act had been fun and exhilarating for him, but he didn't seem to care that he'd hurt her. She'd refused him afterward, even when he'd begged, even when he'd promised to marry her. Marriage just wasn't part of her future. Neither was sex.

She forced her heavy eyelids to open, to see this wild man rising from between her legs, a smile on his face. A wicked grin.

Uh-oh.

When he straightened, Challie did want to pee. Boxers weren't big enough for what he'd grown between his legs.

Heavily veined, his man-thing reminded her of the anaconda she'd seen on a television movie, which had scared her senseless. Hanging free, bouncing, pulsing to its own music, the head was a crest of magnificence. This snake would rip her apart.

"I don't think so. Nope. Uh-uh. Can't do it." She closed her legs tight enough to flatten a biscuit and started to scoot off the counter.

He held her in place. "I won't hurt you. Promise."

Challie shook her head. "You'd better go back to Arizona, get one of those big-breasted blondes. Maybe one lives here. This is out of the question. Never." She just couldn't stop her insides from quivering while staring at all that beauty reaching toward her, enticing her to stay.

He touched her again, ran his fingers up her thigh, stroked softly between her legs, coaxing them apart. Mesmerized, she watched two of his fingers slip inside her to the second knuckle and retreat, repeated, deeper.

She melted. Challie begged him to stop, to keep going, to stop again.

When he stepped between her legs, rubbing the engorged head against her slick opening, she knew her bones turned to butter, oozed over the counter and dripped to the floor. Drawing her knees up, he positioned her heels, spreading her bare feet apart. When he penetrated, Challie sucked in air. At most, one inch of the serpent disappeared inside her body, stretching her, only to reappear.

It hurt. She couldn't take the pain. "I can't. You're too big. Hate pain."

"Just relax. I'll go slowly."

He thrust forward a tiny bit farther. Fascinated by the sight of his man-thing vanishing only to reemerge, Challie relaxed her muscles.

"See? You're not fighting me anymore," Fontana said. "What's changed?"

She licked her lips. She hadn't gotten the chance to watch Amobi. He'd kept her above him at the start, then on her back for the duration. "Curiosity. I've always been curious about sex. We shouldn't do this anyway. Hate pain for nothing."

"Yes, we should. Believe me. It won't be for nothing. We'll both feel really good soon." He slipped inside her again, added more length. "How does it feel?"

She bit her lip. "Better." It wasn't too, too bad. "Much better. Don't push hard."

"I won't." He pulled out slowly, rubbed the glistening head against her swollen nub then gave her more on the next deeper drive.

Each time he retreated, the serpent came out wet, slick. From her juices. Watching made the invasion easier, but he had not completely penetrated. Could she handle it? Oh, but she wanted to enjoy it all if she could.

Donnie began to shake. He wanted to bury himself to the hilt. Virginal goods. Watching her watch him increased his drive. No woman had ever paid attention, and he'd never moved this slowly before now.

With each stroke, he swelled. With each stroke, he neared the edge of delirium. With each languid thrust, he had a hell of a time holding back from jackhammering Challie through the wall.

"Is it getting bigger?" she asked, looking up into his face. "I don't think I can take any more."

Sweating now, he still had a good three inches left, wanted to feel her body against his, touch her very core. "We'll go slow and easy. Tell me what you feel. Tell me what you like. Talk to me." She swallowed several times, but her eyes glazed as he penetrated again. At least he was able to focus. Barely.

"It's so smooth, like . . . like cotton. I feel like it's caressing me the way classical music caresses. Chopin, Schumann, Tchaikovsky."

"I am caressing you. Classical?" It was a style he'd mostly avoided. He had to admit, the slow sensuous movements were as caressing as music. Like the piano music that he'd heard at the mansion.

"Go slower. I like watching," she said, shifting on the counter. "More. Give me a little bit more."

He sank into her another inch, retreated more the next withdrawal, ever so leisurely when on the verge of a cataclysmic eruption. He didn't know how he could continue at this pace. The veins in his cock had expanded. Blood pumped madly, matching the beat of his heart. Fast. Pounding. Nowhere near classical standards, more like heavy metal.

She ran her finger down his wet length as he withdrew, then wiggled forward, balanced on the counter's edge. "More."

Shifting her legs over his arms, he pushed deeper, slightly harder. He touched the tip of her tiny protrusion with his fingertips, pressed down, making solid contact with Duke as he left her cocoon in measured degrees. The ragged hiss was his own.

A trickle of her sweet-tasting nectar followed, dribbled to the countertop, wasted when he should have lapped it up with his tongue. He withdrew and started down to his knees before Duke went on a plundering rampage.

"No! Don't take it away."

Okay. No problem. Bending his knees slightly, penetrating again, he shoved in an up angle, his fingers pressing firmly down on her clit.

She looked up, straight into his eyes. There was something there in those sparkling gray depths, something different when the pupils spread like water. Then he recognized the intensity in her storm gray eyes. G-spot. A second later, the first snap stunned Duke with such violence he nearly came.

"I w-want," she stuttered. Her voice caught on a sob. "All of it. Now. Now!"

On that welcome demand, he surged forward. Impact dragged out a scream. Donnie let loose of her legs and wrapped his arms around her body. "I'm sorry. Sorry." Embedded, he could hardly stand still, wanting to drive home again.

She wrapped all of her limbs around him. Challie lifted on a sleek rise and he forced her hips down, over and over again. The movements escalated to a wicked frenzy, taking them to the next unruly level.

He fought against the blur clouding his vision. Without warning, she clamped around him. Donnie detonated on a mighty roar, drowning out her strangled scream. He kissed her, drank deeply as his world turned upside down and went sideways.

Blinded by the climax's ferocity, legs weak and swaying, he grabbed the counter to stabilize them, balancing Challie with one arm, and continued pounding with pillaging strokes. Until his thrusts slowed to a gentle rocking motion, until Duke lost his ravaging zeal.

Burying his face against her neck, moaning, he dropped tender kisses on her shoulder up to her ear.

As the tremors wore off, their breaths coming in shallow pants, Donnie deposited Challie on the counter, trying to remember if and when he'd climaxed like this before. She'd damn near sucked the life from his body.

Blinking several times, clearing his mind, he remembered one important fact.

Coed pool.

What if she got pregnant? He'd be stuck with a wife *and* a kid. He was too young for a family of his own, too wild for one. Families needed devotion, too much time, when he liked his foot-loose and fancy freedoms. Dedication belonged to other men. Not Donnie.

Unwrapping Challie, he eased out of her warmth. Dynamite snatch, one he'd love to dive into a second time when Duke was capable of getting another rise. In a few minutes. With a condom. Never this again without one. Risky business otherwise.

Leaning back, Donnie asked, "Are you protected?" He flinched at his brusque tone.

"From what?"

Ah, shit. "Pregnancy."

She blinked rapidly. "Protected how?"

Ah, fuck. "Why the hell are you screwing when you're not on the pill or wearing a diaphragm? Something to keep from having babies!"

"You're the one who started this screwing. Why didn't *you* use protection? I'd be cleaning if it hadn't been for you." She wore indignant well and slapped at his chest. "My clothes wouldn't be ripped apart, either." She jumped down from the counter, groaning, tattered shorts hanging like a raggedy skirt.

Donnie tucked away a wasted Duke. He zipped his pants and wrapped his arm around her shoulders. "What's the matter?"

"Nothing."

"Yes, there is. What's wrong?"

"I said nothing." Taking a step, she cringed, noisily sucking in the next breath.

Hell, he'd done it now. She'd fucked his brains out. Now she couldn't walk. He scooped her into his arms.

"Put me down, you big jerk."

He started for her bedroom. Changing his mind, he took her to his room. The bed was bigger and closer to the bathroom. Donnie set her down gently. "Warm water will help. I'll fill the tub."

"I don't need you to draw my bath water," she snapped. "I don't need you." She crawled off the opposite side of the bed and hobbled across the room.

"Challie, come back here."

Instead, she slammed his door, then the one to the bathroom.

Women.

4

"Draw me a bath," Challie grumbled. "I can draw my own bath, thank you very much."

She did hurt. Warm water soothed the soreness. What in the world had provoked her to do such a thing? She was no better than Mrs. Tedesco's friend whose giggles, moans and groans had filtered into the guest room Challie had been cleaning. In the pool house! When she'd gotten enough gumption to leave, really trying to sneak out, Fontana was kissing the woman, his eyes wide open, staring at Challie. She'd had a hard time looking away, drawn to the intensity of his gaze. He was the type to enjoy two women at once. Three, probably. A harem. The shameless devil. As she'd hurried to the door, she'd felt his penetrating gaze piercing her back. Unnerved, she'd sprinted to the mansion.

Hattie had called loose women "tramps." So now, she was loose too, Challie decided. Twice. One black, one white. Well, no more. This was it. This "screwing" was a mistake. Both times.

She leaned back in the tub, rested her head on the rim,

checking her surroundings. The faucet and mirror shined. The floor was beige rather than dirt brown. Tile around the tub sparkled. Fontana had done an excellent job cleaning.

Fontana. She didn't know the man's first name. Lord. She was a tramp. He'd go back to Arizona, bragging how he'd laid the maid working at the Tedesco mansion. If Hattie heard, she'd have a heart attack. If Mrs. Tedesco caught wind of it, Challie figured she'd lose her job.

She slid down into the tub until the bubbles reached her chin. What was she going to do now? No job. No money. No life. Sent back home. And the thought made her want to throw up.

Donnie finished what Challie had started. Even mopped the floor. It was the least he could do.

If he weren't so damn big, she wouldn't be sore right now. If she hadn't demanded all of him, she wouldn't need to soak in the tub. If she hadn't fucked his brains out . . . Crap.

He looked down at the gold watch on his wrist. How long did baths take anyway? What the hell was she doing in there, drowning?

He hurried down the hall and banged on the door. "Challie!"

"What?"

"Oh," he said dryly. At least she hadn't drowned. "What's taking you so long?"

"Can't a woman bathe privately? I like to soak. Go away. Leave me alone."

Then, Donnie heard a suspicious sniffle. "What's wrong now?"

"Nothing. Go away."

"I'm coming in." The door was unlocked since he'd busted the jamb earlier.

"Get out! Get out!" She heaved the bar of soap.

Donnie ducked. The soap hit the wall behind him, cracked in half. Pieces ricocheted into the sink. The washcloth followed. Water went everywhere, splashed across the mirror and, damn it, on *his* clean floor.

What the fuck? Drawing himself upright to his full six-foot height, he settled both fists on his hips. "That's enough."

She had the nerve to fish through the water and pitch a sponge.

He ducked again, just not in time. The sponge smacked the side of his head, spraying him down. "I'll take a paddle to your ass if you throw one more thing." He wasn't beyond giving her a good spanking. Women needed them at times.

Her eyes turned glassy, then narrowed to thin slits. "You go ahead and try."

Luckily, she had nothing left to throw, except the mean look on her face spoke volumes. Were those tears dripping down her cheeks? Challie yanked the shower curtain closed.

What the hell was he supposed to do now? He despised tears, hated seeing a weepy woman. They used them to control a man. Donnie let no one control him. Except Tedesco on occasion. He should leave the bathroom. Go about his business. *Ignore it,* he thought while picking up the soap pieces, sponge and washcloth, which he used to wipe the floor. Yep. Close the door and find a magazine to read. Or a book. There were lots of books on the shelves: mysteries, westerns, nonfiction . . . all sorts of dull, outdated reading material, including several stupid romance novels. Somebody had dragged their old lady here.

Donnie pulled the shower curtain back. "Challie, I didn't mean to hurt you. Don't—" Shit. What the hell was he supposed to say? He didn't know how to stop a woman from bawling. "Weep."

"I don't ever cry."

Her back was straight as a steel beam. Kneeling beside the

tub, Donnie ran his finger down her spine. "Yes, you were. I saw tears."

"Tub water."

"Prove it. Turn around and look at me."

Another sniffle escaped. "I want you to leave me alone."

Like hell. He grabbed another washcloth from the rack, dipped it into soapy water, squeezed some of the moisture down her spine and lathered her rigid body. She finally relaxed; her shoulders weren't bunched any longer, hiding her neck. Knotted muscle had smoothed out. He forced her to turn toward him, but not without a hassle. Challie fought him every step of the way, splashing water everywhere. As wet as his clothes had gotten, he should've stripped and climbed into the tub with her.

She'd tied up her hair in a cute ponytail. A few locks had escaped the thick bundle. Damp, they stuck to her neck and shoulders. When he set them free, the strands curled into bouncy, loose waves. He liked seeing a woman's hair hanging free, but Challie wasn't just any woman. She was going to be his wife, if only for a little while.

They never spoke, not even when he parted her legs and gently ran the washcloth between them, wishing to feel her silkiness with unencumbered fingers.

Once the water had cooled, the bath lost its bubbles. Donnie pulled the plug from the drain. He grabbed the oversized blue-striped towel, shook it out and held it up. With satin-smooth skin drizzling with water, didn't Challie realize how much she turned him on? Shit, he wanted to fuck her again. Duke was ready, manufacturing process complete.

Once he dried her body, he planned to take her to bed. No full penetration this time. No matter how much he wanted to fuck *her* brains out. With a condom. Damned thing better hold every drop of cum he'd stored after the last eruption.

"I need to shower to rinse completely off."

Hell. "What about the bath? Didn't soaking do the job?"

"Baths are only for soaking. After a while, it's like sitting in your own filth. Hate filth."

She hated a lot of things. Did she hate him for hurting her?

"I need privacy."

Well, shit. He'd fucked her. He'd bathed her. Now, she wanted privacy? He wanted some ass. In the shower, if necessary. Did a rinse job for two fit into the equation?

Standing naked without showing the least bit of embarrassment, Challie tipped her head to one side and attached her hands to her hips in a familiar pose.

He got the picture. Donnie's shoulders sagged. Guess what he wanted didn't fit into her linear reasoning. Sighing noisily, he handed her the towel.

She took long showers.

Tapping his fingers in a four-note tune, Donnie waited. The old *Sports Illustrated* was as boring as reading an encyclopedia. When reading didn't take his mind off sex, Donnie just sat there, stroking his cock, keeping Duke in readied condition.

By the time Challie finished doing whatever the hell she had to do that took so damn long, all the hot water would be gone. He'd have to wash himself with cold water, in the sink. Then take her to bed.

She finally emerged. Fully dressed: jeans, long-sleeve shirt, tennis shoes. How the hell could he fuck her in all those clothes? It'd take him too long to peel off the damn jeans; he'd blow his wad before they reached her ankles.

"I'm going to take a walk. I'll make you a snack when I get back." She sauntered out the front door.

What the hell? All this damn time he'd sat here horny and she decided to take a damn walk. Did she even notice he had a hard-on? Did she even care? Oh, no. "I'm going to take a goddamn walk," he mimicked badly. No woman walked away from him. All chased him. All wanted what he had to give.

Except this one.

Fine. She'll be begging for my meat to fill her pussy. Meanwhile, what the devil am I supposed to do with Duke?

Donnie huffed. He got up, wandered into the kitchen and looked out the window.

Challie had never seen such beautiful country.

The sky was endlessly clear. The prairie's cool breeze was refreshing, unpolluted. Animals grazed in the distance. Quiet. Complete silence.

She'd better enjoy the scene while she had the chance. Her homeland was nothing like this place. In South Africa, many tribes lived in rundown shacks. Some owned tents. Unfortunate others survived in the open. But the land and view were never as spectacular as Montana.

She spun circles, arms spread wide, grin on her face, inhaling the sweet scent of Montana. Odds were this visit was her last to the state. Mrs. Tedesco had said they'd probably spend a week or so and Fontana's guests would arrive in a few days. Having visitors would keep her mind off leaving and off what had happened earlier. Every time she thought about Fontana, she sizzled inside. She couldn't think about sex again. For gosh sakes, she didn't know his first name! Of course, he didn't know her real last name either.

But he'd taught her the best of sex and what it's really like when it's really good. She'd keep the memories tucked away in her mind forever.

Yawning noisily, she swatted at a buzzing fly. Challie started down the dirt road toward the hills. A variety of huge trees and fences divided the property. Up ahead, she caught sight of a big, brown cow jumping the pen. She'd never seen one this large before. Or this close.

What was she doing? Flinging her arms around, spinning, Challie looked like a nymph. He'd like her better as a nymphomaniac right about now, tearing off his clothes in a rush to enjoy Duke's manhandling.

Donnie braced his hands against the window frame as he watched Challie. None of the women he'd messed with would want to be here. None would be happy anywhere away from the city. None would ever consider visiting Montana or cow country or find satisfaction on an open prairie unless a prime-time shopping center was nearby.

Filling a glass with the only source of water on the ranch, a well, he decided there were things he liked about Challie. She didn't complain about the hodgepodge of bullcrap other women bitched about: her hair mussed after rough sex, sweating, or nails, or smudged makeup, which she didn't wear. Her face was scrubbed clean and bright, free of enhancements she wouldn't need anyway. She only complained about filth. And, of course, mice.

He had to get a cat, find one while she was on her frigging walk. So much for blistering sex in the next few minutes.

Peering out the window again, he saw Challie running toward the cabin. What the devil?

Donnie met her at the screen door. Across the way, someone had penned the dogs. They were barking their asses off, which usually meant ranch workers had arrived after a long day in the fields. Was a truck full of guys the reason Challie had run? Or maybe the dogs had caught the scent of something in their territory. Ranch dogs ran in packs, working together as well as wolves.

Panting, Challie said, "A cow is loose!"

Hell, he thought it was an important issue. "No big deal. The foreman'll rope her and lead her back to the pasture. They're branded. He'll know it belongs here." He had *her* here now.

"But there's no one around. We can put her back where she

belongs ourselves. Otherwise, she might get hurt. Please? I don't want her to get hurt."

A frigging cow jacking up my game plan. "All right. All right."

Following close behind Challie, long strides to her trotting, Donnie grabbed a rope hanging from the hook outside the main barn as if he knew what to do. Lassoing took talent Donnie didn't have. But a cow, which was probably a calf, cake.

He'd spent several days one colder-than-a-bitch February with Paul and Ray during calving season. He'd damn near frozen his ass off at four o'clock in the morning while the foreman pulled a calf. What a mess.

"You need a bigger rope," Challie said, throwing her arms out wide.

Paul said Ray had purchased several Texas longhorns to breed with a select group of cattle. Donnie hoped he hadn't picked up Brahma bulls. They were way more than he was willing to mess with on a good day, even with backup cowboys who knew what they were doing.

"She was coming up the road," Challie said.

They rounded the corner of the barn and came damn near face-to-face with an effing moose! A huge bull with a rack the size of frigging Montana.

Donnie grabbed the back of Challie's shirt, stopped her cold. "Don't move a muscle," he whispered. "Not cow. Moose. Tramplers, but their eyesight is—"

Challie bolted.

"Bad." Fucking A.

She darted across the road, leaving Donnie in a lousy situation. He had two choices. Make a fast dash back into the barn to save his own ass, knowing the narrow doorway would prevent the moose from entering with a rack this size or . . .

Bullwinkle made his call of the angry wild and charged.

Donnie sprinted. He dove under the rail fence where Challie

hid in a shallow ditch filled with weeds, hay, mounds of loose dirt. Bullwinkle stomped, grunting, generally pissed. Hunters claimed humans frightened these animals.

Latching onto Challie's shirt, Donnie dug in and crawled, dragging her with him under the corral's intricate wood design. Ranch hands used it to load steers onto transport trucks. They were protected here.

Until Bullwinkle tried to crash through the wood.

Challie's hair-raising scream raised mega-sized goose bumps, which sprouted down Donnie's body to the bottoms of his feet. He clamped his hand over her mouth and hauled her into his arms, then covered her body with his own, protecting her the best way he knew how. He didn't know which was worse, Challie's clawing, attempting to skitter away, or Bullwinkle bent on splintering every rotting piece of goddamn wood surrounding them.

He and his future wife were going to die today because he'd failed to keep his cock inside his pants.

Donnie squeezed his eyes shut and closed his ears to the bona fide wail of an angry creature. For the first time in years, he prayed, begging for forgiveness, vowing to change his ways if the man upstairs would let them live another day.

All at once, silence.

Opening his eyes, he spied four brown legs lumbering away. Donnie let out the breath he'd been holding in one long whoosh. Maybe, just maybe, the rumbling noise of a distant vehicle had Bullwinkle galloping off into the sunset.

Nestled between Challie's legs, their breathing rapid, their hearts thumping in unison, he uncovered her mouth.

Terror shined in her eyes. She whispered, "Is it gone?"

"Yeah, I think so." He rolled to his side, taking Challie with him, tightening his arms around her as a shiver sprinted through her body and transferred into his. "Hey, it's okay now."

An old lumber truck roared past the corral, rumbled down the road, gravel clattering against the undercarriage, raising a dense cloud of dust. Several seconds later, the driver tooted his horn—probably at Bullwinkle. Come autumn, during rutting season, big daddy moose might decide to challenge the log hauler's vehicle in a territorial attack. He just might win the match against the antique.

Donnie cupped Challie's chin. "Your face is smudged with dirt." He smoothed his thumb over her cheek where his fingerprints had temporarily branded her soft skin.

"Bath," she said breathlessly.

Fuck a bath. He'd shower her insides with his fresh, scalding juice. Donnie pressed his lips to hers, teasing them apart. She went pliant under his exploration as he delved deeper in a dance as old as Adam and Eve's sexy samba. The moan he heard was his own. When she sighed, the erotic sound kicked his pulse up a notch, popped the clutch on Duke, jerking his gears into overdrive. Slowly, he glided one hand up and down her midriff. He grazed the side of her breast, covered it, found her nipple budded and squeezed the tightness. She arched toward him in offering or wanting more. She wore no bra to hinder his advances.

Donnie unfastened every single button down her shirt and spread the fabric open. Her breathing rapid, her chest heaved. He latched onto her nipple with his teeth, gnawed, suckled, gnawed again. Her legs restless and moving, he slipped his hand down to the juncture between her thighs. The territory was hot, damp. Pressing the heel of his hand to her mound dragged a deep moan from her throat. Challie's legs spread wider, her hips rising to meet the pressure.

In a rush on her wordless call for more, Donnie got his jeans open with one desperate yank. Duke sprang free like an overstretched wire. Thick. Hard. Needy of this woman's stimulating currents. He shoved his baggies down, peeled her hand from his shirt, wrapped it around his cock and forced her to squeeze.

"Tighter," he rasped, hissing out a harsh breath from the sweet torture. "Stroke him." He guided her hand down and up his throbbing length in the same rhythm that his tongue stroked inside her mouth.

"So hard," she said against his cheek. "So big. So hot."

"For you. Just you."

He moved her hand farther down to clasp the family jewels. They were stretched tight, aching. "Keep working me. Touch me everywhere. Do it."

She compressed gently then caressed his shaft from base to tip in a teasing slide. His blood erupted into flaming liquid. She wasn't a newbie, but not a pro.

Donnie jammed his hand inside her jeans, quickly shoved his middle finger into her hot snatch, careful not to hurt her again. When her breath hitched, he began *their* slow samba.

A shortie. When she fastened her fingers around Duke's bulging head, Donnie cruised on the verge of bursting on the next breath. Way too soon. He shoved two fingers inside her slickness, then added a third to match what should be his cock, pumping hard, fast. She hovered on the fine edge of coming apart.

Watching her climax rise to the surface, he did burst. "Goddamn it!"

His body shaking, he came in her hand, on her clothes, her belly and the dirt ground like a geyser after a long dormant season. Weak, but far from empty, Donnie crawled over her body. Automatically, her legs wrapped snugly around his waist. He skimmed his hardness over her sensitivity, feeling her quiver as her hips lifted. That stout little clit wanted this bad. Donnie gave her everything he could possibly give under the current conditions. Dry fucks were a bitch in any circumstance.

Shoving his cock at the denim, working to get a better feel, the first snap occurred. She shrieked, clutching his body with those strong legs when he wished to be inside her feeling the powerful bite. It had stunned him silly earlier, as had all the quick nips afterward in rapid succession. She let loose so freely. Heated dampness teasingly spread over Duke's sensitive head.

Rocking against her, the scent of her potent sex filling his nostrils, jarring him again, he spurted, releasing the last milligram of juice and final ounce of energy. But when Challie's legs sagged, something licked Donnie's bare ass. What the fuck?

He jerked his head around, banged it against the slat above them and grimaced. Frigging Ike. The dog's erect nub of a tail wiggled a mile a second.

"Get the hell out of here!"

Wary, Ike's ears laid back. His tail ceased wagging.

"Don't be mean to him." In his weakened condition, Challie shoved him easily to the side. "Come here, Ike," she cooed. "He's so mean."

When Ike backed away, she crawled toward the ugly hound, butt tooted toward Donnie's face and, evidently, him totally forgotten.

A damn Heinz 57 wins her complete devotion over me and Duke.

Getting his boxers and jeans readjusted was a feat in confinement. He needed to shower. Dirt, pebbles and hay had gotten inside his clothes.

Challie sat on her heels, dusted her hands on her pants while buttoning her shirt. She looked over her shoulder. "I'm taking a bath. Hate filth."

"Together." Perfect for a slick interlude of some serious . . .

"Alone. I don't bathe in other people's filth."

Son of a bitch. No way would he wait another hour, scratching worse than flea-ridden hounds. The bunkhouse was equipped with a small lavatory.

5

Ten minutes later, Donnie bumped into the foreman outside the bunkhouse's front door.

"Thought I saw me a new SUV out back," Charlie Lawson said. The man had a hell of a grip shaking hands, tight enough to make a grown man drop to his knees. "How ya doin', hombre? Ray said you were vacationin' up here."

Lawson sported the thickest mustache on the planet magnified by a square jaw. His eyes were darker than the cheap whiskey he drank—not yet bloodshot today—but Donnie smelled liquor on the foreman's breath, even with a smoldering cigarette hanging from the corner of his mouth. The paunch belly had grown.

"Can't complain," Donnie replied. "How about you? Tamed any broncs lately? Still doing the rodeo circuit?"

Lawson sucked hard off the cigarette butt. He flicked the burning remains to the ground, stubbed it out under the heel of his dusty boot. One long, steady stream of hazy gray blasted from his nostrils. "Not so much no more. Steer caught the leg durin' the rodeo last year."

Labor Day was advertised as "Montana's Biggest Weekend." Technically, it was the Beaverhead County Fair and the Dillon Rodeo. The auction was officially 4-H. Ray bought one or two animals from local kids annually.

When they started across the gravel, Donnie noticed the cowboy favored his right leg.

"What brings you this far north? Fishin'? Bloody Dick's runnin' high this year. So's Trail Crick. Caught a mess of brookies the other day. Thinkin' about an overnight up there by Dad's Lake. You up for it?"

This guy had caught *the* largest trout on the prairie. Hell of a fly fisherman. Funny thing was he never ate his catch. Whenever Paul was on site planning fish fries for parties, he called Lawson—the meat and potatoes man of Horse Prairie.

"I'll think about." Donnie wondered whether Challie had ever fished. "Couple of Paul's friends coming in."

Lawson grunted. He pulled the pack of Marlboros from his shirt pocket, lit another cigarette. Smoked like a chimney, drank like a whale.

"Where's Ray? We haven't seen him since we got in."

Eyebrows lifting, Lawson stared at their cabin, squinting, then back at Donnie. "S'pose he's pickin' up supplies and shit, pissin' aroun' town."

Ray and Lawson weren't the best of friends. Both had issues Donnie would just as soon avoid rather than ask questions. "Anybody around who might have a spare cat? Rodents are trying to take over in there."

"Mice thick as flies on cowshit this season. Think they scared off the black and whites." As in skunk. Those and badgers were fierce creatures. "But all them damn cats we had, I . . . Check deaf Ross. That pretty little filly of his keeps a few."

Just then, someone honked. "*Vamonos, amigo!*"

"Eduardo," Lawson said. "Good, hard worker. Guess it's

time to git along, little doggie." He'd have swaggered if he hadn't screwed up his leg.

Since Challie was bathing and sure to use all the hot water during another shower, Donnie made a quick trip to the neighbors living a few miles downwind.

Lawson was right.

"Thanks, Mr. Ross," Donnie yelled. The old codger couldn't hear a bomb detonate across the road.

"Anytime. Damn cats multiply worse than rabbits. Good mouser, that one. She'll clear 'em out for ya if you keep her inside." Ross had more wrinkles than prunes. A roadmap of blue veins stretched across translucent skin. He'd lived on this ranch most of his life. "Gonna be up here a while? The kitty litter oughta hold you a few weeks."

"Maybe. Got time off for good behavior." And all depended on his proposal, the wedding plans, plus all other stupid shit associated with the supposed big day.

"Well, if ya need anything else, just you holler. And feed the furball table scraps when she run outta mice. The granddaughter don't feed 'em no store-bought food. Keeps 'em healthy."

As the screen door closed, Donnie held the Manx mix in the air. Challie was going to like the tuxedo it wore. Tuxedo. Good name if her new mistress thought so. He tossed the "furball" on the backseat.

By the time he reached the curve leading to the foreman's house, he knew something was wrong. Way wrong.

Donnie sped beyond the graveled lane, slammed on the brakes, filling the air thick with dust, but the gentle breeze whisked it downwind. He swaggered back toward Challie. Marching, suitcase in hand, she ignored him.

He caught hold of her wildly swinging arm, drew her back to face him. "What the hell are you doing?"

"Leaving." She was headed straight into the mountains. Toward Idaho.

"Why?"

With shaded eyes of a raging storm, she said, "You left me alone in that place. Mice everywhere. Hate mice."

God, she really despised the vermin. "I picked up a cat just for you. Come back with me. Old man Ross said she'd clear them out. If not I'll go into town for traps, and I'll take you with me."

Damn it, she couldn't leave. Sure as shit, some local yokel would give her a lift, maybe as far as Butte. She had no business riding with strangers, particularly cowboys.

He tried to take her luggage. She wouldn't give it up.

"Challie." He stepped closer, ran his fingers down her arm, enjoying the feel of her smooth skin. "I promise."

She seemed to think about it. "You'll move the furniture, sweep all the floors? Make sure they're not hiding?"

"Yes. Anything." He could almost see her brain working.

"What about the throw rugs? They've been crawling on them."

He let out a long, exasperated sigh. "I'll beat the hell out of them with the broom. Outside."

She didn't answer right away. Finally, she said, "All right."

She handed him her suitcase. Donnie tossed it in the backseat. He wouldn't have minded helping her inside the Jeep, getting a free feel in the process, but she remembered the running board.

As he climbed behind the wheel, the cat crawled between them into Challie's lap, purring louder than the SUV's engine. "What a pretty kitty."

Any other woman he knew would bitch about cat fur attaching to their designer clothes or jacking with their allergies. Not this one. Challie stroked the animal with loving care.

"How about calling her Tuxedo?"

"It fits," she replied, nuzzling the "pretty kitty" like a long-lost pet.

Now, if he could just get her to stroke *him* with a little tender loving care again. He'd purr louder than the damn cat.

Donnie chuckled to himself. Or raise the roof with a lion's conquering roar.

At the house, she fed Tuxedo a snack first, chopped her food into fine pieces and served it in a glass bowl. Afterward, she made Donnie's pastrami sandwich, added a side of chips and one peewee dill pickle. On a flimsy paper plate. Challie ate less than Tuxedo. Off a real plate. Ike showed up for a shared snack.

While Donnie moved furniture and dragged rugs outside for a good beating, she dusted, gathered linens, washed windows and ignored him. At last, she asked for his help. She'd never reach the vaulted ceiling's cobwebs, even with a broom. He'd worked up a real sweat today.

As Donnie swaggered down the hall, moving on to the last bedroom, Tuxedo darted past him.

The piercing scream that tore through the cabin froze the blood in his veins. He damn near broke a leg on the living room chair. Challie stood on the counter, dancing a little in place, pointing at the rodent clamped between Tuxedo's teeth. Apparently, the cat's new mistress wasn't too happy about her pet's first show-and-tell session.

Smiling, Donnie hoisted Challie down. He carried her into his bedroom and sat until the mouse was set free for a little playtime. Or eaten. Hopefully, the latter. Legs curled beneath her, Challie stayed on his lap.

Duke jumped hard again. Donnie had one hell of a time believing he still carried the all-too-wholesome sexual urge. He should be too beat for sex. Who would've thought he'd ever work this hard? Manual labor wasn't his style. Cleaning house was supposed to be a woman's natural job.

"Why did she bring that filthy creature into my kitchen?"

To share, or to show mama her prize. "She's trying to make you happy." He smoothed a hand over her thigh, sneaked his fingers between them, attempting to make her happy in his own way.

"Bad cat!" Challie snapped when Tuxedo sauntered into the room, sat primly and licked her white paws clean.

Obviously, she wasn't interested in Donnie's subtle ministrations. She kept him in a constant state of arousal and he thought by now she'd be begging him to plug her.

By nightfall the cabin was spotless.

Challie had washed the linens and together they'd hung them out to dry. She remade all the beds after Donnie dragged the twin mattresses outside for airing. She insisted he beat them with the broom handle first.

For dinner, she'd roasted chicken—his favorite—and served creamy mashed potatoes with the best damn gravy he'd ever had. She was a dynamite cook with a dynamite snatch to boot. While she washed dishes, he dried and put them away, figuring the more time he spent with her, the more she'd want him. With several full nights left without another soul in the cabin, the place clean and a cat to take care of the dreaded mice, they had plenty of time to spend in bed together. Tired or not, he planned to make good use of their solitude. All she had to do was ask. He'd give her everything she wanted, plus some. Tonight, they'd burn up the sheets until daybreak.

"It's been a long day," Challie said. "I'm going to bed. Good night." She scooped up Tuxedo, sauntered down the hall. Not to his bedroom. To hers.

Good night? Donnie chewed on that piece of fat. He'd make her beg now. Tease the hell out of her. He knew this game too well. If she thought he'd go after her, he had news for Ms. Smith. No way, even if a hard-on killed him while he waited.

Needing a shower as frigid as a Montana winter, Donnie trudged into the bathroom.

Challie sat on the bed, staring outside the single window into the dark night, and swallowed. Her imagination had always run amok. She remembered the many pairs of gleaming yellow eyes, the sounds of thrashing, marauding, the vivid screams. Wild animals prowled in Montana too. Very few people lived in the vicinity to chase them away. She snapped the shades closed. Fear bred more fear.

She stripped out of her clothes. Hattie had bought her two floor-length cotton gowns for this trip. They were much softer than the old, static-clinging nylon pajamas Hattie had given her when she arrived. Any type of pajamas was a luxury Challie had never enjoyed until moving to the United States. She'd slept naked most of her life, or fully clothed if Papa had ordered, prepared to make an escape if tensions reached a volatile degree. Shivering, she discarded the undesirable memories and hung her clothes in the small closet, then switched off the overhead light. The cute antique lamp provided soft glowing illumination.

Today, she'd aired out the cabin of its stale odors, but the night air was chilly after the warm day, much cooler than her homeland's sweltering nights, even cooler than nighttime Arizona. She drew the heavy blanket up to her waist, snuggled under the clean sheet, smelling its fresh scent.

The cabin was quiet except for Tuxedo's constant purring. She perched on the bedside table until Challie switched off the lamp. Tuxedo tiptoed across the pillow and curled up close to her back.

Lifting her hand, Challie only imagined seeing her fingers. There was nothing to fear from darkness when life in her village was so much scarier. Candlelight had done little to illuminate the small room she shared with Grandmama in the shanty. Shadows had danced on the walls. Warfare and killers had owned the streets.

Here, only she and Fontana were in the cabin anyway. What if something terrible happened? Who would know? What if a lion broke through a window while they slept? Or a wild band of monkeys? Who would help them? She shuddered at the images she'd had since childhood.

Then, howling split the quiet night. Challie scrambled out of bed, snatched up Tuxedo and hurried out of the room.

He knew it.

Donnie knew she'd come begging him to plug her. He smiled, hearing Challie's rap at his bedroom door, and turned on the lamp.

"Come in."

She peeked inside, clutching Tuxedo. Where did she shop for clothes and lingerie? Hadn't anybody mentioned sexiness to her? Victoria's Secret? Frederick's? Damn.

"Something is howling outside."

"Coyotes."

She took a tentative step. "Can we sleep in here? I hate howling."

Name one thing you don't hate.

Donnie yanked the sheet back. Women were so coy sometimes. She wanted him and was too afraid to admit it. The games people play.

"Tuxedo can sleep between us."

Like hell. "Tuxedo needs to sleep on the floor to catch the mice," Donnie replied, knowing she'd agree hearing the plural of the critters.

"She didn't eat them all?"

"Not a chance." He chuckled when she dropped the cat and charged toward the bed.

Keeping to the edge of the mattress, she pulled the sheet up to her chin. "Can they climb up here?"

The right answer would keep her right up under him. "Maybe."

"I'm getting my clothes on. In fact, I'm sleeping in your tank."

Donnie dragged her across the bed and into his arms. "Tuxedo won't let them."

Damn, she smelled good enough to eat. She'd wasted more water after dinner bathing. Without him. But her skin wasn't wrinkled or dry or cracked. How many baths did a person need every day?

Draping his heavy leg between her thighs, he pinned her to the mattress, cuffed her wrists, lifted her arms above her head and pinned them together with one hand. He dragged her gown's hem above her breasts.

Duke bounced against her leg for two beats then reared up toward the object of his search, poised, in striking distance.

The look in Challie's eyes was palpable.

Beg. You get nothing until you beg. Drawn to her heat, he pressed the head of his cock to the edge of her fire.

"This is a bad idea," she said. "I've made two too many mistakes in my life. I shouldn't make another one."

Like hell. Sex with me is not in error. He delved his tongue into her ear. She squirmed, legs moving restlessly. She was one minute from begging. He knew it. *God, please, not a second more.*

Her wiggling set off new sensations. Donnie ached to get inside her. He bit a path down the tendon of her neck, moved farther and latched onto her nipple, sucking noisily, teasing her with his teeth.

"Stop it."

Not a chance. She vibrated against his skin. He wanted her to beg, wanted to fill her, but when he lifted his hips to settle between her legs, she clamped both tightly around his thigh.

"One more time," Donnie whispered. "Just once. I won't hurt you."

"But, I don't know—"

He kissed her silent, thoroughly, and her legs lost their grip. As Donnie moved up, over and forward, they fell open like petals of a flower.

He eased into her heat, anticipating the intoxicating pleasure to come. She was wet, not soaking, but enough for him to make her wetter. If he held back, let her take the lead, she'd work *him*.

Sliding out, Donnie rolled to his side, taking Challie with him.

6

Challie forced him onto his back. Straddling his thighs, she sat upright and all ten fingers gripped his bobbing man-thing. She squeezed. He sucked in air.

Amobi had taught her what to do, when to do it and never to let up.

She'd know when the timing was right, when to take him into her body. Fontana would lose control first, as she had.

He was wet and sticky from her juices and she stroked his man-thing from the dark nest of hair to the very tip and down again, squeezing. Within seconds, the first pearly drop appeared on the bulging head. She spread the liquid around the crest of beauty with one fingertip.

When she squeezed again, he stopped her hands.

"Enough," he said, panting. "I don't want to lose it too soon. I can't take much more."

She pushed his hands aside. "Yes, you can," Challie murmured.

She had full control, watching his staff of pleasure bounce against his rippling abdomen. How did she manage to take him completely inside her the first time? But even with accompanying pain, sex with Fontana was wonderful.

She ran her fingers up and down the length in a gentle caress. Hot, like his hands. Hard, like a tree trunk.

Her body quaked with excitement. Unfurling, surfacing, causing her skin to tingle. Soon all his splendor would fill her. He knew what she liked, knew just how to set her body free. But she wanted him on a feverish path, the same way he'd coaxed her into their first time.

"Challie?"

"Hmm?"

This would be her final mistake in life, but a gratifying error. By next week, Mrs. Tedesco would send her home. Challie would carry a few wonderful memories of a man she knew only as Fontana.

"Do you give head?"

Huh? Her hands stilled. She was well versed in the English language, but . . . head? Not wanting to appear ignorant again, she said, "No."

His groan was deep, resonating. "Will you one day?"

She thought a moment, suspected the day would never arrive. "Maybe some day. Yes."

"Challie?" His breathing sounded as irregular as if he'd raced a mile across desert sands.

"Hmm?" She continued stroking him. Another liquid drop appeared.

"I'm gonna come soon."

"Not yet."

As his legs shifted on the bed, he reached for the headboard's wooden supports and wrapped his fingers around two. The muscles in his arms flexed, smoothed, flexed again. Squeezing his eyes shut, his stomach muscles tightened. Sweat spontaneously sprouted on his forehead. His hips bucked. Twice.

"I can't wait any longer," he rasped.

* * *

Donnie was well aware of every touch, every movement of her hands: fingers clasping, guiding. Pressing her hands against his chest, her heat surrounded him as she took him in with agonizing slowness. She sighed as her plump ass descended by a mere inch or two. She lifted, sank only partially, lifted again. Circling her hips, she angled differently and purred as Duke glided into tightness on a smooth slide. She was killing him.

Her hips in perpetual motion, Donnie raised his hips to greet her on the next teasing down stroke. Except, she kept him from full penetration. Then she lifted off his body, had Duke thumping against his belly.

Ah, shit. He'd reached the brink of detonation, needed release. They both needed release.

He rolled Challie beneath him. She'd taken him to the point of no return and, from what he could see, hear and tell, without pain. Staring into her eyes, he saw no fear, no regret for what she'd done. She'd primed him just for this. He'd give it to her. Everything. Drain himself dry.

Wrapping her legs around his hips, she said, "Now. I want you now."

Oh, yeah, she needed a real fucking. He'd screw her witless, have her screaming his name. He wanted to hear it from her own sweet lips as he penetrated her tight passage, wanting her to remember it was he who had fucked her into delirium.

"Who's fucking you, Challie?"

She bit her bottom lip.

Frustrated, Donnie growled low in the back of his throat. "Who's making love to you?"

She squeaked out a groan. "Fontana."

He resisted descending into her tightness, circling his hips, teasing her, and she writhed beneath him. "My real name, say it."

Terror shined in her eyes. "Mr. Fontana."

Christ. She didn't know his first name. For some reason, he wanted her to know everything about him, wanted her to accept the man controlling her now. He had control.

"Donovan," he said in an odd voice, shaking from holding back, wanting to drive his cock home where it belonged. "Donovan. Marcel. Fontana."

As his full name tumbled from her lips, he shoved forward with one maddening thrust, piercing her, and plundered her mouth.

He smacked against her with driving force while his tongue matched the assault with the same commanding rhythm. He couldn't get enough. The head of his cock was overly sensitive to her natural heat and her tight squeezes pushed him to a frantic plateau. If he continued at this rate, he'd bust one before Challie.

Never. They'd travel together, reach for the same stars. He had to stop, had to hold on to his senses.

Withdrawing completely extracted a hostile "no" from her. Like him, she was needy. He would give her everything he had to give.

In a frenzied display, Donnie sat up, lifted her hips from the bed and drove home. On a gasp, her fingers tore into his arms, held on fiercely.

Oh, yes, she wanted this, but he wanted more.

Rabid now, wild, maddened, sweat dripped down his face and splashed on her soft skin, branding her. She was his now. Greed was a bitch and he wanted everything. All for himself this time.

Her body. Her mind. Her soul. And all of her glory.

He let loose of her legs. His hips in motion, he watched his cock slide in and out, watched her juices flow freely. She moved with natural finesse, matching his thrusts stroke for stroke. She was wringing the shit out of him, never letting up, increasing the tempo with blinding speed. Together, they did it all. Together, they worked hard toward the inevitable.

And then it began, gathering force with acute ferocity, stimulated by the woman who had tortured him into a savage animal. Donnie willed it to stop, wanting her to go over the top with him, at the same time, through a powerhouse of ecstasy.

"Not without you," he ground out. "Not without you coming with me. Look at me. Look at me, goddamn it!" He had to see her eyes, see what filled them. Shoving a hand in her hair, he twisted the thick mass in his fist.

Her gaze locked with his. At first, something indefinable shined there. Then something touched his very core that made his heart pound harder.

"Donovan! Donovan!" She clamped around him in a tight grip, hatching an explosive climax.

"God," he roared, and Challie reared up screaming.

Minutes passed, the sound of their heavy pants the only noise.

Spent, Donnie lay sprawled across Challie. She'd drained him of every ounce of juice, every damn milligram, and sapped him of strength. The pungent scent of sex filled the room. Breathing in the aroma, contented, he ran one hand up her midriff while licking the crevices of her ear.

She giggled.

Damn, he liked the sound and gave her reason to giggle again. Hardly able to move, he knew he weighed more than she could bear. Donnie rolled to his side, drew her back against him and spooned her body. When she wiggled, Duke woke.

How the hell could that possibly be?

At this rate, she'd kill him in a short time, but it'd be a damn happy death. Donnie smiled.

"How do you feel?" he whispered.

"Marvelous," Challie replied. "Alive. Like I just finished listening to my favorite concerto."

Tightening his arm around her waist, he said, "No pain?"

She shook her head, sighing.

A quiet minute went by while she stroked his arm. He caught her hand, measured his own with hers and laced their fingers together. She had delicate hands with long, slender fingers. "I forgot to use a condom again. You make me forget everything, except being inside you."

Challie lifted her shoulder slightly. "I won't get pregnant. If I do, you don't have anything to worry about."

"What do you mean?"

"I'll take care of it somehow. I won't cause you any problems."

He sat upright. "Take care of it how, and what damn problems?"

Rolling to her back, she caught his gaze. "Don't you see? We're worlds apart. I'm a maid. You're—"

"I'm what?"

"—different," she finished simultaneously.

Different how? A woman abuser in disguise? A playboy on a destructive rampage? Okay, sure, he'd fucked way more than a shitload of women, but he'd never abused one. He was no different from the next guy with a hot-to-trot libido. If other men had his rod, they'd screw every woman in sight who wanted a taste.

But his sexual prowess couldn't be *the* different that Challie was talking about. She would never allow him to make love to her if he beat on women. She'd all but threatened him earlier over a simple paddling.

Make love?

Ah, hell. He remembered the look in her eyes, moments before they plunged over ecstasy's cliff. He also remembered how his heart thumped, seeing hers shamelessly displayed on an invisible sleeve.

"Soon," Challie said. She reached out and ran her fingers up his hard-earned six-pack and farther up to his chest. Every muscle along the path twitched, settled down. "Things will be different. You'll have guests."

"So? I don't give a damn about Thompson and Moretti."

He knew both men well. Gary Thompson, distribution supervisor, was quiet and easy-going. Roman Moretti was Paul's best friend from way back. For a guy who skipped college, Roman competently managed all of payroll and personnel at PT Industries.

She frowned a little. "What do you think they would like for dinner their first night? Prime—"

"Forget the guests," Donnie snapped. "They can make their own damn meals." She'd changed the subject a little too quickly for his taste. "Why are you so worried about guests? We were talking about—"

"A busy week. I'll have a lot to do."

Yeah. Taking care of me, making love to me. A lot. Day and night.

"It's late. We should get some rest." She drew the tangled sheet up and over herself.

"Challie—"

"Good night." She turned her back on him.

Donnie's jaw went slack. He did not like being ignored. "We need to finish this discussion."

"Sleep, Donovan Marcel Fontana." She yawned hugely, enough to crack her jaw. "Sleep."

She remembered, and Donnie's smile spread across his lips.

With the lamplight glowing, he could see she breathed deeply, already dead to the world. Knocked out before they finished discussing "different." When he turned out the light, sleep forgot to claim his senses.

What exactly did she mean by different?

I'm a man, with flesh and blood and feelings. A beating heart, one hammering against his ribs suddenly, one on the verge of some emotional shit.

Moonbeams lit the bed. Propping his chin on his hand, Donnie stared at Challie while she slept restlessly. The sheet slipped down to her waist. He drew it up to her shoulders, tucked it around her body.

If he moved closer to her, he'd probably wake her. If he woke her, he'd make love to her again. If he made love to her, his heart would surely get too damned emotional. Hell. How did this crap get started? Love at first sight was bullshit. It just didn't happen. Lust. It had to be lusting after her tight sexpot.

He scooted to Challie's side of the bed and wrapped one arm around her waist. She sighed, contented just like him.

And she slept like the dead, didn't respond as he'd expected, as he expected all women to react.

He tried rousing her subtly, kissing her shoulder and neck, which dragged out a menacing grumble from her. Duke exerted a little stout pressure from behind. Challie scooted to the opposite side of the king bed. When Donnie tried a tender caress, tantalizing the little nub between her legs, she slapped his hand.

By dawn, no less horny, he drifted into an exhausted sleep.

Loud purring woke her. Tuxedo walked up her body. Challie opened her eyes. She'd slept so well last night.

Today was going to be another beautiful sight. The sun glowed behind thin curtains, lighting the room brilliantly. The digital clock said seven o'clock. An hour later than her usual rising time!

Putting Tuxedo aside, she slipped off the mattress quietly, stretched full length, arms over her head, fingers clasped, twisting side to side. Starting today, everything would be different. Life in general.

Challie tiptoed to the door. She took one last look at the room, then at Donovan Marcel Fontana. Naked, he slept on his back, one leg bent at the knee, the other outstretched, arms opened wide.

He had a beautiful body. Muscled and sleek. Eventually, some lucky woman would caress him at her leisure, whenever she wanted to touch him, for the rest of her life. Pinning Donovan down for marriage might take a little time, but his future wife would be happy in the end. He was a good man. Sweet, attentive, a helpful partner and excellent lover. Just never her bed partner again. She closed the door. She had things to do. Challie would not disappoint Mrs. Tedesco.

Showering quickly, she dressed properly in a shapeless, ankle-length, gray jumper. She French-braided her hair into a single thick piece of art. Loose hair never worked while cooking in the Tedesco mansion. Hattie had jumped all over her one day for making that particular mistake, but Challie had refused to wear a hairnet like an indentured servant. Even if she was one.

She smoothed her jumper free of wrinkles and twirled in front of the mirror. Yesterday, she'd found a red-checkered apron. Homemade biscuits sounded like a nice change. Taking a deep breath, cleansing her mind for the day ahead, she opened the bathroom door.

Challie yelped. "Mr. Fontana, you nearly scared me to death." Why was he up so early? She'd expected him to sleep at least another hour.

Forearms braced against the doorframe overhead, his well-defined, in-the-flesh body was sexier than the god women fantasized about coming to their bed. She allowed her gaze to wander downward. A male well endowed, carrying a robust masterpiece of desire when fully aroused. She shivered, remembering how well they'd fit together, how wonderful his man-thing felt inside. It twitched, lengthened, swelled. Challie frowned, wondering how men made them move without assistance. She thought to ask how.

"What's with this *Mr.* Fontana bullshit?" His gaze traveled up and down her body as he lowered his arms. "What the devil is that you're wearing? What the hell are you doing out of our bed this early?"

"Our?"

"Ours!"

Challie flinched at his tone.

"And you're supposed to be there when I wake up, not sneaking around showering alone, then dressing in this thing," he said, flicking the fabric at her shoulder. "What in the hell have you done to your hair?"

Goodness. He was angry because she'd left his bed. Really angry. Then, she realized exactly why. Challie bristled with righteous indignation.

"Why, you—" She slapped him, hard, snapping his head to one side, disgusted, more disgusted and ashamed of herself for her own licentious behavior. "I'm not your whore, Mr. Fontana, your tramp or your bimbo. I may be your servant for now, but I will never be at your beck and call for *that*," Challie snapped, pointing, unwilling to stare at his man-thing again.

His face turned red as the Devil's skin. She took a tentative step backward. Striking him was surely the final insult, certainly terminating her employment. Once Mrs. Tedesco heard . . . Challie might as well hop the next outgoing mice-infested cargo ship. She had enough money to get to the coast. By bus, not airplane.

Grandmama would've been happy to see her had she survived the fever, although no one else in the village would care whether Challie lived or died. She would sink to an outcast again, shunned because of her too-light complexion, because of her tainted bloodline.

Fighting back tears gathering in her eyes, she'd promised herself never to cry again once she arrived in the United States, not when she had a chance at a new life, a chance at happiness doing what she loved most. And she'd blown it. She'd slept with a white man, fallen in wistful love overnight like a teenaged girl after her first kiss. She'd destroyed all hope of future happiness. If she had any kind of luck, it was all bad from the moment she was conceived.

Her mother sure hadn't wanted her. She'd given up parental rights, left Challie's father to raise their daughter on his own. When he died, her grandmother had taken Challie in, given her the love she desired from a caring mother like the other children at her school. But Grandmama had grown old and her health had withered.

Challie had known for months her grandmother would join her son in the heavens and leave her granddaughter to face a life of lonely solitude in a village ravaged by famine, political unrest and disease. A place where her father had returned after living years in the United States, studying then practicing medicine. A small village he'd fought valiantly to save from devastation and death and the homeland he'd journeyed back to with a tiny baby in his arms, expecting her to stand tall and proud.

"I didn't mean for it to sound so intense, Challie. I'm sorry."

She blinked rapidly. Sorry, when she had attempted to slap him silly? Of course! She gave her head a sound shake, clearing the impossible thoughts brewing inside her brain. He was stuck in Montana with her. Guests arriving. Two more males. A pair of his friends. Fontana needed someone to cook and clean: a servant for the next week or more.

She may be a servant now, but not for long. She had her father's wishes and footsteps to follow. She had pride. She *would* stand tall.

But if she had the nerve, she'd have each one of the macho men throwing up. What did she have to lose now anyway? Absolutely nothing. She had everything to gain through talent and determination. Maybe her mother didn't want her, but somebody out there wanted Challie Baderleen to play concert piano. Somebody wanted to pay her money enough to send home to help the poor, the destitute and the dreamless.

Straightening her back, Challie lifted her chin defiantly, glowering. "Breakfast. Twenty minutes." She elbowed him aside and stomped toward the kitchen.

7

Donnie slapped the wall. A string of filthy curses, combining Italian, French and English followed. As always, he'd said or done some stupid macho shit.

He'd treated women like second-class citizens, exactly how Tedesco's cronies handled their wives or girlfriends. But Donnie hadn't intended to mistreat Challie. She'd misunderstood. The women he'd dealt with expected shitty behavior. Some suffered more than verbal abuse by their old man's egos. Most just lived with it. Unlike his French-born mother. Donnie loved her like crazy, even when she stood up to his possessively arrogant father. After forty-two years of marriage, Pops claimed that whenever he saw the rolling pin, he changed his way of thinking.

With those thoughts in mind, now what?

He wandered down the hall toward the kitchen. Challie was hard at work. Flames heated a skillet. On the counter sat a rolling pin. She quickly worked dough there. He swallowed. Attempting to seduce her would probably get his face slapped again or a rolling pin upside the head. Pops never did say how much it hurt. Mom wasn't nearly as strong-armed as Challie or as diligent with a target from a distance. A good twenty feet away, Donnie opted to stay right where he stood.

Someone banged at the front door.

Challie ignored the pounding, which meant she knew he was standing there. How? Not one floorboard creaked, and he was barefoot.

"I'll get it." Pissed at the intrusion, he snatched the door open.

"Glo-ry be!" the young woman said.

Something about her was recognizable. Big blond hair, big blue eyes, bigger tits. Pretty young thing. She wore a blue-plaid shirt cupping her breasts like hands, skin-tight faded jeans, snakeskin boots. Behind her, a badass red Dodge Ram sat out front.

"Sugah, I've been missin' you for eleven long months. A good racehorse stays on a cowgirl's mind."

Now what the hell was she talking about? Donnie's mouth dropped open. He followed her gaze and saw what she saw. "Uh, excuse me."

He closed the door and charged into the bedroom. Shorts didn't keep him from hanging out. He found jeans and zipped them as he raced back down the hall.

"Can I help you?"

"I know you couldn't've forgot all about me, honey. Jennifer Ann Ross." She opened the screen door, stepped inside.

The lightbulb flashed on. The rodeo. Roar of the crowd. A rocking nooner in the back of her grandfather's old station wagon. She was a brunette at the time. So why was he embarrassed? Any other day, Duke would be standing proudly at attention with a "pretty young filly," as Lawson had mentioned, offering her hot wares again.

"Is there something I can do for you, Jennifer? I'm pretty busy."

"I can sure think of one or two."

He heard a loud crash. In the kitchen? Was it the skillet or the rolling pin?

"Sorry. Didn't know you had company. Wouldn't've stopped by otherwise. Gramps thought you was up here all by your lonesome," Jennifer whispered. "Got the wife with you, cowboy?"

Sort of, but, yeah, he'd told Jennifer that he was married to keep things simple and distant.

"Hardly," Donnie heard and spun around.

"I'm the temporary maid. Would you like the job?" Challie asked. "I'll trade you. Granted, I've only ridden two horses in the last four years. A black stallion and a lame white nag."

Oh, shit. The sarcasm in her tone stung worse than a pesky horsefly. Donnie looked down to make sure she hadn't brought the rolling pin.

His jaw went slack. *Wait a minute. Is she comparing me to some idiot she fucked first?*

Every jealous molecule in his body divided. Lame white nag? He scowled. Her ass was hay and he the combine—once he got rid of Jennifer Ann here.

"Well, now, sounds to me like you're free as rattlesnake on the prairie again. Got a hoedown startin' this afternoon. You interested, cowboy? Shindig's s'posed to last all evenin'. 'Course, we ain't got to stay for long if you got somethin' better in mind, somethin' wilder. Like another hard ride. Doesn't have to be on stable ground either."

Jesus. She was bold as the day was long. "Actually, I'm unavailable. I've got a few things to take care of."

"I can wait."

"Before noon."

"Figures. Maybe another time." Jennifer Ann shrugged. She turned her back, walked off and let the screen door swing shut behind her with a loud bang.

"Lame white nag?" Donnie said in a deadly voice as he spun around.

The front door slammed with gale-wind force. He threw the latch.

Challie folded her arms, stood her ground until he advanced on her. With menacing forward progress, Donnie matched her backward steps down the hall. She started to say something, but evidently thought again and clamped her mouth shut.

Good damn thing. He was in no mood for lip. No mood for . . .

She tried to dart into the bedroom.

He caught her arm on the fly and hauled her back. No way could she run from him. She had no place to hide. He'd chase her ass across Horse Prairie, if necessary. Lame white nag.

Pressing her back into the narrow alcove, Donnie wedged his knee between her legs, had her off the floor or standing on tiptoes.

She slapped at him, but he snagged her wrists, cuffed them to the wall above her head—like a trussed hare—and held on with one of his hands.

"Still thinking about your black stallion now?" His voice sounded oddly different to his own ears, filled with hostility, laced with acute jealousy. "Who is he?"

Icy contempt glared back.

"Was he a good fuck? Better than me? Does he live in Phoenix?"

At this moment, he didn't care what answers she gave and, if she did answer, Donnie didn't hear it. His ears roared with hot blood, anger steeped in jealousy.

He raised his knee higher, ground it against her body in undulating circles. She whimpered. And began the ride. Oh, yeah. He helped. With the scent of her frustrations wafting around them, he helped a lot more. Her breaths came in shallow bursts. Donnie yanked her ugly gray tent up to her waist. He found his favorite hot mark. Challie swallowed, panting. But something he'd never seen before shone in her eyes. Something that shook him to the roots of his hair.

He shrugged it off an instant later.

Donnie unzipped his jeans and pulled out his taming rod. Tugging her panties aside, he pressed the head to her heat. "Was it better than this?"

His nostrils flared, he inhaled the fragrance of her sex and penetrated slowly. Watching her eyes glaze over, Donnie released her wrists. He had Challie exactly where he wanted, sizzling with need, burning with desire, pliant.

He gripped her hips and lifted her body several inches. Her nails sank into his shoulders as he pressed her down, inch by thick inch until he filled her, hissing out a breath between his teeth. Donnie repeated each movement with gentle force. She was sopping wet, slippery, but tight.

Her strong legs closed around him. He pumped harder, bending his knees, straightening, banging her against the wall. Banging hard. She climaxed. The tumultuous orgasm squeezed his cock in a greedy fist. He plundered her mouth in mid-scream, but he held back an accompanying explosive nut, started over before she caught her next breath.

Knowing the very spot to push her over the edge, he used his fingers in a joint assault. Donnie worked her until she came unglued, until he could no longer contain the quaking building inside his own body.

It wanted freedom.

"Nobody touches you. Nobody but me makes love to you. Nobody!"

He drove upward, hard, nailed Challie to the wall and unleashed the power he'd harnessed like a mighty beast.

They detonated.

"Goddamn it!" he roared, pounding his fist against the wall.

* * *

Challie had trouble catching her breath, trying to hold on to Donovan's head, shoulders, anything to keep from dissolving, her orgasm in full-consuming bloom, stimulated by the man holding her imprisoned.

My God.

Spent, her legs slipped down to his sides, but she stayed impaled solidly in what she imagined resembled a dangling, limp puppet or ragdoll. He continued thrusting hard.

Minutes passed before he lifted his head, sweating, smelling utterly male. He backed away, carried her to his bedroom and followed her down to the mattress without losing intimate contact.

"We need to get this thing off."

She assumed he referred to her jumper since he pulled frantically at the garment.

"I'm not finished with you yet. Have to touch you everywhere, every inch. Brand you. Raise up."

Brand?

When she didn't move, he dragged the jumper over her head then sacrificed another pair of panties with one yank.

"I'm not yours for the taking," she said. "Or for your hot poker."

"The hell you say. You heard me. M-i-n-e. Mine. I'm just as possessive as my dad. Nobody touches what belongs to me."

"As in chattel?" she argued. America was no different from her homeland. Women were property even here! She shoved at him with no effect then sucked in air.

His man-thing was hard. Pulsing. Scorching.

Not again. No.

But his eyes glared a surefire warning that blatantly ordered, "The hell you say."

Minutes later, weak, slumberous and barely able to move, Challie understood the term "well-pleasured."

She opened her eyes, feeling the bed shift under Donovan's

weight. He wrung out the washcloth soaking in a ceramic basin and bathed her skin. At last, he smoothed it between her legs. The heat eased the slight tenderness from their lovemaking. Yes, making love is what he'd called it. Not that nasty-sounding F-word, not screwing, not sex. Making love. He had an insatiable appetite for the delicious act.

When he finished cleansing her most private possession, he pressed a kiss to each of her thighs and licked his tongue over her sensitivity.

"Stop," she said.

"I like the taste of you."

"You like the taste of any willing female of the species."

"Challie—"

She held her hand up to stop what she knew was an exclusive male retort. "Sex is what men enjoy most of all about life. You just happen to be a man with a special talent that women can enjoy too. I don't have a problem with your . . . your loose behavior, Donovan. I also don't have any expectations of you."

"Do you have expectations about anything at all?"

He sounded displeased for some reason. "Of course, I do."

"Just what the hell are they since I'm not included?"

Displeased was too mild to describe his tone. Slightly angry fit better. But why? He'd gotten what he wanted, a willing woman who held no strings of obligation.

"The symphony. I'm a pianist. The only thing I've ever wanted badly is to be recognized, loved for what I do as a concert pianist, for who I am."

He huffed without amusement in his eyes, then he stared back into hers, frowning. "Was it you I heard playing at the Tedescos'? I'd stopped by there to pick up papers for Paul a couple of times, thought somebody left the CD player on."

She had no idea anyone other than Hattie had heard her music.

The Tedescos owned a lovely, restored Steinway Model A

grand. She'd practiced whenever possible, as much as possible. Hattie's old player piano wasn't nearly as fine-tuned as the Tedescos' satin, ebony-finished instrument. On the other hand, Challie's life wasn't worth a dime and all her dreams would go up in smoke if the lady of the house ever found out that she'd dared to practice on their antique.

"You won't tell them, will you?" she asked, nervous. As long as Donovan sealed his lips about their short-term escapade and her piano playing, she would stay gainfully employed.

"Tell the Tedescos you can pound the daylights out of a set of eighty-eights? You bet your sweet ass I will. Paul is chairman emeritus of the Phoenix Symphony. He'll flip inside—"

"No!" Challie sat upright.

Hattie had told her about Mr. Tedesco's tenure with the Phoenix Symphony. Challie needed more time to practice, time to plan. She was an unknown, unestablished pianist with an ear for music and tone. Fingers able to blaze across a keyboard with ease.

She'd taught herself to play on a broken-down Steinway at school while listening to the vinyl records her schoolteacher owned. Miss Tamor knew she had an extraordinarily talented pupil, a musical genius, and worked with her. She'd taught Challie as much as she knew, taught her to read music.

The final gift from her father was the refurbished Baldwin he'd found for sale. She'd cried for a week, but she'd wept longer and harder after his death. She'd practiced every day for hours. At her father's memorial service, she'd played two of his favorite melodies. Challie was eleven years old at the time.

"Why not?"

"It's complicated. Please, don't say anything."

"But—"

"Please, Donovan."

He cupped her chin with one hand, frowning. "Are you sure? With Paul—"

"I'm absolutely sure." Although, by the look in his eyes, she wasn't sure he believed she had any talent whatsoever.

Someone banged on the front door.

"Why is it every time I try to have a decent conversation with you there's always an interruption?"

Challie fell back on the bed, rolled to her side and lifted an eyebrow. "Jennifer Ann back for the hoedown?"

He pinched her butt. "Get dressed. It might be one of the workers. Maybe the foreman."

8

Donovan's hearty laughter filtered into the bathroom. Challie unbraided what was left of the French plait then brushed her hair with a vengeance. Taming the wild mane . . . Good Lord, she'd forgotten about the biscuits, rather, the bricks by now. She hurried toward the kitchen, but Donovan caught hold of her arm.

He introduced her to Ray, Mr. Tedesco's eldest son. She had no idea this man was so much older than the Tedesco's other children. Slightly taller than his father's height, Ray was huskier, with a full head of dark brown hair. Kindness sparkled in his intense brown eyes.

"It's very nice to meet you, *bwa* . . . uh . . . sir."

He tipped his cowboy hat then removed it altogether. "Likewise."

Donovan frowned. "His name's Ray."

Hattie would flip if she heard her niece use his first name. Challie smiled.

"Does Meredith keep her piano tuned? Challie here—"

"Excuse me. Would you like to have breakfast with Mr.

Fontana?" She stared at the floor when Donovan scowled. "I'm making eggs, bacon, homemade biscuits."

"Sounds like a winner," Ray said. His voice was soothing, unlike his father's gruff tone. "Since Meredith and the kids are gone, I've had to cook for myself. Get tired of microwaved oatmeal."

Challie hurried into the kitchen. And just in time. The oven was smoking. She yanked the burnt bricks out, dumped them into the trash and opened the window, waving her hands.

"Can she cook?" she heard Ray whisper.

"She's a dynamite one. I had her tied up earlier. Forgot she'd started breakfast."

Challie groaned under her breath. *Please don't say any more.* "Would you like your eggs scrambled, fried, poached—"

"Whatever's easiest for you," Donovan said. "You need help?"

"No!" She bit her tongue for barking the word, appalled.

"Spitfire," he said loud enough for the world to hear. "About the piano."

"Would you like grits or potatoes?" Good Lord. Donovan would not let up. She never should've told him about her dreams. "I can fix corned beef hash if you'd rather not eat bacon."

"Whichever," Donovan said. "Make it easy on yourself." He turned back to his guest. "I want her to see your place, give her a chance to try out—"

"How about a big omelet?" Challie said loudly. "Cheese, tomatoes, onions, pep—"

"Damn it, I'll fix breakfast!" Donovan snapped. He swung around suddenly, fists at his waist, eyes narrowed. "You can talk to Ray about playing the piano."

"You had no right to mention—" She flinched at her own hot-tempered comeback.

"Time-out," Ray said, looking from one to the other, "before this squabble goes any further."

"I'm sorry, Misters Tedesco and Fontana." Any more strikes against her and this job was history. She went back to her duties.

"Let's step outside," Ray said. "Cool off."

The screen door slammed shut behind the two men.

Nervous, Challie broke the first three yolks when she had intended to make homemade Benedict Arnold eggs. No, he was the infamous traitor. Benedict's eggs. No . . . Who cared? Flustered, worried about her future, she'd planned to impress the men with food, make them forget about her outburst. Now they were stuck with the regular, and revolting, scrambled mess. Or omelets.

She put two skillets on burners then started chopping, shredding, pulverizing everything that looked good.

By the time Donovan and the ranch owner wandered back inside, the table was set.

"Coffee?" Challie asked, smiling.

"For the love of God. There's only three of us. You cooked enough for an army battalion," Donovan said.

A gallon of juice, milk and four types of jam were ready for consumption. She'd placed the basket overflowing with hot biscuits on the sideboard. An enormous turkey platter, containing two skillet-sized fat omelets sided with crispy bacon, corned beef hash and a slab of ham, overpowered the center of the table.

"Breakfast is for you and your guest," Challie said, pouring coffee.

"I don't know about anybody else," Ray said. He pulled out the nearest chair. "But damned if I won't make a big dent in everything here. Meredith put me on a diet last month." He smiled broadly and grabbed four biscuits. "Cat's gone."

"Can I get you anything else?"

Donovan stood in place. "You can sit and eat with us. We're not invalids."

"Oh, I forgot butter." She hurried to the refrigerator. "Can't have biscuits without butter and honey."

"Have a seat, Challie." He dragged the chair back.

"Yeah," Ray said. "Join us. The cook should always eat with the crew."

"I'm really not supposed—"

"New day." Donovan pressed her down into the chair. He found another plate in the cabinet and silverware for himself. "Now, it's time to dig in."

Ray led them to the back door of his home. He said the family rarely used the front entrance. It and the deck were on the opposite side of the house, facing west and the beautiful mountain range.

"Those are the Bitteroot Mountains," Donovan said. "We'll drive up to Lemhi Pass sometime this week so you can see where two explorers—"

"Lewis and Clark," Challie announced. She'd loved studying history almost as much as she loved playing the piano. "They started in Missouri. The expedition lasted from 1803 to 1806. They never would have made it very far without the Shoshone/Hidatsa woman, Sacagawea. She was familiar with the native tribes and aided the explorers in translations. She married a French Canadian, Toussaint Charbonneau. They had a son named Jean Baptiste."

"Damn," Donovan said.

"Son of a bitch," Ray added, chuckling.

"Captain Clark also kept a slave. His manservant's name was York, a prisoner for life."

After a quiet moment, Donovan asked, "Were you ever a teacher?"

"Never," Challie replied, staring at the ground. She had tutored three young people who were unafraid of her. They lived in the same village as Amobi.

"No way in hell I'd remember all those details."

"I learn quickly," she said. "Important details stick with me." All details, really. Some people would say she was born with a photographic memory.

"Names and dates are my worst. Mom has to remind me of Pops's birthday. When's your birthday, Challie?" Donovan asked.

That was a part of history lost to her. Her father had admitted not knowing the exact date, but he knew the month and year of her birth. "I was a March child. What a lovely room, Mr. Ray."

"How many times do I have to remind you his name is simply Ray? And how can you consider a mudroom *lovely*?"

Sighing, the ranch owner said, "Let's move on."

The next room was the play area for adults and children; pinball machines, toys and a pool table were the main clutter. From there they moved to a fabulous open kitchen then an impressive family/dining room. A gallery of floor-to-ceiling windows framed the mountain range. Warmed by radiant heating, maple-colored hardwood floors ran throughout the ranch house, Ray explained. Kitchen cabinets and built-in bookshelves closely matched the wood grain. Leather covered most of the furniture, and above the massive, stone fireplace hung an elk's head. Family pictures were everywhere: smiling faces, togetherness, friends, hugs, joy.

Challie felt the same old pinch of jealousy seeing genuine love float through this house—this home—on one constant wave. She chastised herself silently. Her grandmother had given her unconditional love like her father before his death.

As they rounded the corner, she filled her lungs with air. Forget the big-screen television, Challie zeroed in on the black grand piano. "Ooh," she crooned quietly. Wiggling her fingers, she'd love to get them busy on the keys.

"Want to see the rest of the house?" Ray asked. "The master suite is particularly remarkable."

How long had she stood in place, staring? "Yes, of course. Such a beautiful home."

"Meredith worked as an interior designer until we moved to Montana." He started down the hallway then stopped. "Coming?"

"Challie?" Donovan queried.

She blinked rapidly, still mesmerized by the piano's beauty. "I'd love to play the room." She shook her head. "*See* . . . which room?"

Ray smiled. "The master. We'll come back here right after."

The suite was spacious, spectacular, with the same paramount view as the main family area. French doors led to their private deck housing the hot tub and sauna. But their lavatory, rather, his and her bathrooms and closets put together, was nearly as large as Hattie's apartment.

"Meredith believes all rooms should be comfortable living space filled with custom-made furnishings, including the bathrooms," Ray said, opening an enormous armoire filled with fluffy towels and toiletries. "She's got this thing for wood."

"If ever I'm rich or famous, I'll contact your wife to decorate my home, but on a much smaller scale," Challie said.

Donovan moved to her side. "Yeah, big homes can be a pain to care for."

"My one-person household won't require much space, though," Challie replied. She shrugged her shoulders when Donovan frowned. "Even if my aunt would like to live with me." She ran her fingers over the black granite countertop, which coordinated with the bathroom's décor.

"The shower connects our bathrooms. Dual entrances, steam, multiple showerheads, scheduler for individual heat, etcetera. As you can see," Ray said, "Meredith opted to have a soaking tub on her side. Why, I don't know, since we have a hot tub."

"Woman thing," Donovan replied. "Challie takes long baths alone."

She hissed loud enough for him to hear, drawing a wicked grin.

"I see," Ray said, glancing from Donovan to her. "Shall we move back to the family room?"

Thanks to Donovan's big mouth. She elbowed his ribs when Ray went out the door.

Flinching, he whispered, "Why the hell did—"

"You know why!" Challie walked off.

In the family room, Ray pointed to the piano. "Donnie says you play."

Darn him. "A little."

"Meredith is pretty good. Tina bought the Spinet—"

"Steinway. Circa 1886."

Lifting an eyebrow, he said, "Exactly. She bought the Steinway for Meredith's enjoyment when we visit. The wife would like our daughters to learn when they can sit in one place long enough. They'd rather ride horses with dear-old dad." His face glowed with a broad smile, obviously proud of his children. "Want to give it a try? Our Petrof is better."

One of the finest, a Model I. So much money in one instrument. But she'd love to lay her fingers on the keys and bit her bottom lip to hide her smile. "I really shouldn't."

"You've been itching to get to this piano ever since you saw it. Go ahead. Show me what you can do."

How could she resist? Challie climbed the pedestal to the grand. She ran her fingers down the ivory keys. It was beautiful. Sitting, she scooted the bench closer, rubbed her hands on her gray jumper, then fisted and stretched her fingers. She hadn't played in a week.

Sucking in a nervous breath, she asked, "What would you like to hear?"

"I don't know any classical tunes," Donovan said. "Ray, got a piece you're impressed with these days?"

"Classical? I was under the assumption she played the modern works like Meredith."

Embarrassed, Challie said, "I love several genres, but classical is my favorite."

"Your choice, then."

Donnie had his doubts about the Great Pretender, including her admission to playing at Paul's home. He'd admitted having no real knowledge of her abilities. Anybody—even he—could bang out a mean "Chopsticks" melody.

He'd been to all of one concert, the one and only time he'd worn a penguin suit. The pianist was good. The audience had naturally applauded, no standing ovation. But the player's qualifications fell short compared to Challie's dazzling talent. Obviously, Ray was awed. His mouth hung open, his eyes bulging in amazement. Earlier, before breakfast, he'd questioned whether she had any talent at all.

Challie would have brought down the roof performing on stage. Her fingers skimmed the keyboard as if they were part of the ivory. Totally into it, she rocked and swayed to the music.

"She's good, isn't she?" Donnie asked.

"Sshh." Ray leaned back on the leather sofa, his legs stretched out, his hands propped behind his head, his eyes closed. He kept one booted foot in motion with the downbeat.

Minutes later when Challie struck the final chord, Ray got to his feet, clapping loudly. "Bravo! Bravo!"

Cowboy or not, he and Meredith had attended the same concert with Paul, Tina and Donnie. Evidently, his love for classical music hadn't changed.

Donnie puffed up prouder than the dominant, crowing

rooster, knowing he would soon marry Phoenix's bright new star. There was no doubt in his mind Challie would accept his proposal. Weren't all chicks into marriage and nesting? The single women he'd dated were always hinting. Meeting their parents, whom he avoided at all cost. Bridal showers, needing a man's opinion on what he'd like to see a woman wearing. His answer was "nothing." Weddings. He had attended one in his life. And baby showers. He knew how babies were made and that they cost big ducats in the long run.

"Good Christ. Has Dad heard her play? Of course, he has." Ray started toward the kitchen. "I'm calling him right now. The old man was holding out on me, damn him."

Fear rose steadily in Challie's eyes. Why, Donnie had no idea. "Hold up. Paul doesn't know."

Ray picked up the remote phone. "What? Oh, this is too good. Love throwing the old man new curves. Let's see, speed dial number . . . I hate this mess. Meredith has everybody on the planet written here. Not in alphabetical order." He ran his finger down a tablet.

"But don't you think my . . . don't you think Challie ought to have some say-so? I mean, it's her life you're talking about here. Don't you think telling Paul should be her bomb, if she chooses to drop it?"

It took a few moments for Ray to replace the remote. "You're right. Although, I can't understand why she'd want to wait and not audition now. Of course, she's in Montana at the moment." He paced back and forth along a six-foot path, rubbing his jaw, looking like the cat that caught the mouse, planning a major game he anticipated winning. "When you're ready, Challie, I can manipulate a few channels. It's not easy to go it alone with the officers and board, even the conductor. Or with my father."

Donnie winked at Challie. Her shoulders lost the stiff tension.

Thank you, she mouthed.

She had her sassy ways, but when she blushed and shyly looked away, Donnie's heartbeat raced at maximum velocity.

Donovan had maneuvered her into sleeping with him last night. With fear.

"You lied to me," Challie said.

"It wasn't a lie. I did see a mouse."

"Where?"

He grinned. "Outside."

She punched his arm. "I can't keep sleeping with you. What if your guests or—"

He kissed her. Goodness. He had the power to erase her thoughts, have her legs spreading bonelessly wide, craving for his body to be inside hers. She loved the taste of him, the feel of him. Everything about Donovan Marcel Fontana.

She came to her senses quickly, reining in the searing lust he always invoked, broke away from his warm, teasing lips and tongue. "Mr. Fontana, I will not be seduced by you any longer. I have to get up, bathe and make breakfast. It's already seven thirty."

"Donovan. Yeah, but my batteries have recharged. A snack will hold me for a while," he murmured and latched onto her left breast with his teeth, sending high-voltage shock waves through her senses.

Arching toward him, she laced her fingers in his hair. She knew this was wrong, but she was unable to stop his progress. Donovan slid between her legs, kissing a starburst path down to her belly. He licked the button to her existence, blew a hot breath, spreading heat through her physical and mental being, causing her muscles to go lax, her core to quiver, her mind to go blank.

But when her stomach growled loudly, for a moment he

stopped his exploration. The second rumble brought his head up at lightning speed.

"For Christ's sake." His eyes narrowed to the thinnest slits she'd ever seen. "You hardly ate any breakfast yesterday, you nibbled at lunch and last night you claimed you weren't hungry."

"I don't need much to survive on."

"Survive?" He crawled off her, then the bed. "You're starving yourself!"

"One meal a day is plenty," she replied, snappish. "I've survived on much less." Here they go again, arguing. She hated arguments.

"Get dressed."

"I'm taking a bath," Challie sassed.

"Fine. Bathe then get dressed."

"I'm not *your* slave, Mr. Fontana."

"Donovan. I'll paddle your ass if you don't get your buns into the bathroom so we can eat."

Yanking on the top sheet, Challie finally got it free. She wrapped it around her body. "Breakfast. Twenty minutes." She stomped away. "Men."

Spiteful, she took an extra ten minutes longer. Challie continued mumbling as she came out of the bathroom. "Gets on my last nerve." She dumped her nightwear on the bed. "I'm never sleeping with another man. Don't care if all the mice in the world are under, over or—"

She sniffed the air. Her stomach growled noisily. Challie came to a dead stop. Donovan was at the stove, barefoot, wearing baggy jeans. Every lean muscle in his back stretched, tightened and stretched again.

The table was set for two. Juice, milk. When he swung around, their gazes collided.

"Breakfast," Donovan said. She loved his smile. "Hope you like boiled eggs."

"My favorite." Cooking was her job. "Um, sorry, I should have made you breakfast first, before bathing."

He pulled out two chairs. "I might be a chauvinist, but I'm not a helpless invalid. Sit. Toast got a little dark. Bacon, too."

"I like my bacon crunchy."

Except this stuff was scorched. He'd scraped the charred bread and swathed it in butter. When she cracked the egg, the white oozed over the fragile shell onto her plate. Challie swallowed several times, her gag reflexes at full throttle. She could do this. Donovan had made her breakfast, had done more for her than any man. Other than her father.

She tore the toast into small pieces for soaking. Each slimy bite slid down her throat slower than the last. "This is really good."

"Yeah, it is. Chef Fontana didn't know he could cook beyond a burger or two. Coffee?"

"Sure." She started out of her chair. If she could just make it to the sink.

"Sit."

Challie closed her eyes, begging her stomach to keep her cookies . . . er . . . soggy toast where it belonged. When Donovan turned his back, she made good use of several paper napkins. "I didn't realize how hungry I was. Thank you."

"Tell you what," he said, filling her mug. "From now on, I'll fix breakfast every other day, giving you a break."

She swallowed again. She couldn't take another meal of his cooking. "This is my job, but I'll switch lunches with you." Anybody could make sandwiches, no stove necessary.

"Deal. As a bonus I made lunch already. We'll borrow one of the four-wheelers and toss a line a ways down Bloody Dick. Even on private property, we need to stay undercover without licenses. Have you ever stream fished?"

There were no lakes near her village. "A few times," Challie replied, keeping her eyes on the darkest liquid she'd ever seen.

Her grandmother had taught her the woman's way to catch dinner.

She sipped from the mug. Gracious. This tar would poison all the prairie mice in Montana. Even she knew the coffeepot used filters. Breakfast was far from perfect, but Donovan had made the effort to please her. The simple gesture brought a smile to her lips. "Mmm. Perfect."

"I'll run through the shower. We can head out when you're finished eating."

The second he turned the corner, Challie dumped the gritty contents of her coffee mug down the drain and trashed breakfast.

9

Donnie picked up the ranch phone on the third ring. Most of Horse Prairie was a cell phone dead area. "Yeah."

"So, how have the happy newlyweds done these last couple of days?"

Oh, shit. Paul. "Uh . . ."

"Consummation complete? Everything in order? I was able to hold off the cops, told them I sent you out of town for a few days with your fiancée. They're waiting to interrogate you and Challie."

"Um . . ." What the hell was he supposed to tell him?

"Don't make a liar out of me, Donnie. Silence is not always golden."

He fell into the nearest chair. Raking his fingers through his hair, Donnie said, "Everything's cool, Paul, with a few minor technicalities I'm handling."

"What minor technicalities?"

"Well," he said quietly, looking down the hall, making sure Challie wasn't within earshot. "We haven't signed the license."

Dead silence filled the phone line. "Have you or have you not completed the ceremony?"

He hadn't found the balls to broach the ultimate question. Challie was talking about living in her own house—with her auntie. "Not quite," Donnie replied lamely.

"What the hell are you talking about? What the hell are you waiting for? Christmas? The cops will have your nuts crystallized and hung from the office tree by then. Your holiday season will not be in good cheer."

"It'll get done. No problem." He heard a door close down the hall. "It'll happen. I gotta run, Paul, and make good."

"Call my private line the moment you've signed the papers."

Donnie stared at the receiver after hearing a click. Tedesco never cut anybody any slack. All business, no bullshit, subtle intimidation. He'd surely make good on a threat.

As for Challie, Donnie had made some headway, just not enough to pop the question. Yet. Tonight he'd ask. Maybe. And just maybe she'd answer in the affirmative. If not . . . the thought had his body sweating BBs, but seeing Challie dressed in tight jeans and blue blouse had Duke on the rise.

"Are we ready?"

Oh, hell, yeah. Just not for fishing.

"Or is there something Mr. Tedesco wants you to do instead?"

How the devil did she hear from the back of the house? She'd hear mice squeak a mile away. Donnie shoved off the sofa and went to the kitchen table. "Lunch box. Gourmet," he said, holding up the day pack. "Four-wheeler's in the equipment barn. So're the rods and reels. Spinners, too, if you don't fly-fish."

"I don't." The woman never hid her sour faces.

"I'll teach you how it's done. It's all in the wrist action." He held the screen door open.

"I'd rather not."

"Yeah, well, we fish for our own meals," Donnie said, chucking her chin. "But, I don't mind sharing all I have with you."

Ike trotted over to Challie's side. "Can he come?"

"Absolutely not. He likes to splash and swim. We'll have to hightail out of here without him watching. Stupid dog'll follow us otherwise."

"He's not stupid. Ike, stay."

Damned if he didn't lie down on the deck under the table. She had a way with animals. Except for Bullwinkle.

"Why are you carrying a gun? Hate guns."

"Insurance." He hoped like hell they wouldn't run into the loping moose again. It'd take a helluva lot more than the .38 tucked in the back of his jeans.

It was a beautiful, clear day. Not a cloud in sight.

Arms wrapped tightly around his waist, Challie hung on for dear life while Donnie raced the four-wheeler down the dusty road, fishtailing and spewing pebbles in all directions. When he waved at the neighbors speeding in a Ford three-quarter ton going the opposite direction, she gripped him tighter. Donnie gave the racer more gas.

He stopped near the bridge. Rushing water moved down the stream then leveled smooth as glass. Pockets of hungry fish swam in this creek.

"Is the water cold or warm?" Challie asked.

"Chilly as always. I don't recommend wading unless it's necessary." He slung the day pack over his shoulder, untied the rods and handed one to Challie. "Do you know—"

"I've fished before, don't need instruction."

"Sounds like a challenge. I'm game if you are." She nodded sassily. Fishing was his second-best pastime. Nothing would ever top sex. "We'll start here, work our way downstream. Stay close. If we get out of eyeshot, follow the creek back up to the bike, or holler, especially if you need help.

"Lawson said the trout were biting good. To make the contest worthwhile, keepers must be a minimum fifteen inches. We'll see who catches the best. For your information, I yanked out an eighteen-inch bruiser last August."

"Boasting is not very becoming of you," Challie said.

"Truth always hurts in the end." He leaned down, kissed her hard. "Winner names the price and terms." Damn, she tasted good. He went in for a second taster, but Challie backed away.

"And when you lose?"

"Won't."

"Braggart," Challie mumbled. She tucked a plastic bag into her back pocket.

An hour later, Donnie shouted, "Come to papa!"

The big brown fought like a bucking bronco, up in the air, down into water, up again. Damned if he'd let this bugger go easily. The beast was in the winner's circle, *the* winner. No way would Challie catch anything this large on a spinner.

He found her upstream in a wide pool he'd fished earlier. "What are you doing?"

Her rod was propped against a shade tree. Bent over in thigh-deep water, Challie said, "Quiet."

"Are you playing? Or is the tub at home not deep enough for bathing?"

"Leave me alone. Go fish."

Fine. Great. "Another hour and we do lunch at the bridge. Don't holler for me when you slip into a hole." Women. Can't take them nowhere without back talk. Should've left her ass at home. Yeah, right, when he had plans to nail her on the prairie.

Donnie didn't get far when he heard gunshot echoing through the valley. Rifle? They sure as hell didn't need stray bullets whizzing by their heads.

"Challie!" He tore across the unstable ground, over rocks, swinging rod and day pack. "Challie!"

She raced toward him, thank God. "Donovan, did you shoot at something?"

"No. It's rare to hear gunfire outside hunting season. Maybe one of the ranch hands scared off a skunk or porcupine. It happens."

"I hate guns. Can we go back? I'm done fishing."

Sure. He'd won the bet. She'd have to accept the terms of his win. Sex in the country. Donnie grinned, lifting his catch by the gills. "Told you I was king."

"That's it?"

"One, but it's enough for the championship. What'd you catch? A sack of minnows?" he asked, staring at her bag. "Which means, I win. As for my terms—"

Challie dragged one from the plastic attached to her belt loops. "This is fish for cooking. You lose, Donovan Marcel Fontana. I caught this one, the smaller of the two, when you finally left me in peace."

Holy shit. He'd have to get a tape measure. This monster might take Lawson's title. How big was the second shark? "By hand?" he asked, incredulous. Well, shit. This just blew his original game plan.

"There's no better fishing than a woman's way."

"You must be part Indian. Chippewa? An ex-foreman's wife is Chippewa Cree. I've seen her catch by hand. Slick as shit. She rubs their bellies. You did the same?"

Another gunshot broke the silence, closer this time.

"What the hell?"

"It's near the ranch house," Challie said. She almost left him in the dust running back toward the four-wheeler.

Less than three minutes later, they rounded the corner. He came to a sliding stop when Charlie Lawson fired again. Ike yelped then fell silent.

Challie screamed loud enough to stampede cattle. Donnie tried to stop her, but she hopped off the four-wheeler and ran toward the downed dog anyway. No doubt, Ike was dead.

Holstering his rifle on the saddle, Lawson dismounted the

big paint he always rode. He lit a cigarette as usual. As sweaty as the horse was, the cowboy must've chased the hound halfway across Horse Prairie.

Challie fell to her knees beside her favorite dog. She stroked the animal's head. Donnie knelt and wrapped his arm around her shoulders. She looked up at Lawson. Not one tear had fallen from her eyes. Rage filled them as she shrugged Donnie's arm away, stood and faced the cowboy.

Donnie got to his feet as well. Something fierce, something sinister shined in her gray eyes.

"Do you still have your gun, Mr. Fontana?"

"Donovan, and, yeah, but it stays with me." No way he'd let her commit murder, even if the cowboy deserved the death penalty. "Why?"

"Because I want you to shoot him." She kicked dirt and stones at Lawson's boots. "Shoot him like he did this defenseless hound!"

Lawson stepped back, tipping his black hat off his forehead. Actually, he appeared fearful. Not of Donnie, but of the little woman who advanced on him. "I caught him swingin' again. He's a stray mutt anyhow."

"I don't give a damn!" Challie shouted. "Shoot him, Donovan. He deserves it more than any stray mutt, the *mutt*."

When she jabbed her finger at Lawson's chest, Donnie wrapped his arms around her body and lifted Challie off the ground. She kicked, squirmed worse than a wild child in full-blown tantrum. He'd have shin bruises for weeks.

Tossing the half-smoked cigarette on the ground, Lawson said, "Get her out of here, Fontana. I don't need no damn woman problems. If you can't tame her, let me show you how."

He set Challie down. Holding her wrist, Donnie restrained her behind him and stepped up to Lawson, got in his face up and personal like. "If you so much as lay one hand on her, country boy," he replied in a no-nonsense tone, "or even look at her stupid, you'd best bend over, pucker up and kiss your ass good-bye."

Mumbling under his breath, Lawson stomped away. The paint danced in place as he mounted the horse. Lawson reared him like the Lone Ranger and galloped away.

"What about Ike? We can't leave him here," Challie said, panting. "We have to bury him."

"Go inside." He had a gentle hold on her wrist. "I'll take care of it."

"I want to help. I buried Porky."

She didn't elaborate, but Donnie figured the animal had meant a lot to her and had tragically died somehow by the way she'd clutched her fist to her heart. "Let me get a shovel."

"And a box, so bugs and other animals won't get to him. Something to protect him." She blinked away the mistiness in her eyes.

Ike's burial became a major production. Donnie dug the grave near Challie's bedroom. Ceremony, prayers and the cross he'd fabricated with two wooden stakes nailed together. She printed Ike's name with a black marker pen.

The afternoon crept by slowly. Challie fried fish, cooked red rice and steamed spinach for his midday meal. She skipped eating, skipped conversation and bathed again. The bedroom became her safe haven.

Donnie wondered how long she would grieve. He'd checked on her at three thirty. She was sitting on the bed, staring out of the window, staring at Ike's grave site. He checked again at four. She hadn't moved. At half past the hour, he carried Tuxedo into the room. Challie sat in the same place and, for the fourth time, she didn't acknowledge his presence.

Frustrated now, missing her sass and spunk, he scooped her into his arms, stretched her out in bed with Tuxedo and climbed in beside her. He rocked her for a good long while. She'd taken this harder than he had expected, and she hadn't shed a tear.

Funny how he didn't get a boner. Any other time, he'd have stripped her naked within seconds, obliterate the pain she was suffering with persuasive, gentle enticement.

"I need you," Challie said seconds later.

Duke woke.

"I need you to erase my heartache," she added. "My terms for out-fishing you. You said winner names the terms."

Donnie chuckled to himself. She'd beaten him fair and square. By hand, no less. And she'd ruined his greatest plan to save his butt. Next time. He'd honor her request today with playful teasing and tender lovemaking.

"Hard. I want it hard. Fast. I want you to drive the ache from my heart, body and my mind," she demanded, rolling to her back.

O-kay. Whatever his lady wanted, his lady got.

"I want—"

He kissed the words from her lips, delved his tongue deep into her mouth. Forget stripping her. She wore loose shorts, flimsy top, no bra. Donnie freed Duke. He was ready for the raid. In due time. He worked Challie relentlessly. And it wasn't long before she was sopping wet. Ready, begging.

Yanking her shorts and panties aside, he drove inside her tightness like a stud racehorse mounted his mare, pinned her to the bed with his body on the first powerful invasion, took her breath away. But she matched him stroke for stroke, egging him on. When he pounded, she met him with equal animal ferocity. The growl he heard was not his own. It was fierce, angry.

She flipped him to his back, continued on a violent path, rising, dropping, rising again. She wouldn't let up, wouldn't let him break rhythm. Tossing her head back, she groaned, deep, resonating, a sound edging more animal than human. When she looked into his eyes again, something wild glinted in the gray depths. She rode him harder, goaded him with tight squeezes and teasing relaxation.

In the next instant, a sudden spasm stunned his dick to the edge of release.

"Jesus! Jesus!" And he nearly came off the bed.

Rearing up, Donnie shoved his hands under her thighs. He raised Challie then dropped her down his stout length, over and over again until she splintered, screaming at the top of her lungs, burying her face against his neck.

They were far from finished. Each successive snap punctuated his libido. Rolling Challie beneath him, he continued pounding with punishing strokes at maximum velocity. Until he emptied.

She'd drained him, took all he had to offer—all she wanted—and then some.

Minutes later, hot, sweaty and believing he'd hurt her with uncontrolled savagery, Donnie started to withdraw slowly.

"Stay," she ordered. "Stay inside me. I need more."

More? He thought he'd fucked her brains out already. Well, she'd screwed him blind. "Give me a minute."

For two days, Donovan kept her on her back or above him, constantly in his arms. Except when she'd insisted on bathing and the times they'd both required nourishment. It took that long for Challie to slip totally out from under the blue, what Donovan called, funk, no matter how hard he'd worked at putting a smile on her face. A smile for one reason only.

But he truly was making her fall in love with him more than she already had. So foolish for a tramp lacking status or future. Once they returned to Arizona, he'd forget all about the Tedesco maid. He'd move on to the next woman willing to satisfy his insatiable prowess.

In less than a month, she'd digressed from a *damned* Orphan Annie to illegal immigrant to the belittling honor of alien tramp. Her grandmother was surely spinning the wooden casket in her grave. As for her father, she'd shamed him beyond redemption. For two days she'd thought only of her pain and heartache while grieving the loss of another loved one, had forgotten the moral values her family had instilled all of her life. Well, no more. This foolish sex business with Donovan had to stop. Today. Now. She was a proud young woman and she had scruples! She would not be called any man's pleasure toy or *anybody's* whore. Her own village people would have booted her out of the tribe, sent her into exile. Uh-uh. She had nowhere else to go if Mrs. Tedesco fired her, no life worth living.

She had plans for her future, difficult as they were.

Mr. Ray sounded ready and able to help, but she wasn't prepared to "drop the bomb" yet. She needed more practice, more time on the keyboard, time to chase the jitters from her capable fingers. Her hands shook now, thinking about Mr. Tedesco's harsh expression, his disenchanted eyes, seemingly disgusted simply by the sight of her. Why did he dislike her so? She'd shown dedicated loyalty ever since her employment under his wife's careful directives.

From behind, Donovan's arms slipped around her in a soothing embrace. He planted a lingering kiss to her cheek. "I'm rejuvenated, ready for round twenty-one."

Feeling his familiar hardness against her derriere, she shook her head. "I'm taking a walk."

"It's dark. Can't have you walking the countryside without an escort. Without me. Let's skip walking for high-powered exercise."

"Dusk. Short stroll, Donovan. Need fresh air. Alone," she added quickly, turning in his arms, witnessing the spark of irritation shading his hazel eyes. "I won't be long, back in time to feed you dessert."

"My choice of sweets."

"As long as *I'm*," Challie emphasized, "not on your menu."

She wasn't on the dessert menu last night nor was she the early-bird special this morning.

Challie had locked the door to her room to keep him out, to stop another seduction he would surely win. Donovan had cursed navy streaks, even threatened to paddle her ass. She had ignored the sarcastic warnings; he wouldn't dare. Sleepless, she'd heard him test the doorknob several times during the night, heard him griping.

At daybreak, she closed both doors to his room. Naked and beautiful, Donovan had slept restlessly from the looks of the twisted sheets and, obviously, in need of a woman. His arms were clasped tightly around one pillow clutched to his chest. He was fully aroused.

Maybe Jennifer Ann . . . The young woman was definitely interested. Another visit by her, she would fall victim to his magnetic power and his body again.

An untried taste of jealousy crept into Challie's senses. She shook her head to dislodge the emotional jarring. She had no right to jealousy, certainly no rights to any man.

She sneaked her usual morning bath, quickly rinsed under sprinkling water, dressed and went for another revitalizing walk to wipe away silly thoughts brewing from sensual daydreams. Fresh air cleared the cobwebs from her brain, but kneeling beside Ike's grave resurrected a thousand memories. Nearly all rushed forward to present day.

The men who had witnessed her father's murder had watched the same assailants kill Porky, the family dog and protector. They'd roasted the only goat her family owned, and the killers had left Porky to scavengers.

Challie found the fat puppy one day—abandoned, hungry and whimpering. Her father never resisted when she begged for anything requiring little or no money. Growing up without siblings was difficult for a little girl, harder for any child without friends or playmates. Porky had greeted her happily when she'd come home from school every day of his short life. Just like Ike had become attached to her. Now, he was gone.

She laid her fingers on the cross. It wiggled. Donovan would hammer it back into the ground. The next second, she heard footsteps and wondered if he'd heard her showering.

"Frettin' over an ugly-ass mutt." The voice was deep, the words slurred, the tone mean and nasty.

Challie kept her focus on the cross, but from the corner of her eye, she saw the half-filled liquor bottle this man held by its neck. Less than one foot from her knee, his lighted cigarette landed in the grass. Luckily, morning dew had moisturized the prairie overnight. Sucking in a quiet, shaky breath, she held it. When her hand began to tremble, she wrapped her fingers around the stake to control her unsteadiness.

Stay calm. Don't give him reason to show ugliness.

"You where you s'posed to be," he continued. "On yer knees, wench, like a good l'il alien. Know what alien is, alien?"

Don't answer. Ignore him. Maybe he'll go away. Maybe he'll disappear, vanish with the breeze.

She closed her eyes, wishing to fade away as she had wished so often as a child when threatened. She'd eventually found a world of her own in music. No one touched her in her private fantasies.

"You hear me, bitch? I'm talkin' to you!"

He jammed his filthy paws into her hair, yanked her head back. When he leaned down, Challie nearly gagged, the stink of his foul breath fanning over her face.

"Don't be thinkin' you too good, missy. You ain't nuttin' but trash. Untamed trash. Know what I do to trash?"

She had what she needed now, clutched tightly in her hand.

"Hey!"

At the same moment Ray yelled, Challie swung the cross. She smacked the dog killer's right knee. He screamed louder than excited women who yelped for joy and he toppled over as Ray trotted across the grass.

"What in the hell are you doing, Lawson?" Ray grabbed the drunken cowboy's shirt lapels, dragged him to his feet. "What the *fuck* are you doing?"

His face blazing red with fury, Ray shoved the foreman, sent him stumbling backward. "Get off my property. Pack your gear and get the hell off my ranch. You're fired. And don't let me see you on Horse Prairie again."

Bare-chested and barefooted, Donovan came flying around the corner of the cabin. "I'll kill you, Lawson. I'm gonna rip you limb from limb."

Ray caught him by the arm. Holding him back didn't look easy. "Back off, Donnie. Calm down."

"Donovan, please, don't."

"I've got the situation under control," Ray said. "Get out of here, Lawson. Now or I let him loose."

His gaze flew to Donovan's angry eyes. Lawson swallowed then he refocused on the ranch owner.

"What about my money? You owe me."

Ray pulled his wallet from his hip pocket, plucked several bills, tossed them to the ground.

Sneering, the cowboy snatched up his money. He counted the bills then grabbed up his dusty hat and limped away, moaning.

Challie let out the breath she'd been holding. Donovan was right there lifting her to her feet, embracing her.

"Are you okay? Did he hurt you? I just happened to look through the window. I swear I would've—"

"Hate fighting."

Chuckling noisily, Ray hooked his thumbs through his belt loops. "She might hate fighting, but she tagged him good, nearly broke the idiot's leg."

Donovan hadn't released her. He continued stroking her back.

"Never did like the SOB," Ray continued. "Dad hired him before we moved here. He'd hinted Lawson would hang himself."

When Donovan had no reply, the ranch owner went on. "Dad's funny about people. He gives them a fair shot then gives them a length of rope when they screw up. Sees if they knot the noose and take the leap."

Challie listened, but Donovan didn't. She wasn't at all sure what Ray meant. Knot the noose and take the leap? What did that mean?

"He even eggs them on. Some people don't know when to step back, take a look at the situation and make changes."

Uh-oh. What if Mr. Tedesco was watching to see if she'd make the ultimate mistake? Hanging herself.

"Actually, he's not as shitty as he makes people think," Ray continued. "All talk and a nipper of a bite. Unless somebody does something really stupid."

Donovan cupped her face, his palms warm against her skin. "Are you sure you're okay?"

"Absolutely." Seeing the ranch owner watching every move closely, Challie stepped away from Donovan. She would not make the error Mr. Tedesco expected.

"Well, then." Ray grinned broadly. "This calls for a celebration. Dinner tonight. My place."

"What would you like?" she asked. He'd had a hand in helping her. Without his interruption, no telling what Demon Lawson would have tried.

"My treat. I'm chef. Salad, steaks, baked potatoes, the only stuff I can do well."

Lord. She hoped he cooked better than Donovan's scorching technique.

"I'll have Eduardo and his wife, Antonia, up. You'll like her."

Unused to being surrounded by men, Challie loved the thought of female company.

"Doing something nice for our ladies would be good," Donovan said.

She really must set him straight. She was not his lady. His temporary tramp? Yes . . . er . . . was. Girlfriend? Hardly. Wife? Only by magic or miracle. Like if her mother suddenly appeared before her eyes. Like that would ever happen after twenty-nine years. The shameful woman couldn't possibly recognize her own daughter. Probably didn't know her child's name either. Who cared?

"Haven't seen old man Ross in a while," Ray said. "Guess I ought to invite him and his granddaughter, Jennifer, over."

Bile swam upstream from Challie's belly, searing her throat.

10

She'd distanced herself from him all afternoon and Donnie couldn't figure out why. They had conversations, but every time he moved close to her personal zone, Challie found something to do far away from him. Was she angry with him because of Lawson's stupidity?

The moment he'd seen the idiot, he couldn't get out of the house fast enough. Livid hardly described the emotions consuming him. Murder had saturated his mind, but he'd reined in the fury at her request.

"Mr. Ray wants us to arrive by five thirty," Challie said, breaking into his thoughts.

"Ray, plain Ray. But, yeah, he's all into punctuality like his dad." He wished she'd wear something different. How many drab drapes did she own? Two were hanging on the clothesline. "You know, we'll probably sit on the deck. Might be better if you wore jeans."

She shrugged. "My jumpers are comfortable."

And butt ugly. Once they married, or beforehand, he'd take her shopping. No woman of his was venturing out in public wearing funeral gray. Naturally, he'd pay for it and help pick out sexy stuff worthy of a second or third eyeballing. She really should show her shapely legs beneath today's hot miniskirts, wearing high heels.

Her hair hung loose. Fine time to crush it between his fingers while he delved his tongue down her slim throat. Too late. She turned her back and walked off.

"Do you think we could at least leave together, arrive at the same time?" When she didn't respond, he caught hold of Challie's arm before she stepped off the porch. "Look, I'm sorry I wasn't Johnny-on-the-spot when Lawson started his shit. I can only move so fast. Did you expect me to dive through the window? Is that why you're pissed at me?"

"I'm not . . . angry with you."

"Well, what the fuck is the problem? This is the first time I've been able to touch you since this morning, goddamn it. I don't like this kind of shit. When we get—" Hell, he hadn't popped the question yet. What better time than tonight? "When we get over to Ray's, you can at least *act* like you enjoy my company. And we're not staying all evening. We need to have a serious conversation."

Wrenching her arm free, Challie turned tail and ran.

"Son of a—" Donnie mumbled darkly.

He started after her, tempted to tackle and spank her sweet ass, but a beat-up Camaro chugged into the parking area, abruptly halting his pursuit. Just what he needed, somebody to catch him chasing her down.

More rust than green, the Camaro rumbled like an army tank, spitting black smoke when the driver cut the engine. Donnie's first ride, won in a craps game, had been a used '88. Hottest wheels on the highway. In fact, his first piece of . . . history.

Tall and slim, the Mexican guy climbed out of the vehicle, went around to the passenger side and helped the woman out.

Waddling, she was fat with kid—or plural—ready to drop the onboard load anytime. Her yellow floral dress stretched tight around her expanding abdomen. Sliced fruits filled the clear bowl she carried.

"You must be Donnie," the guy said. "I'm Eduardo Castillo. My wife Antonia."

He nodded and shook their hands. "Pleasure meeting you both."

"And the *señorita* running from you?" Eduardo angled his head toward Ray's back door. "Challie?"

Well, shit. "She wasn't running from me, actually."

"Oh, no? Could've fooled me." Antonia was five foot nothin' like Challie. With sparkling brown eyes, great smile, husky voice and polished face surrounded by shoulder-length, lazy waves, she put the *X* in exotic.

"She's just hungry. She's making the salad, doesn't want to hold up dinner." *Lying sack of shit.* She'd bolted like a frightened hare.

Antonia tsked, and Donnie knew *she* knew he'd lied. Jamming his fingers into his front pockets, hunching his shoulders, he said, "All right, yeah, she was sprinting from me for some odd reason." Why, he had no idea.

Challie immediately made friends with Antonia.

Ray was all smiles when he answered the door. As he led everyone to the great room, he said, "Nice to have a little company. Gets lonesome in this big house without the wife and kids. Anybody want a drink? The bar is open and full, gentlemen. Ladies, can I get you something—scotch, bourbon, martini, juice, lemonade? I went grocery shopping."

Now was a good time to show his best qualities, Donnie thought, to impress. He'd worked seven months as bartender for a local New York pub. How many parties had he attended with Paul and Tina? Maybe his manners weren't as cultured as

Paul's refinement, but he was not a complete idiot. Challie seemed more receptive when he put his ego on the back burner.

He filled two tumblers with ice and lemonade and put together lightweight bourbon and waters for the man of the house and himself. Eduardo requested cold Modelo.

"Challie and I can make the salad," Antonia said. She thanked Donnie for both tumblers. "It'll give us a chance to get better acquainted."

"Well, all right, then," Ray said with a smile. "I'll bust out the snack platter. Delicatessen Sophie made one up special on short notice." He'd claimed the woman, a sixty-something widow, had the hots for him ever since his first visit to the supermarket.

Males needed their egos tweaked on occasion. Donnie's pride could use a major boost after today's less-than stellar appeal.

Why did Challie run from him? He'd only said they should have a conversation. What was up with that after they'd indulged in high-powered sex? Should've meant something to her. Typically, he'd walk away from a woman before hour twenty-four. Risky business otherwise. As in common-law marriage in some states. *Might work,* he thought, while staring at Challie's ass as she followed Antonia into the kitchen. If he knew the statutes of Montana.

Donnie jiggled the ice cubes in his glass, finished off the cocktail. He made the next one stronger. When he looked at Challie again, she was ignoring him as usual. He swallowed a fortifying amount of liquor.

". . . sense, *amigo*."

Blinking rapidly, Donnie snapped his head around. "What?"

"Alcohol," Eduardo replied, "only alters one's common sense."

Yeah, he knew all about the deadly poison. He'd limited his

consumption to three hard drinks after zoning out on his seventeenth birthday. Drinking cheap, cherry vodka would put the hurt on God. Intimacy with another porcelain bowl was no longer in Donnie's repertoire.

"When a woman's got control of your brain," Eduardo finished.

Well, hell. How long had he been staring at Challie while this know-it-all stared at him?

"Don't fret, *amigo*. We've all been down *El Diablo*'s path." Nodding toward the kitchen, Eduardo continued. "Antonia. I nearly killed a man because of her. Tequila can turn a fellow into a mean son of a bitch, the reason I only drink *cerveza* now. After the incident, she reduced me to a sniveling idiot."

Donnie snickered. No woman could possibly make him snivel. Beg? Maybe for pussy. Snivel? Fat chance.

"I believe, pussy whipped is the term nowadays," Eduardo murmured.

Ray pointed to the snack tray, thank the man above for the interruption, and motioned toward the deck. At least the host wasn't talking any shit. "So," he said and put the tray on the round wrought iron table. He got comfortable in a lounge chair. "How's it going with Challie? Have you made any headway? Pretty woman."

For Christ's sake. What was it about married men? Did they know everything? See everything?

"Eduardo, did he tell you how talented she is? She works the ivory on our Petrof."

"She works him, too," Eduardo replied.

"Nobody works—"

"Yep, she's got his nose," Ray said. He sipped on his drink. "Should've seen him this morning, ready to go to war with Lawson for messing with her. Thought I might have to call the prairie posse for backup."

Just put all my business in the streets. Thanks a helluva lot, Tedesco. "It was only because—"

"I told him about the PW blur," the other loudmouth said, cocking an eyebrow.

Just leave me out of the damn conversation. Donnie tipped his chair back on two legs, rocking, his pissed level increasing as the seconds ticked away. "I always maintain—"

"Been there. Done that," Ray replied. He grinned. "My vision still blurs."

"Me, I'm blinded most of the time. Just have to accept it, get used to it. Deal with it."

They looked at Donnie, skinnin' and grinnin'.

Fuck you both. He hadn't intended for the chair to smack the deck so hard or to set the glass down harder. Liquor spilled over his hand, dripped through the table's itty-bitty holes. "Nobody works me, goddamn it, and nobody gets my nose. As for your stupid blur—"

The sick yokels had the nerve to laugh.

Since neither one of these hardheads felt inclined to change the subject, Donnie said, "So, who's the next foreman?"

"Blind Eduardo."

Jesus Christ. Ray couldn't let it drop. To Eduardo, Donnie asked, "What about Antonia? She looks like she's ready to have the baby anytime."

"Three weeks," he replied. "Haying's almost finished. Doctor says it'll take another six weeks before I can lose my eyesight altogether."

For the love of God.

The sliding screen door opened. "Your friend Mr. Ross has arrived," Challie said to Ray, then she looked squarely at Donnie. "And Miss Jennifer."

Crap, he thought, having hoped Ross and his granddaughter had declined the invitation. Or better, that Ray hadn't asked them at all. "I'll light the charcoal, get the grill ready," Donnie said and started toward Challie. She about-faced and fled. What the devil was this shit about?

"WNB," Ray said, following him to the door.

"What?"

"Working. Nose. Blur." Eduardo's raucous howl beat a tickled hyena's laughter.

"Bite me," Donnie mumbled. "I'll show you how far away from the truth you are."

"Oh, yeah?" Ray said. "We've had a gas grill ever since we moved here. You've grilled burgers on it every time you've come to Montana."

Fucking A.

Old man Ross, donned in his usual bib overalls and using a single crutch, hobbled through the kitchen. Behind him, Jennifer Ann.

Thin straps held the red minidress in place. Her hefty hooters were on display in two rolling hills, her shapely legs flexing in red high heels. She strolled right up to Donnie, backed him into the corner of the counter and pressed against him. "Hey, cowboy."

"Jennifer."

Ray said, "Donnie, mind grabbing a six-pack of ginger ale from the commissary? Ross drinks it. Anybody else want soda?"

"Pepsi," Antonia said. Her husband raised his hand, agreeing.

"No problem." Donnie weaseled away from Jennifer. She had talent—bold as the day was long. Keeping her at bay was going to take effort.

He hustled out to the commissary. When he strode back inside, Jennifer blocked his path between the *lovely* mudroom and playroom.

"Seems like you're tryin' to avoid me, cowboy." She pressed her body to his again.

Both hands were occupied with six-packs. "Actually—"

"You know, I've been dreamin' about that hard cock."

"Jennifer—"

"I want it fillin' my pussy. How about you, cowboy. You ready to get it on, a quickie to satisfy us both?"

If man's body contained BBs, Donnie figured he was sweating machine-gun fire. She ground her hips hard against his. For some unknown reason, he looked down the hall. Challie glanced their way for a split second and turned her back as if he didn't exist.

"Jennifer Ann! Come on in here and help these women git this food ready."

"Shit," she hissed, stepping back.

Silently, Donnie thanked Ross for the intrusion.

At the dinner table, Paul Bunyan's axe couldn't slice the mounting tension brewing against Donnie's ego.

He pulled out a chair for Challie. She sat in the one Ray offered instead and, damn it, he sandwiched her between himself and Eduardo. Jennifer Ann took the chair he held. When Donnie tried engaging Challie in conversation, Ray changed the subject and dragged Antonia into the chat. Exasperated, Donnie smiled in her direction. Straight-faced, Challie looked away. This was simple, frigging neglect. On the other hand, Jennifer Ann gave him too much attention—walking her fingers up his thigh, playing footsy . . . He scooted his chair farther around the circular table, crowding Ray.

After dinner, Donnie volunteered to help Challie with kitchen detail. Good old Eduardo stepped into her place, grinning. She praised his expertise and, again, ignored her future husband.

Wait until he got her butt home. They had some serious yakking to do. He was not the man to ignore.

"Jennifer Ann, time we git on home now. Forgot to bring my pills. Thanks, Ray. Next time we'll do a shindig on my ranch. Jennifer Ann can put a meal together."

"Gramps, you know I don't like to cook."

"You will if you want to keep that dang truck I bought." The granddaughter's bottom lip damn near dropped to the floor.

Donnie took the opportunity to hit the head. No way would he walk her out and risk a frisking. When he thought it was safe, he went back to the kitchen.

Gripping the edge of the counter firmly, he inhaled deeply, blew the air out in one long steady rush through his nostrils.

"What's your problem?" Ray asked. He stood in the doorway between the hallway and galley.

"I don't have a problem. Why?"

"Because you're wearing a sour glower again, blowing steam through your ears. I can feel the heat from here. What the devil's the matter with you?"

While Eduardo's pregnant wife had watched comfortably from the leather chaise lounge, her husband had snuggled beside Challie at the piano. Donnie's future wife was attentively teaching the guy to play a few chords, speaking quietly, touching him and shifting his fingers on the keys. A little too intimately. Donnie sucked in another pissed-off breath.

Moving into the kitchen, Ray said, "He's married and he's in love with his wife. Antonia encouraged him. She's got her eye on old man Ross's piano."

Donnie deflated noisily. He was so damn sure no woman would ever get away with working him. Or get his nose. As for the blur, hell, pussy was known to blow a man's mind, even the best of men.

"A lot of guys have joined the club. Why should you be an exception, Donnie? Look at Dad. He thinks he wears the color of power. He'd swear on the Bible he had control of everything going on in his life. But you know who's really wearing purple? Tina. She's so good, she makes it look like he's king, makes him think he's king. Same goes in my household. I've just learned how to deal with it. Like Dad, you're trying to deny your emotions." He slapped Donnie on the shoulder. "Put aside the bravado. Open your eyes. Get in touch with your feminine side."

"I don't have a damn feminine side," Donnie replied nastily.

"Bullshit. Every person on the planet has *XY* chromosomes. And the *X* always comes first. You know the *X* means woman, don't you? Even the Bruce Willis wannabes have a feminine streak. Get over it."

Challie began playing, catching everyone's attention.

"God, I wish Meredith were here to listen with me." Ray wandered over to his favorite chair and lowered himself onto the leather. Scooting down, he propped his hands behind his head and stretched out his bulky legs.

The novice piano player left the bench. Eduardo went to his wife when she reached her hand out toward him. He cozied up beside her. Her hand atop his, they massaged her swollen belly.

I don't have a damn feminine side, Donnie proclaimed silently. *Never had one, never will.*

But he couldn't deny the WNB club was calling his name, loud and clear. Drawn to Challie, he sat on the piano bench beside her, keeping some distance between them. If she suddenly stopped playing and left the room, he knew it would scrape deeply at his ego—bad. If she did leave, how could he propose if she hated the sight of him?

She played like a pro. Three tunes. She *was* a pro and completely oblivious to his nearness. Challie had the room under her magic, its occupants mesmerized.

Who had taught her to play? Where was she taught? Why

was she waiting to debut when she could easily steal the show? She'd win the hearts of her listeners. She'd gain notoriety, move on to stardom and travel. What would happen then?

What would happen to *them*?

He expected his wife to stay by his side as other wives stayed with their husbands. But, okay, she could play for the symphony, maybe go on short tours. Day tours. Paul would get her the finest business organizer. He'd make sure she was set, taken care of, managed. *Paul only knows a bunch of damn men,* Donnie thought, as jealousy made another nasty appearance. Emotion unbecoming of a bona fide bachelor.

Clapping and bravos ended his musings. He joined in the salute with gusto, adding a cheer of his own. "Yowza!"

Was she blushing? For the first time, he realized Challie carried a quiet shyness he'd grown used to in short time. The broads he'd fooled with in the past would take center stage, applauding themselves if they had any endowment to speak of, but most of them only had one or two talents, he noticed, ones Duke understood well. Those dames were no comparison to Challie's subtle charm. Now, if he could just slow his heartbeat to a confirmed bachelor's unemotional tempo.

"Play it again, Sam," Donnie yelled. She made him proud.

Clapping ceased. Everyone looked at him, including the greatest pianist.

Ray said, "Sophisticates say encore."

Well, shit, he'd blown it—until Challie giggled. He loved the sound.

"I think I'd better get Antonia home," Eduardo said. "She tires easily these days." His wife's glare didn't change his mind. Obviously she wanted to enjoy more of Challie's talent. Antonia didn't budge.

On the same page, maybe only the same chapter, Donnie was ready to get his fiancée-to-be home. Stretching his arms overhead, he checked his watch and said, "It is getting late. Thanks for inviting us." He intended to talk with Challie about their future. Tomorrow. After a long, blurred night.

"My pleasure," Ray replied. "As much as I'd love to hear Challie play until her fingers blistered, I do have some accounting to catch up on."

Ray helped Eduardo get his wife on her feet, a challenge and struggle for her. She hugged Challie. From the looks of things, they'd become good friends. And a smile filled with happiness spread across Challie's lips.

How many girlfriends had she found in Arizona? When did she have time? She spent most of her daylight hours working at the Tedesco mansion. Women needed friends or confidantes, unlike guys, who seldom needed bosom buddies except when drinking, which always led to lying. At least Challie had Antonia for a friend while here.

They waved to the Castillos as their car rumbled away.

Donnie grabbed Challie's wrist, started pulling her toward the house, but she dug her heels into the dirt and gravel, skidding them both to a stop.

"What are you doing?" she demanded. The harder she tried breaking free of his grip the tighter his hold.

"We," Donnie emphasized, "are going inside for privacy. I thought we'd never get rid of the Castillos. The evening wasn't dedicated to girls' night out. Not the way I'm wound up." He was horny, and Duke was already pumped for a home invasion, an endless raid.

Struggling with her reluctance, he got them inside, pushed her up against the door, he slammed and locked it. Donnie went on the offensive.

Challie went on the defensive. She shoved him backward. Twice. "What? A quickie to satisfy us both?" And she shoved him again.

Oh, shit. She'd heard every word, which meant she knew he and Jennifer Ann had knocked off a piece. "We didn't do anything."

"You would have if Mr. Ross hadn't called her." She shook her head, huffing. "That's your prerogative. That's your style."

Somebody banged on the damn door.

"I didn't chase after her. She cornered me!"

"Maybe your legs didn't move, but your man-thing," she said snottily. "Never mind. There's no reason to discuss it. It's your business. You're an adult. You can do as you please with whomever you please."

Bullshit. Okay, Duke had woken. He didn't order him to rise. Long-term training. It was automatic. He never would've screwed the cowgirl again.

Donnie opened his mouth to say so, but somebody hit the door hard.

Damn it, every frigging time they tried to talk—or argue—there was an interruption. "Don't go anywhere," Donnie said. "We're not finished with this." He went to see who had come a-banging. They weren't expecting company. God-forbid if the caller was Jennifer Ann.

"What the hell took you so long to unlock this thing?"

11

The man's voice dipped as deep as the subterranean depths.

"What's it to you, Gunther?" Donnie said sourly. "Why are you guys here so soon? Where's Thompson?"

This idiot was a jerk, an imbecile, a forty-something asshole who called himself tough and a lady's man. They were equally built, but Gunther's background was dirty-blond Scandinavian. His managing techniques as warehouse supervisor were just as cold and unfeeling as his ice blue eyes, matching the light blue shirt, if they weren't hidden behind mirrored shades. They seemed to glow after dark. Donnie didn't like the PT Industries vampire. The feeling was mutual.

"He couldn't make the trip. I took his place," Gunther replied.

These two guys showing up just ruined his game plan.

"What do you got to eat in this place?" Moretti asked. "I slept all the way here and I'm starved." Roman was shorter than average with a thick mop of graying hair.

"It's a little late for dinner, but I can make sandwiches,"

Challie piped in. She moved beside Donnie, staring at the linoleum.

"Challie. Challie. Challie," Gunther said, his tone dropping on each word, which brought her head up fast. "I'll take anything you have to offer, darlin'."

Motherfucker. Donnie stepped in front of her to keep this fangless critter's eyes from roving over her body even though she wore the ugly tented shit again. "Did you come all the way here without luggage?"

"It's in the car."

"Then I suggest you go get it," Donnie snapped.

Gunther cocked his eyebrow. "He sounds testy, don't he, Moretti? Problems, Fontana?"

"Only one," Donnie replied, sneering. "You."

"Come on, Gunther," Moretti said, latching onto the vampire's shirtsleeve, leading him away. "Don't start any shit."

"I don't like him," Challie whispered. "Somehow, he reminds me of Mr. Lawson. His tone."

"He's a butthead like Lawson." *The bastard,* Donnie thought, watching Gunther open the car trunk. "Keep away from him."

Twenty minutes later, Challie stacked a plate full of sandwiches on the table.

Moretti dove in with both hands before she filled the iced tea glasses. Apparently Gunther expected the man to clean the plate. He grabbed three halves. Chair tipped back on two legs, rocking, Donovan watched her busily at work. He winked. She frowned.

"Whatcha gonna cook for breakfast, Miss Challie?" Moretti asked.

Did he always talk with his mouth full? "Whatever you would like," she replied and set the iced tea pitcher on the table. "Would you care for chips?"

He nodded jerkily. "What about lunch tomorrow? What're we having then?"

Overweight men should never worry about eating. "I'll decide tomorrow."

"And dinner?"

For gosh sakes. He hadn't finished . . . She turned around. Well, shoot. The sandwich plate was empty. She hustled to make more, using the last slices of pastrami, honey ham and bread. Somebody would have to grocery shop soon. Naturally, she didn't have a driver's license. Or a car of her own. The way these people ate, no wonder Hattie had packed so much food.

"So," Moretti continued. "What's for dinner tomorrow night?"

Something to satisfy his bottomless pit. "Rib roast. Prime."

"Like you?" Gunther asked. He sucked juice from a fat dill pickle. "You give head, Challie darlin'?"

"You son of a bitch." Donovan's fingers twisted into Gunther's shirt before his chair hit the floor. "I ought to knock the shit out of you." He drew his fist back.

Gunther grabbed his arm with one hand, forming a sizable fist with the other.

"Hey!" Moretti yelled, dropping both sandwiches, scraping his chair back from the table.

Challie stared at Gunther, at the pickle, then at Donovan. Head, as in sucking on . . .

She burst out laughing. Anything to stop an old-fashioned brawl like the Old West used to have. Broken mirrors, shattered furniture and bloodied bodies should stay in that century, kept on the prairie landscape. She hated fighting.

All three men stared at her. Not one moved.

Finally taming her laughter, Challie glued one hand to her hip, pointing her finger at each male. "Let me tell you all something before you go any further. A—no fighting. Or B—you'll wish I never cooked. And C—Mr. Gunther, it is none of *your* business." Satisfied, she marched out of the room.

"Feisty little thing, isn't she?" Moretti said, picking up his sandwiches, jamming them together into a Dagwood-style meal. He took a huge bite. "What did she mean by 'you'll wish I never cooked'?"

Donnie shrugged and let loose of Gunther's shirt. His intended prey's hands fell away. Yeah. She was feisty as hell. He liked her spunk. "Watch your mouth, Gunther, or we'll end up at the local doc's office."

"To fix your pretty nose?"

"Better. To extract my foot from your ass." He followed Challie to the bedroom.

She was folding a blouse. Other items were already in her suitcase.

"Challie—"

"Hate fighting." And back to those hate expressions while ignoring him.

He closed the door, moved closer and wrapped his arms around her from behind, pinning hers. Leaning down, he whispered, "No more fighting. Promise."

"Hate macho." She shoved his arms away, spun around. "Head?"

Oh, shit. She had talent not only for playing the piano, but also for a mean, challenging glare. Donnie stepped back.

"You wanted me to—"

"It's a natural human act," he cut in. "I just thought—"

"You and your stupid friends thought wrong! I bet you all planned this, didn't you? You devils thought I'd give every one of you some damn *head*."

He didn't like hearing her curse, but Challie went on a rant.

"Is that why they sent me here with you, so you could break me in like a milking cow to milk you?" She slapped the blouse on the bed, picked up a figurine from the bedside table and drew it back.

Donnie caught her wrist in midswing. The ceramic ballerina crashed to the floor, splintering on impact. He had to say something. "No, not true. We—you and I—came here to get married." Damn it to hell. This was not how he'd planned to pop the question. What question?

Challie's eyes grew to saucer size. Then, she fainted. Donnie caught her before she hit the floor. So much for the happy bride-to-be. As he lifted her into his arms, the bedroom door flew open. Both Gunther and Moretti stood there, mouths hanging open.

"What'd you do to her, you dumb bastard?" Moretti shouted. "Shit, Fontana, you didn't have to knock her out. What the hell's the matter with you? I ought to take your ass outside and beat the living hell of you! See how you like it."

Jesus. The man really thought he'd cold-cocked her. "She fainted. I didn't lay a hand on her."

Moretti's face flushed bright red. "You got your hands on her now! Put her down."

Donnie kicked the suitcase aside. He put Challie gently in bed and smoothed her hair from her face.

"Get a wet washcloth, Gunther. Water too," Moretti ordered. "Include a whip if you can find one."

Donnie scowled. "Like I said, I didn't hit her."

"Oh, she just picked up some heavy glass shit and tried to knock her own damn brains out, huh? Get real."

"She tried to throw it at me. I just stopped her."

"And then you hit her over the head."

Gunther leaned his shoulder casually against the doorframe, holding a glass and washcloth, smirking.

"If you didn't want to marry the woman," Moretti barked, "all you had to do was leave the state or even the damn country."

Frowning, groaning, Challie was coming around. Donnie smoothed her hair again.

"Get away from her." Moretti's voice seemed to blow the room apart. He was a cantankerous old devil when riled.

"She's my . . . I'm staying right beside her."

"Hate shouting." She covered her face with the pillow.

"Are you all right?" Donnie asked.

"Of course she's not!" Moretti stomped across the floor. He shoved Donnie aside. "Here, Challie, drink some of this. I know this jerk put a nasty knot on your head. I brought a cool washcloth to ease the pain. Get you some aspirin and ice soon as we drag this lousy little bastard out of here."

"I did *not* hit her." Christ, everybody thought the same ridiculous shit. He'd never hurt a woman.

"Hit me?" Challie pushed the pillow away and sat up, eyes narrowed. "Nobody hits me and gets away with it."

"See?" Donnie hissed.

"You don't have to cover for him," Moretti advised. "Tedesco'll nail him once he hears. I ought to call him right now."

Ah, shit. Donnie groaned, worried about his livelihood and his jewels. With Moretti's protection and Tedesco's threats, much trouble brewed.

"He don't like none of his men smacking women around," his accuser said.

"He didn't touch me. I think I fainted." She glared at Donnie as she stood. "Over something he said."

Hauling Donnie to his feet by the shirtsleeve, Moretti asked, "What the hell did you say to her, you little bastard?"

"I'm leaving." Challie stood, rubbing her temples. "Headache. Hate arguing."

"Now look what you did. Come on, Miss Challie, let me help you to the kitchen. Don't want you doing too much."

Moretti was only thinking about his gut. "*I'll* help her," Donnie snapped.

"Get out. All of you."

She didn't really mean for him to leave. Impossible. They had wedding plans to make.

"Out!" she ordered, stamping her foot.

Tripping over each other's feet like The Three Stooges, they stumbled through the doorway. When Donovan turned back, mouth hanging open as if to say something, Challie glared him into closing the door.

Lord. Weariness weighed on her.

She lowered herself slowly to the bed again and curled her fingers into the mattress.

How could grown men act this way? Arguing, bickering, fighting. She thought she'd left all craziness behind. Males were no different here than in her homeland.

When the men bearing guns came to their village shanty, commanding her father to join with them in retaliation, Challie hid. They'd hounded him oftentimes. Papa finally gave in to their demands. He left with the renegades. His *comrades* brought him home on a bloodied, filthy blanket. Murdered.

Papa was a man destined to save lives. A doctor. Nimble fingers. But someone had taken his life instead. Challie could only imagine what fear he might've harbored when death stared him in the face. It had to be much worse than the frightening few moments with Donovan, feeling his muscles flex under her fingertips, seeing his nostrils flared, anger burning wildly in his eyes.

He was a gentle man. Most times. Sometimes.

But she knew he hadn't harmed the Pearson woman. She'd seen her storm out of the bedroom, cursing Donovan. He'd walked away from her.

The second time, Challie had gone back inside the upstairs bedroom unnoticed. When she peeked out again, Pearson had allowed a man to caress her bottom. He wore a gold ring on his little finger. She would never forget the ring, not one with sparkling jewels. His face was hidden behind the door. Then he pushed it shut.

Donovan hadn't worn a ring that she'd seen this trip. Challie sighed. She had no idea what happened in there. Something did. Something terrible.

She wished the cabin had a piano for her enjoyment. Playing provided the only solace to ease the anguish gathering in her heart from long-ago memories of her father and grandmother and the disconcerting thoughts she had now. The pain wouldn't be so hard to endure if she had someone to lean on, a mother who shared the same aching heart. A parent to give comfort and love.

Or a good man to hold her, to banish the nagging pain.

She shook her head at the preposterous thought. She had a career to pursue and her mother to find and neither plan included male company. Having a good man around meant . . .

Meant what?

She'd never *had* a good man. Two sexual partners didn't qualify as having male companionship. At least, not for long. Besides, both relationships had revolved around her sexual curiosity. Only Donovan had the power to culminate more emotion than her inquisitive brain cells normally produced.

She curled her fingers tighter into the mattress.

"What did he say?" Challie burst out. "Get married?"

She marched into the kitchen.

"You," she said, pointing her thumb at Donovan. "Outside. Now."

"Your ass is in big trouble," Gunther said. She so hated the sound of his snickering.

When Donovan scooted his chair back. Challie heard Moretti whisper, "Hope this don't disrupt meals."

She spun around. "You'll be lucky if you *get* another meal!"

"Damn. She has good ears," the man said.

"And you eat too damn much," Gunther replied.

Challie heard every word of the exchange. Yes, she had an excellent sense of hearing.

She straight-armed the screen door and let it fly back into Donovan, thinking that she should've flung it back into his face.

"I like the way your hips sway when you're angry."

Challie continued onward, stomping toward the old wooden barn. She wanted no one else to hear what she had to say.

"They fit perfectly in my hands," Donovan said, following. "The rest of your body fits perfect to mine too."

The nerve of this man. Was he expecting her to swoon again, fall into his arms, believing every word coming out of his mouth?

At the barn door, she spun around, kicked up dust and hay in the process, spraying his tennis shoes. "Marriage?"

He stepped back, eyes wide open. "A wedding."

"A wedding? Why would I ever consider marrying you? Why would you want to marry me?"

He swallowed a half dozen times. "Harmony?"

"Harmony? Have you gone crazy? We have no harmony. We don't have one damn thing in common!"

"Don't curse at me, Challie," he said. "I don't like it when you curse."

"You curse worse than a sailor on a slippery ship deck. I've heard them too. You have a filthy mouth," she yelled, poking his chest with each word. She had him backing away.

"I won't anymore. Promise. Once we're—"

"You can curse all you want. We're not getting married. Today, tomorrow or any other day."

12

Oh, hell, Donnie thought despairingly. She was angry now, but she'd go ballistic knowing why they needed to wed. Women enjoyed courtship, love, marriage and a happily-ever-after kind of hell . . . er . . . thing, ride off into the wild-blue-yonder type of sh . . . uh . . . deal.

Donnie didn't know how to court a tennis ball.

All of his adult years, even some teenage ones, had been strictly focused on fuck . . . uh . . . intimacy. Except for the job. No love, no emotional bull . . . attachments, not one monogamous relationship. He couldn't deny sex had been his ultimate goal in life, sleeping with every available broad worth his . . . worth Duke's time. Now he was hip deep in trouble, needing to marry this woman to keep her from talking to the cops. A woman who had all but said, "bite me." So what now? Somehow, he had to tell her the truth. Maybe she'd understand. Maybe she'd reconsider.

When Challie took a step around him, he hauled her off the ground and tossed her over his shoulder like a sack of Idaho potatoes. Hundred and ten pounds soaking wet.

"Put me down, damn you!"

He opened, then pulled the barn door closed and carried her up the steps leading to the loft. Pounding his back, she kicked worse than an agitated bull and yelled some nastiness deserving a good spanking. In fact, a hell of a butt whipping.

"One more piece of filth out of your mouth, I'm burning your behind."

"You touch me and it'll be the last time you lay a hand on or push your man-thing inside a woman, you bastard."

She was furious.

He was pissed.

Filthy language was meant for men only. And calling him a bastard? What's up with that? He had a mother and a father. Both names were on his official birth certificate. Oh, yeah. Time for a strap at the very least.

He reached down to unbuckle his belt, realized he didn't have one on. At the top of the stairs, Donnie swung around, looking for a place to set her down. She cursed indignantly, although some phrases weren't technically correct. Things like uncle of a bitch and grannyfucker sounded weird. She got the point across with volume.

In one corner, four hay-bale columns nearly reached the ceiling. His only options were the floor, covered with a thick layer of straw, his lap or two other single bales. He opted for the floor. Donnie dropped to his knees, dragged Challie from his shoulder and flipped her over to her stomach.

He lifted his hand. She rolled to her back. What he saw in her huge gray eyes wasn't anger. Worse. Fear. The same wild-eyed terror he'd seen during his jealous tirade. Christ Almighty. His heart thudded like an Indian tom-tom. He had no intention of scaring her, no reason to have her believing he'd hurt her.

He lowered his hand, ran it up her ankle then her calf. She

jerked away. "Challie, I'd never hurt you. Don't be afraid of me."

"I hate you."

He'd blown it, but they'd shared something more than the hate she claimed, something much better. He couldn't stand for her to hate him.

Donnie relied on the intimacy that bound them together.

She tried to scramble away. Holding her, he inched forward on his knees. She raised her hand, but Donnie caught her wrist, yanked her against his chest and devoured her lips in a sensuous assault. Challie fought him, pulling his hair, slapping at his shoulders, trying to scream, trying to bite. Until he lowered her to the straw-laden floor, covered her body with his own and slid between her legs.

Moving his hips in a dance she would remember, he thrust his tongue into her mouth to a well-known ritual he craved. But unlike other intimate times, he took it slow. Leisurely tormenting, grinding against her, fitting their bodies together. He was bone hard in seconds when her legs came up, circled his waist. She squeezed. His growl started way in the back of his throat and he ground his hips harder, straining, rocking. He wanted inside her. But not yet. Not until she let him know when.

Donnie unlocked her legs. Shifting to one side, he lifted the hem of her jumper, found warmth and wrenched her panties free. The territory left open was wet. Slippery. Claiming her lips again, he slipped his middle finger into her heat, twisted and withdrew. Her hips bucked. She groaned. He did it again, thumbed her clit, massaged and received a low-sounding sigh for his efforts. Adding the second finger and more pressure to her G-spot earned a whimper.

She broke away from the kiss and said, "Donovan—"

"Not yet," he murmured.

Her breathing was shallow. Uncontrolled.

"Still hate me?" Without a response, he repeated his question.

"Yes." She sounded unconvincing.

He shoved his fingers deeper, pressed harder on her clit, circling his thumb. "Do you?"

Before she responded, he moved down between her legs, caught her sensitive nub between his teeth and sucked, at the same time delving his fingers into her sexpot. And he sucked more. Her hips came up. She clamped her thighs around his head.

Sinking his teeth into her, a whimpered cry filled the barn then she cried a solid "No." She was ready.

Donnie slid back up her body, unzipping his pants, and his cock sprang gloriously free. He wrapped his fingers around the jutting thickness, pressed the gleaming head against her opening. He moved forward a fraction, withdrew again, tormenting her with rapid thrusts. Straw fell from his clothes onto hers as the scent of her sex wafted around him. Struggling for his own control now, struggling more to keep his sanity intact, he waited for the right moment.

She trembled. He'd reached prime time. Rolling Challie to her stomach, he dragged her hips up, balancing her on her hands and knees, and spread her apart with both hands. Thrusting slowly, carefully at first, he finally shoved into her tightness in one commanding surge.

Challie yelped, but not a hurtful sound, not enough to stop him. He would, if she'd demanded he cease the invasion. He held her steady, fingers digging into her hips when she clamped around his length.

Drawing back, he waited a mere second, then surged again, skin against skin, heat to sweltering heat. She purred, circled her fine ass, teasing him. Nothing would stop him now, he plowed on, over and over, gave her more than any woman could ever want while primal pressure built deep within his own body. On the verge of demanding freedom, her arms crumpled from his onslaught.

"Up, damn it." He tagged her butt with an underhanded slap, soothed the sting when she yipped. "You want this, I'll give it to you, good and hard, but I want something in return."

"No!"

Blinded by his own greed, the need for this woman had surpassed overwhelming. She knew exactly what he'd risk asking. She *knew* it.

Donnie drew her up again and thrust harder, stayed motionless, then shoved her hips forward and dragged them back to meet him, smacking against her with domineering command. He'd fuck her brains out for denying him one appeal, knowing she'd gone far beyond the junction of no return.

On the threshold of losing all restraint, he pulled out, flipped her over to her back and spread her legs wide. And waited. "You know what I'm asking," he said with a suffocated breath.

He'd never let himself get so riled, so far gone. No woman had ever possessed him into making unrealistic demands during a frenzied union.

She grabbed his hair with all ten fingers. "You bastard. You bas—"

He drove home, burying himself to the hilt, the deepest penetration, and plundered Challie's mouth before the scream left her throat. Pounding harder, their bodies slid across the hay-covered floorboards.

"I'm gonna come. I w-want," he said on a ragged whisper. "Want you for—" He lost his thoughts. "Come with me."

Challie urged him on with purrs of acceptance, encouraging whispers and equal stimulation. Locking her legs behind him, she kept him where she wanted, kept him in place, feeding her own greedy appetite. And his, when detonation brewed hot and vicious and only moments away.

With an orgasm on the brink of eruption, her senses narrowed, finely tuned and on a streaking, white-hot fiery path, she fought to hold back the agonizing shriek rising in her throat. She snapped around him and shattered. Losing her breath, she bit his shoulder and imploded. Challie hung on with every ounce of strength she had while he shook in her arms, while they traveled to a private paradise well beyond reality on a carefree romp.

He gushed, a thrilling sensation during the peak of bliss. Squeezing their bodies tightly together, she raised her knees, spread them wider, lifting her hips. He ground hard against her sensitivity and sank deeper, prolonging her chaotic climax.

But, he was not finished.

Dragging her off the floor onto his thighs, he lifted and shoved her down his still-hard length, starting a brand-new round of tantalizing, sleek sensations. Challie couldn't stop herself from helping.

Swinging around on his knees, balancing her with one arm, he crawled toward the bales of hay. Bouncing wreaked bedlam on her senses. When Donovan lowered her over one bale, he said, "We're not done. I want more, lots more."

So did Challie. She circled her hips to the same tune they'd dance to, but then he pulled out, extracting a hostile hiss from her when her insides still shimmered. He pulled a foil package from his pocket. The small balloon hardly covered his man-thing. Why was he using it now when he'd never worn one with her before?

"I want to make love to you everywhere. I want to put it right here." He touched her where she'd never been touched by anyone.

Challie shook her head.

"Yes."

He held on to her hip with one hand. Two fingers went into

his mouth, came out glistening. Challie started to tremble. Would he force her into this madness?

Squirming backward with nowhere to go, she said, "No, Donovan, please."

"I won't hurt you. I'll go slow, easy. You'll like how it feels. Promise. It'll blow your mind, blow both our minds."

He stared so hard into her eyes she wanted to give in to him, wanted to give him anything he asked for. Challie bit her lip. He was touching her where she needed his touch most of all and she nearly forgot his gentle testing of the *most* private part of her body.

"Let me." He stroked again, deeper, and the startling sensation raised the hair on her head. "If it hurts you, I'll pull out. I won't go any further. Can I?"

He didn't wait for her answer. While Donovan worked at convincing her, he held himself, rubbing the crested head against her throbbing nub, sliding his hand up and down the length of his erection. The skin was taut, stretched and deep red. He pressed his man-thing to *that* place.

Something quivered in her belly, and Challie closed her eyes. He promised to stop if the pain was too much. When his warm fingers left her body, her eyelids fluttered open.

Drawing her knees up, setting her heels on the hay, he spread her legs. "I want you bad." He moved so slowly, leisurely penetrating a measured degree, retreating, but her breath hitched on the next invasion. "I want you, Challie, but I won't force you. Just relax."

He spoke softly, enticing her. Hearing the tone of his voice, she did settle down. He whispered words of encouragement, told her how beautiful she was, that she would enjoy the union as much as he would. That this was the ultimate sexual act between two people. Hands vibrating against her skin, he looked down at his progress. His man-thing was hot, scorching. Rigid.

She squeezed her eyes shut again as he penetrated slightly

deeper, circling, teasing. The next stroke was different, upward . . . onward . . . and then his fingers toyed with her stiff protrusion.

Challie swallowed and opened her eyes, saw Donovan's face hovering above hers. He kissed her, ran his tongue over her lips.

"See? You're cuddling all of me. Was it so bad?"

Never. Nothing was ever bad with Donovan. "No," Challie whispered, shaking her head.

He captured her lips in a searing kiss then slithered backward and glided languidly forward again, once, twice, three times. Challie's eyesight blurred, crossed, and she responded to the filling movements with a purr.

Arching, she whispered. "Yes," and smoothed her fingers delicately up his arms, up his neck, and into his hair. "Yes. More."

He shifted her legs over his arms, cupped her bottom, sank deeper, and held still. Pulsing, he pulled back as slowly as he'd moved forward, but he returned to her on a sleek stream of ecstasy, bombarding her narrowed senses.

"Faster," she commanded.

The scent of him was so male. The taste of his kisses, the feel of him joining with her, the sound of his feral growls as he moved with smooth deliberation, following her orders—all heightened the acute awareness of the lover holding her imprisoned with his body. Captivity she now welcomed.

"Faster," she said again.

Something different, something buried deep inside rose to the surface. Something fierce and mighty she had no control over. Challie curled her fingers into the solid muscles of Donovan's arms. She couldn't stop the rising, didn't want it stopped now. *It* wanted freedom.

"Dono—" she managed to squeak out on a sob. "Donnie?"

Perspiration beaded his forehead, dripped down his cheeks and onto her clothes. He let loose of her legs and his strokes intensified, his hands manipulating her hips. "Do it. Blow my mind."

He smacked against her with staccato thrusts, pounding relentlessly. "Take it. Take it!"

She did. On a vicious clamp. The tempestuous rising wrenched a strangled scream from the cavernous depths of her inner being, and Donovan pitched forward on a tortured bellow.

Heart thumping furiously, blood roared in her ears. Challie's legs spread bonelessly wider as he rocked and rocked more, the hard planes of his stomach tormenting her hypersensitive nub with violent pleasure. She left the planet, the galaxy, stormed through the universe on the savage ride to an uncharted territory.

13

"Fontana!" someone yelled.

"Are they here?"

"Don't see 'em."

"Maybe they're up in the loft doing the nasty. I heard something when we crossed the yard. I'm going up."

Oh no! Challie's marvelous journey suddenly reversed directions, fading. "Donovan," she whispered frantically, squirming. She tried to get her feet under him, couldn't. "They're coming! Get out, Donovan. Get off of me."

He didn't move, continued shaking violently, groaning his familiar sounds of fulfillment against her neck, his breath hot on her skin.

"Leave 'em alone. Married couples are supposed to get naked. I'm just worried about dessert. She promised."

Married?

"Yeah, well, they haven't tied the knot."

"So?"

"I got a plan."

"What plan?"

"Nothin'."

Hearing the barn door shut, Challie caved in to relief. Until Donovan's weight caused uneasiness.

Pieces of hay stuck to his hair. She plucked and flicked them away. When he didn't move, she yanked on a thick lock.

"Ow!"

"So you are alive."

"Barely," he replied. He rose to his elbows, balanced his forehead on hers. "Exhausted. You wore me out, brutally. Blew my mind. Temporarily went deaf, dumb and blind."

Challie lifted his head with both hands. "You're a terrible man. You always make me lose myself when we do these luscious acts." The last was so different, electrifying. It had blown her mind as well.

He nipped at her chin, easing gradually out of her body, igniting another glimmering tremor. Challie tensed, sucked in a quiet breath and tightened around him.

"Don't do that again," he warned.

"Tickles."

"It'll turn into more than just tickles." He slid forward and backward twice more, quickly lifting her hips on each smooth stroke, hissing. "See?"

Ooh, Challie purred silently, tightening her legs, drawing him back to her again, encouraging, for a third time. But she really shouldn't. Wouldn't. She pressed her hand to his shoulder. Donovan withdrew slowly, steadily, completely.

Frowning, he asked, "Did you bite me?"

She lifted his shirt collar, ran her fingers over the scores left behind on his shoulder—her brand. "Teeth imprint. I had to do something to keep from screeching the first time." The second loud shriek had a voice of its own. Challie yanked on his ear for laughing. "Hush. Your friends might be outside the door. Did you hear them talking?"

"Distant tones bleeding into the frenzy. I was on Planet Ecstasy with you. Didn't want to leave there." Cupping her face, he kissed her nose, her cheek and nuzzled her ear.

She hadn't wanted to leave their special place, either. As usual, all good things must end. Maybe even the ache she was now feeling.

On the other hand, she wasn't sure what to make of Gunther and Moretti's conversation other than their reference to marriage, which was absurd. "You must tell them we're not married, tell them we're not *getting* married." They were his friends, which seemed fitting for him to explain.

"Challie," Donovan said. Furrows creased his brow as he rose up. He readjusted and tucked away the object of her satisfying imprisonment. "We need to talk."

Already she missed having him inside her, but she sat up, flinching, and smoothed her jumper. Her torn panties were crumpled on the floor. Challie sighed. Why did he always rip her underwear apart? At this rate, she'd run out of lingerie before they returned to Arizona unless she found a needle and thread somewhere in the house. Thank God for pockets.

"There's nothing to talk about."

"Yes, there is."

"Donovan," Challie said impatiently. "I'm not marrying you. No matter what. I don't know you. I can't marry a man I don't know. You don't—"

"You do know me. Better than anybody. Better than any woman."

"I know your body. I know how good you feel inside me. So do a lot of other women, much better than I do. Marry one of them."

Slowly, she got to her feet, raked her fingers through her hair since the braid had come loose. She dusted straw from her clothes. Hearing his sigh, she refused to look at Donovan. His hazel eyes could easily draw her back for another sensuous round of untamed sex. On a straw-covered floor. In a barn! She grabbed her panties and stuffed them into her pocket.

Yep. She was a tramp.

The man could entice her into the naughtiest sex by looking at her with those gorgeous eyes. Or displaying his strong body and his beautiful magnet of pleasure. Just thinking about it made her ache to have it buried inside her again.

She needed to get a grip on her emotions. She'd already fallen in love with him like a silly young girl. What do they call it? Infatuation. By the time they returned to Arizona, the fascination would wear off anyway. It had to. He'd go back to carousing with every woman he could find. Every woman available whether they were "available" or not. And she was no different from them, throwing her legs open on a whim because of Donovan and the magnetic power he wielded.

Besides, he didn't love her. How could he? He didn't love anyone but himself. How could she marry a man who didn't love her? More importantly, her destiny did not include marriage, no matter what the reason.

"Hear me out. Please."

"Donovan Marcel Fontana, there's absolutely nothing you say that will change my mind." She started down the stairs, careful, achy. "I have to make dessert or Mr. Moretti might pass out from starvation. Cooking is my job but, Lord, the man eats more than hungry lions."

She left him sitting in the loft and never looked back.

Yawning hugely, Challie crossed the path back toward the cabin.

Goodness. She was tired, weak, needing naptime after a strenuous workout. Donovan had worn her to a delicious frazzle, but all naps had to wait. Bath. Okay, just a shower.

Peering through the screen door, she didn't see either macho fellow in the living room. Challie went inside and tiptoed to her bedroom.

Short minutes later, she stuffed her dirty clothes into a plastic bag, still thinking. Why did Donovan want to marry her? She should've given him a chance to explain. He'd realize the absurdity of a marital union. Marriage meant commitment between two people, according to Grandmama. A monogamous relationship in America. She doubted Donovan had ever stayed with one woman for long. More than likely, two at a time. Probably three. He did like—love—having sex with married women too.

And tramps.

Men had the nerve to call women whores, sluts and tramps. What awful name was given to loose men in this country?

Hmph. No one had ever mentioned that particular scenario. Hattie spoke badly about loose women, never loose men. She even mentioned something happening long ago with Mrs. Tedesco, but she didn't elaborate on the issue. Was she a tramp before marrying her husband? If she was, how did she manage to capture the love of a rich man?

It didn't take long for Challie to figure it out.

Beauty. Mrs. Tedesco was one of the most beautiful women she'd ever seen. Delicate as a rare orchid. Graceful, refined, well bred from good upbringing. Charming. Educated. Trim as the classic hourglass after birthing two children. The very type of woman Donovan needed as a wife.

Challie tugged at her ear, then held her arms out and looked down at herself dressed in dull gray. She shook her head.

Short. Small breasts, wide hips. And firm muscle, just like her father, Grandmama and Aunt Hattie in some ways. They were tall, robust people with sharp, dark eyes in comparison to hers. Delicate? Far from it. She had good upbringing, but not the refined qualities that Mrs. Tedesco possessed. Plus, she lacked status and advanced education. Without Hattie, she would be living as the next homeless beggar in this country. Destitute.

She'd always tried to look her best. Clean clothes, hair somewhat styled, standing proudly. Always proudly. No one other than Hattie knew her background. No one cared. She intended to keep her secrets close at hand.

Spreading the jumper out from her sides, Challie looked at herself once again.

What in the world did Donovan see in her to ask for her hand in marriage?

Donnie hadn't moved far. Sprawled on his back in the loft, knees drawn up, he stacked his hands behind his head and chewed on a piece of straw, staring at the ceiling. There were holes in the wood like the holes in his life. Something was missing.

Why the devil didn't Challie want to marry him? Women were always into money and how many dollars a guy earned, where he lived, what kind of car he drove. Well, he had it all. How could she turn him down? Did Challie realize all he had to offer? How could she? She admitted she knew nothing about him except for his body. Maybe she believed he couldn't provide for her.

That must be it.

He went down the stairs and straight-armed the barn door. She'd better be prepared because he was on a mission.

Challie . . .

Donnie came to a dead stop. What the hell? She might know nothing about him, but he didn't know diddly about her. Like her *real* last name. He kicked a stone from his path. Would she tell another fib?

Okay, okay. You gotta do this right, buddy. Maybe it's the reason she turned me down. I made no effort to learn her name or learn anything about her. Dumbshit. And stop the cursing! You promised to clean up your mouth.

Donnie veered to his left. He had to get it together first.

14

Last evening Donnie spent a few hours alone, walking the ranch grounds, burning the rubber soles off his Nikes, thinking aloud. He'd found the courage to pop the ultimate question, but it didn't happen. Begging didn't help either. Challie refused to sleep with him while Moretti and Gunther were in the house. She refused to unlock the bedroom door.

He'd slept little again, tossing and turning. In fact, she'd said they would *not* sleep together again. It wasn't a booty call pissing him off. He simply wanted her close by, in their bed, wrapped in each other's arms. Tonight, he'd kick the good ole boys out, transplant them to the bunkhouse and gain some solitude with his fiancée.

Fiancée. Yeah, right. Today he had to get down on one knee, pop the question for real. Paul was sure to call, expecting success. Or making another threat.

He glanced at the digital clock. Seven on the nose. The boss was preparing for the day ahead. Tupa, his bodyguard, was probably polishing the Silver Cloud, readying the limo for the morning ride to PT Industries' downtown office. Paul would embrace his wife and children as he said good-bye. Come evening, Tina would meet him at the door, crystal highball glass in hand, welcoming Paul home from a long day of making big ducats. Tedesco lived the perfect life.

Donnie heard the bath water running. Challie. He stacked his hands behind his head, imagining her bent over the tub testing the water's warmth. He ought to join her since they hadn't slept together, get a few intimate moments alone. He knew better.

Once they tied the knot, all this crap would have to change. He'd show her how husbands and wives lived, kind of like Paul and Tina or his mother and father when Mom wasn't ticked. Pops had a way of pissing her off. But he loved her like crazy, would protect his wife and kids with his life—same as Paul—but Mom ruled the roost, no matter what. Probably because of the skillet. Or the rolling pin. She kept Pops in line.

Challie was full of guff, too, backed by a powerhouse pitching arm.

The shower came on. He doubted she'd ever been truly dirty, except when Bullwinkle tried to kill them. Her parents must've had one helluva water bill each month. The only saving grace was she ate like a bird. Chicks worried too much about their weight. She . . .

"Challie, Challie, Challie."

Son of a bitch. Donnie hopped off the bed. Damn Gunther could piss off the gods. Hopping from foot to foot, he got his jeans on and yanked the bedroom door open. Vampires were supposed to sleep during daylight. "Breakfast isn't ready yet. I'll holler when it is."

"You cooking today, Fontana? I take my three eggs sunny-side up. I also want a rasher of swine and crispy hash browns. Homemade pancakes sound good, too. Don't forget the coffee. Strong."

Sneering, Donnie got in his face. But from the corner of his eye, he saw tension building in Challie's shoulders. An argument-in-progress did funny stuff to her. He grabbed her arm, dragged her into his room beside him. To Gunther he said, "Then I suggest you go to Dillon, because the only swine on the ranch is you."

Donnie slammed the door before the vampire snapped a nasty comeback.

"Stop dragging me around like I'm the toy you stole!" Challie said, working to wrench free. Luckily, she held an arm full of clothes, towels and toiletries. "I'm not your ragdoll."

He chucked her chin. "I'm not a thief, but you're a doll just the same." Donnie wrapped his fingers around her small fist, brought her hand up and kissed her knuckles. "We need to talk for a few minutes."

"No, we don't. I've got to get breakfast going before Mr. Moretti wakes, then clean the kitchen and make lunch so he won't starve before dinner, for which I must get the sauce simmering early. I don't have time to talk," she said, extracting her hand from his.

Her lifestyle was too crazy. The woman never took time to relax. Except when playing the piano or when he kept her in bed, sated.

"Antonia is picking me up at ten."

"What?"

"We're going into town."

"I was planning to take you sightseeing, lunch in the country, horseback riding. I've already planned our day."

"Your day. I have my own plans. We'll be back long before dinner. Besides, Mrs. Tedesco is my boss, not you, and she gives me one day off a week. Today. I'm sure Misters Moretti and Gunther would enjoy—"

"Bullshit."

She walked off, straight out the door and down the hall to her room.

Son of a bitch. She had a bad habit of walking away in the middle of their conversations. Arguments.

Overnight, he'd dreamed up all sorts of activities. Lemhi Pass. Shopping in Salmon, Idaho. Horseback riding across the prairie while she clung to him. Drinking a bottle of wine and eating lunch beside rushing water somewhere. Spending the day together and getting to know each other. Popping the question and cementing the union on a fluffy blanket before the ants ran them out would be great before they went to the justice of the peace. Maybe Paul would allow them to take the plane on a Caribbean jaunt. They'd heat the sea to boiling while honeymooning.

That man's mouth had gotten on her last nerve. Did all men in this country speak with forked tongues? She bit her bottom lip. She'd used appalling language a time or two, or three, during justified anger. Well, never again.

Like Donovan, Mr. Tedesco had lashed out at people with the foulest language. He trimmed his words when his wife entered the room. Or his children. Mrs. Tedesco would quietly chastise him into silence. Challie had heard it happen once. He was putty in her hands, begging for forgiveness. The same night at dinner, he'd presented his wife with beautiful jewelry—earrings, necklace and bracelet. Rubies, according to Hattie. Boy, Mrs. Tedesco had her husband wrapped around the first knuckle of her pinky. The woman had more precious gems than jewelry stores. She hardly ever wore the stuff except for important nights out. Why own the jewels? Why not return them, use the money to help those who needed assistance? Challie would.

In the kitchen, she scrambled the last of the eggs since there weren't enough for fried ones to feed each man. She went through another chop and annihilation ritual, used everything possible to stretch the meal. Biscuits, fried sausage links and bacon. They needed groceries. These men would eat a person out of house and home.

And where was the money coming from? Challie had arrived in Montana with a whopping twenty-eight dollars and change. She'd spent a good portion of her wages, the most she'd ever earned, on clothes and toiletries after arriving in the United States with little more than a tattered, brown suitcase full of memories. The rest of her savings was hidden in Hattie's sofa.

She'd buy rudimentary staples, the cheapest available, and spice them up with seasonings. Or maybe she could borrow from Antonia until she went home, then mail her the money once she received her next wages. When was payday? Next week? How long were these men planning to stay in this state eating like hyenas?

"Smelling good, Miss Challie. I love everything you cook."

Sighing, she closed her eyes.

"Can I help somehow?"

Challie twirled around. "Thank you, but, no, sir."

"The name's Roman. How 'bout I set the table, speed things along?"

"I'll take care of it," Donovan said. He went to the cupboard, retrieved plates. "What else besides silverware?"

"I don't need anyone's help."

"Napkins." He found them in the pantry and set four place settings on the table.

"I'm not eating."

"Like . . . yes, you are."

"Exactly, Challie. We eat, you eat," Gunther added.

But there wasn't enough food. "I ate earlier while cooking."

Donovan moved into her space. "No, you didn't. I've been watching you," he whispered.

Darn him. "Snacked. Breakfast isn't my favorite meal. Sit. All of you. Eat while the food is hot." She scooted around Donovan, used hotpads to drag out the biscuits from the oven and dumped them onto a plate. Perfect. She wished Donovan would stop watching every move she made. "Would you get another platter, please?"

"Done," he replied, but Gunther beat him to the cabinet. "Buzz off!" Donovan snatched the platter from Gunther's hands.

"Bite me, fuckface!"

"Damn you two!" Moretti snapped. "Why do you start shit at mealtime?"

Challie gripped the oven's door handle. Closing her eyes, she prayed for strength. These men fought worse than little boys over toys. Grown men never grew up, did they? Arguments progressed to heated words, on to fistfights, then killings. Blood. Gore.

Sucking in a quiet breath, waiting for the next unruly plateau, Challie realized all was quiet. She turned around, stared at each man standing beside a chair. Silenced.

"Can I help put the food on this?" Donovan asked, holding the platter with both hands.

"I'll get cream, sugar, butter and preserves," Moretti said.

"Cups and saucers," Gunther put in. "Coffee smells good. Fontana, you want some?"

"Yeah."

They scurried around the room.

Good Lord. She wouldn't believe it if she hadn't seen it with her own eyes.

After setting the platter on the table, Donovan pulled out a chair. "Ladies first."

Challie shook her head. "Really. I'm not hungry."

"At least drink coffee with us, Miss Challie. We can chat about the day ahead. Looks like a beautiful one, clear as a bell. Good Q-ing weather."

Huh? Q-ing? She guessed he wanted to know when he'd get his next meal. Hattie had mentioned lasagna. A big baking pan of the Italian dish should half fill the man's bottomless pit, which reminded her of garlic bread—fresh bread. More money. Push come to shove, baking a few loaves wasn't a problem.

Would the people working inside the big supermarkets barter as they do on dusty roads in her country? Hattie had never said. She bought all the groceries, for home and for the Tedesco castle. And she'd never traveled to Montana, where everything was miles away.

Somebody in town should know about this Q-ing business. Or Antonia might clue her in on the word.

She shook her head at Mr. Moretti's insistence. "I was thinking of baking lasagna. Will the Italian dish satisfy you?"

"Mm, mm, mm. Got my mouth watering already, Miss Challie. Yep, lasagna is my favorite."

"Name one food not your favorite," Gunther muttered.

While they devoured everything in sight, she seared meat then mixed in aromatic seasoned sauce for simmering.

The kitchen was clean by nine thirty. Lunch was in the refrigerator. Dishes were washed and put away. Challie hurried through another shower. Antonia would surely wear a dress, and she donned her favorite blue denim jumper and sandals.

In the living room, she asked Donovan, "Would you or one of the other men mind stirring the sauce on occasion, making sure it doesn't burn while I'm gone?"

"I'll do it. Moretti would scarf it all down before you get back. Just what are the ladies doing today?"

"Shopping. We need a few items from the market."

"Grocery shopping with all the stuff we brought here?"

"For essentials like lunchmeat, salad mixings. Bread, eggs, milk, cheese, etcetera." The list was long.

"Guess the good ole boys killed it," he said, rising from the couch. "Did Tina give you money for food?"

"Um . . . Not exactly."

"Not exactly? How the devil do you plan to shop without cash?"

"I was going to ask Antonia for a loan." Embarrassed, she looked away until he tipped her chin up with one knuckle. "I'll pay her back out of my wages once I get home."

Scowling, he dragged out his wallet. "You'd borrow from a new acquaintance and not ask me?"

The only hundred-dollar bills she'd ever seen were the ones she'd given to the orphanage, the ones Hattie had given her for the flight to America. She would never ask Donovan for money, for anything. Bartering for the groceries, forty dollars was plenty. Okay, she could borrow twelve dollars. "Too much."

"Take it anyway since Moretti's in hog heaven here. Here's my ATM bankcard just in case. PIN is my birth date in reverse." He mumbled four numbers. Born August fifth. "If you need more cash."

She'd never seen a plastic card before, let alone used one. Hattie paid cash, or wrote her name and the amount on rectangular pieces of paper. IOUs, Challie imagined.

"What else are you planning to do besides grocery shop?"

"Antonia said she needed a manicure. She wants to go to some sort of a salon." For what, she had no idea, nor did she know what a salon was.

"Whatever she has done, you do the same. Here." Donovan added another one hundred dollars, and when Challie refused to take the money, he stuffed the bills and plastic card into her pocket.

"She has a doctor's appointment at eleven. I really don't need your—"

"Buy her lunch. Did she say when you'd be back?"

Hearing a car's approach, Challie said, "She's here. Sometime early afternoon, I think."

Frowning, Donovan peeked out the window. Five seconds later, he said, "Oh, yeah, she's coming around the bend. All right. Good."

He walked her outside, greeted Antonia and questioned her about their return time. What did he expect them to do, leave the state with his money and plastic card?

They were having a splendid day, gabbing constantly.

Challie had learned about salons. Actually, the owner of the business, Mrs. Ricki, mentioned the latest buzz was gauging whether to expand the facility into a full day spa, something Dillon had never had. Something Challie had never seen. She'd quietly asked her new friend about "buzz."

Antonia enjoyed one day of pampering every month: manicure, pedicure, eyebrows waxed. *Ouch,* Challie thought on the first smear and snatch. She opted out of the painful-looking technique. On the odd months, the beautician trimmed Antonia's hair. Challie trimmed her own tresses when needed.

From there, they went to Antonia's doctor appointment.

Simply amazing. Doctor and patient allowed Challie to watch the workings of an ultrasound. She'd never seen raw pregnancy, a woman's naked and swollen abdomen. Antonia's belly button was nonexistent except for the dark shadow left behind. Where had it gone? But, growing inside her friend's big tummy was a tiny baby. He was sucking his thumb! He moved.

"Want to feel Miguel in action?" Antonia asked.

"Can I? Does it hurt?"

"Sometimes, when he's restless. Usually, he gets very antsy

after I eat spicy food. Put your hand here." Antonia guided her hand in a circular motion.

"Wow," Challie said with a smile. She wrinkled her nose, drawing her hand away. The goop was wet and sticky like oozing blood.

"Use the sink over there," the doctor said. She was a quiet, gentle woman. "Let's get you up and dressed, Antonia. I want to see you next week. Challie, it was certainly nice meeting you."

"Likewise." Ray sounded so much more sophisticated saying the expression.

After Antonia finished dressing, she said, "I'm starved. Let's have lunch at Sweetwater Coffee. They have lighter fare. Doc says I need to cut my intake, at least, less fattening stuff. I gained three more pounds. Makes forty-one so far."

Huh? Forty-one pounds? How much would the baby weigh? "Is there a limit?"

"Weight gain is different for every woman during pregnancy. My problem is I crave ice cream. Eduardo buys it from Schwan's if we can't get to town *and* the driver is on Horse Prairie, but it's expensive. We're out." She grinned. "The ice cream shop is right around the corner from Sweetwater's."

"Sneaking ice cream is how you reward the doctor for your care?"

Antonia tsked. "There's also a flower shop. They sell all sorts of cute knickknacks. I've had my eye on a centerpiece for our table. One day, it'll go on sale. After window-shopping, we'll drive around Dillon. Not much to see really. Then, the grocery store before I get too tired."

"We can skip the tour." Donovan had said he would take her sightseeing.

Outside Sweetwater's, they ran into Ray. He paid for lunch, saying he enjoyed their conversation. He truly missed his wife and children. As for grocery shopping, he insisted they use the ranch credit card. Challie was a frugal shopper when prices in America were steeper than craggy mountains, but the marketers refused to barter. Antonia stopped an imminent squabble with the man stocking vegetable bins. The tomatoes were atrocious. *He* should have paid *them* to take the fruit off their shelves. Same for the wilted lettuces and all other pathetic *mboga* (vegetables). And, oh, the *mkate* (bread). She was appalled when the cashier handed her the bill. Antonia snatched it away. She signed her life away on the dotted line.

Anyway, Donovan would be happy that she'd saved his money.

"What does Q-ing mean?"

"Barbequing," Antonia replied.

"I'm not familiar with that term."

Frowning, Antonia said, "Cooking all sorts of meats and foods on a grill. Where are you from? Mars?"

Uh-oh. Everyone in her village cooked the few meats they could afford over an open pit or in the ground. Barbequing, or Q-ing, was simply called cooking.

"I've been meaning to ask anyway. Your accent sounds a little like a Brit's. Where were you born? You're not from this country, are you?"

She'd tried so hard to tame her accent. Challie felt compelled to tell the truth with Antonia keeping her beautiful eyes pinned to hers, newly waxed eyebrows arched in tandem.

"Well?" She grabbed Challie's hand and squeezed. "Don't worry. If you managed to slip into the U.S. unnoticed, I won't tell. Lots of people from all over the world want to live here."

"A small village in South Africa."

"*Ay, chihuahua*. You're far away from home. Does Donnie know? He's so protective of you. Eduardo says he's under the spell. What part of South Africa? Have you seen a real lion?

What about meerkats. They are so cute. Did you go topless? I watch the Travel Channel. Some African women . . . Never mind. Is English a second language?"

Goodness. Antonia asked too many questions, and, yes, women in her village bared their breasts without shame. "I was raised speaking Swahili, and I studied English in school and at home." Her father had taught her more than the basics. She was considered an advanced student.

"Wow. We'll take the long way home. I want to hear all about how you got here and . . . everything."

15

"This Amobi guy proposed? Do you want to marry him?"

"I'm not marrying anyone," Challie said. "My dream is to play concert piano so I can send money to the orphanage, to my people."

Finding her mother was a huge problem without knowing the woman's name or the hospital where Challie was born. One day in the future, she'd hire an attorney or private investigator. Knowing her birth month, maybe there was a chance to find the runaway mother. That is, once Challie had gainful employment.

"Okay, but what if he comes looking for you? What if he demands to marry you?"

Shaking her head, Challie smiled. "Where I come from, the oldest son must follow his parents' wishes. They chose the wife for him."

"An arranged marriage? Ugh," Antonia replied, wrinkling her dainty nose. "Backward."

"True, if you're from another country." She couldn't agree more. "It's our culture, our way of life."

"And his chosen wife, how does she feel about it? Does she want to marry him?"

"I don't know her. She's from another village. Where I'm from, women have few rights. Men have their jobs. Women have their position." Lower than cattle. Cook, clean and have babies, whether they wanted to function in either arena or not. Village men were allowed to have more than one wife. Most did. "It's nothing like America."

"Hmph. That's too bad. Tell me, is this Amobi guy a good catch?"

Challie twisted in the car seat, facing Antonia, feeling relaxed talking with her. "You could say so. He's a steward on a cargo ship. Without him, I never would've made it to the United States."

Amobi worked much like William Still, who others called The Father of the Underground Railroad. He would only risk one stowaway at a time. The trip across the Atlantic Ocean typically lasted two weeks, but occasionally storms extended the journey. Sometimes in the middle of the night, he would sneak bread and leftovers to her.

Challie had arrived at a port in Detroit. They'd sailed up the St. Lawrence River. The scenery was beautiful, the air crisp. Getting off the ship wasn't as easy as getting on. Once she cleared security with falsified papers—masqueraded as a male shipmate, her hair tucked beneath a skullcap and hat—she melted into the masses.

Amobi had given her maps to follow. Hitchhiking with strangers sounded scary. Bus rides were less intimidating. After arriving in Phoenix, she was lost. Luckily, Hattie had answered her phone the third day. Challie was out of money and food with nowhere to go. She'd slept in the bus station, huddled in restroom corners.

Hattie never did mention where she'd disappeared to, or

why, when Challie had left a message. Funny, after her arrival, other evenings her aunt had vanished for hours at a time.

"Okay, but what about Donovan?"

"What about him?"

"He's—"

A muffled popping noise cut off her words. The car swerved across the gravel road.

"Oh, *Dios mio*!" Antonia struggled with the steering wheel.

"What? What?" Challie braced her hands against the dashboard. Thank God for seat belts. The vehicle slid dangerously close to the bridge's metal barrier.

Antonia brought it under control, came to a stop before they skidded into the ditch. "Flat tire, darn it. I told Eduardo we were running on bald ones."

"So, what do we do?"

With a blank look on her face, Antonia said, "Change it. I've watched Eduardo do one. Sort of. It doesn't look very difficult."

"If you say so. I've never driven a car. I didn't know tires had to be changed."

"Well, aren't we a pair?" Antonia opened her door. "All we have to do is get the jack out, the spare tire and boost the car off the ground. Then, somehow, we have to remove the screws to the flat. Finally, we reverse the process. Simple."

Boost the car? Challie wasn't so sure. They looked awfully heavy. Tires didn't look light, either. And, when Antonia opened the trunk, she wondered where the spare tire was hidden.

"I'll kill him. All this junk." Rags, jeans, tools, all sorts of clutter. "Tire's in the bottom."

Unloading the junk didn't take too much time. Getting the tire out took a lot longer. Challie climbed into the trunk to take the brunt of the weight. Antonia had no business lifting anything. What if she went into labor? They were in the middle of nowhere, the nearest farmhouse well over a mile away. Too far for Antonia to walk.

Finally, they managed to balance the tire on the trunk's lip. Challie shoved it with her feet. It landed with a loud flop.

"*Caramba!* It's flat."

Maybe she'd said some kind of a curse word. Challie had a better one for the situation. What were they going to do now?

"This is just great," Antonia said, looking at the sun then her watch. "It's almost five, but even if Eduardo and the crew are still in the fields haying, I forgot to bring the walkie-talkie." She cringed. "He won't be happy with me. With us. We're already three hours later than I told my husband."

"I guess I could run to the farmhouse we passed and ask for help. Will you be okay alone?"

Just then, a vehicle came over the hill, dust swirling behind it.

"We're in luck," Antonia said, squinting. "Looks like Rusty. He's our ticket home. If we hurry, I'll beat Eduardo back to the house."

As the truck approached, Antonia waved her hands wildly. The driver stopped. "Got a flat, huh?" he asked. "Last week I tried to tell Eduardo it was gonna blow soon. Figures the piece of junk waited until two women were in it. Who's the new filly?"

Challie looked behind her.

"This is Challie. Challie, Rusty Lockhart. He works the ranch we passed. Challie's from South—"

"Arizona," she interrupted, frowning at Mrs. I-Won't-Tell Castillo. She should've known better than to lay her life at an acquaintance's feet.

Rusty opened the door. "Might as well change it for ya."

"Spare's flat."

"Figures. Guess y'all better climb inside so's I can get you home."

"Would you mind getting our groceries?"

"I can get them myself," Challie whispered, frowning when Antonia shook her head. "I don't appreciate someone calling me a horse!"

Antonia chuckled. "It's a polite term in Montana, meaning he thinks you're good-looking."

Challie stared at the driver. He was somewhat of a handsome fellow—gentle brown eyes unlike Donovan's fierce hazel ones, thin mustache, dark hair trimmed close to his scalp beneath his cowboy hat. Well-barbered.

"Get in," Antonia said when Rusty opened his door. "I need to ride by the window or I get motion sickness."

Challie maintained airspace between herself and the cowboy.

"I'll swing by the fields so's you can get the husband out here. I can get him back to town for a new tire."

"Oh, no. I'll tell him later," Antonia said. She winked at Challie. "We don't want to bother him right now. Haying."

Rusty grunted. He looked over at Challie. "So, you from south Arizona. Never been to the state before. What part of south Arizona?"

"Phoenix." Challie did not want to have this conversation with a stranger. "*Natoka* . . . I mean . . . Where are you from?"

"Idaho. Born on a ranch outside Twin Falls."

"Beautiful countryside. Impressive mountains. It's the only U.S. state bordered by six others and a Canadian province. Montana, Nevada, Oregon, Utah, Washington, Wyoming, and British Columbia," Challie replied. She was going by what she'd seen and read in an encyclopedia owned by the Tedescos. They hosted an amazing library of information. "Only one hundred twenty-eight miles from Twin Falls to Boise, the capitol. Six hundred thirty-four miles to Coeur d'Alene, where the lake is spectacular. The Snake River runs through your town, and the gorge and park are stunning. The bridge, Perrine Memorial—"

"Challie," Antonia whispered, nudging her ribs. She shook her head.

"It's all true. I read it—"

Shut up, Antonia mouthed.

Oh. Had she talked too much?

"So you've been to Idaho," Rusty finally said. "Been all over the state, it seems."

"Uh . . . not really."

"Sure know a lot about it."

He slowed for the turn at the three-way intersection, looked both ways, continued rolling and made a right onto the paved road Challie remembered. Up ahead, she could see Red Butte, her landmark. Traffic on this road was as thin as in her country.

"We had a good rainy season this year. Folks say Phoenix is drier, hotter than hades," Rusty said. "Is that true?"

Every man she'd met so far cursed fluently. Particularly Donovan. Not Rusty. No other man had asked about her life or about where she lived. And that made Challie smile. "It's quite a bit warmer than Montana. The temperature between the two—" Antonia poked her again. "It's hot there."

Five minutes rolled by in silence.

"Maybe one day I can take a ride way down south to Phoenix. Might even stop in and ask you to show me around town since you know the lay o' the land."

She knew all about Arizona, but Donovan would be his best guide. He seemed to get along with everyone other than that Lawson character. And, of course, Gunther. They were worse than archenemies, for some odd reason. Had they chased after the same woman in the past? Donovan was intimate with so many ladies. Was Gunther the carousing type, chasing everything wearing a skirt?

"Mind if I give you a holler, maybe take you to lunch or dinner in one of them fancy restaurants? Got none in this here county."

Donovan . . . Challie scowled. This was the third time Antonia had elbowed her ribs.

Rusty wheeled the truck onto the dirt road leading toward the ranch. The wind had picked up. Trees swayed, ground cover fluttered. All sorts of birds took flight.

"Ain't trying to be forward or nothing, Miss Challie. Just trying to be a gentleman to a newcomer. Country folk like that in these parts. How long you visiting for? I'm going to town day after tomorrow 'round noon. How 'bout we have some lunch and do a little chow talk?"

Chow talk? "Huh?"

"Get to know each other," Antonia whispered. "It's his way of asking for a date. Are you going to accept?"

Date? She'd never been on a date! And she hardly knew this man.

"Somebody's in a mighty big hurry," Rusty said.

A small brown cloud plumed skyward.

"Dang people need to learn how to slow down. They don't know we're on this side of the hill. Might have an injury onboard, though. Hard to get ambulances way out here in time."

Rusty steered to the right shoulder. The speeding vehicle shot over the hilltop like a bullet and raced by them.

"Could be heart attack. Barney's wife had one last year. Helicopter picked her up and took her to Missoula. She died anyway." Rusty stared through the side-view mirror for long seconds as he eased back onto the road. "Ladies, looks like we got company. They headed back this way."

Challie and Antonia looked over their shoulders as the blue

streak whizzed by again. Swerving in front of the truck, it cut off Rusty's progress. He slammed on the breaks, skidded to an abrasive halt.

Both doors opened on the blue vehicle.

"Uh-oh," Antonia said.

"Ain't that Eduardo? Y'all in luck."

"I don't think so," Antonia replied as Donovan and her husband started back toward them.

"Lock the doors," Challie whispered. "Put your window up."

"He'll break it," Antonia replied. She hissed. "See how he's walking? It's his angry swagger."

"Who's the city boy?" Rusty asked.

Challie almost said "The devil." His face was as red. All he lacked were horns, hooves, pointy tail and a pitchfork. Donovan braced his arms against the driver's door. Eduardo leaned into the passenger side.

"Where the hell have you been, Antonia? Where's the damn car? We've been calling all over town, the hospital, the sheriff and the highway patrol. What if you'd gone into labor? Why did you *not* take the walkie-talkie?"

"We, um, had a flat, *jíto*."

He said something in their language that sounded vulgar.

"The spare was flat too."

Eduardo said another ugly word in retort. "You tried to change the tire and you're pregnant? Have you lost all—"

Antonia groaned, rubbing her belly.

"What is it, sweetheart? Is it the baby? We're going to the hospital."

"No, I'm fine," Antonia replied. She grabbed Challie's hand, squeezed it lightly. "It's just a twinge. Can we go home now? I'd feel better lying down in quiet. It's been a long day, *jíto*. I'm tired."

Ooh, Challie thought, her friend was telling a fib. Swallowing, she risked a glance at the entity glaring through the driver's open window. Glaring at her. She swallowed again. He was grinding his jawbone or sharpening his fangs.

Eduardo gently helped his wife out.

When Donovan started around the front end, Challie yanked the door closed, locked it and rolled up the window.

"Now why'd you go do that?"

"Him." She pointed at Donovan as he yanked on the door handle.

"Unlock this thing!"

"You know him?"

"Not well." She scooted closer to Rusty.

"Woman, I will bust every window and drag you out. Then I'm tearing into your behind in front of God and everybody. Unlock it."

At least he hadn't cursed her, embarrassing her. Challie crowded up to Rusty, still fearful.

"Your old man is ticked."

"He's not my old man. My father's dead."

"What?" Rusty shook his head. "Anywho, I think it's time you got out. This is the only transportation I own. Can't afford a new one. And this man looks like he means what he says. The glass is thick too."

Trembling, Challie asked, "Can you give me a ride home?"

"Don't look like a good idea."

"Challie, you have exactly three seconds to open up."

"I'll pay you twenty-five dollars," she said, staring expectantly at her protective savior. Leaving her with three singles to last until next payday.

Rusty seemed to contemplate her request. "Guess I could. Don't like domestic violence and I sure ain't gettin' involved in nobody's fight. Where to?"

"Phoenix."

"On the count of three, I rip it off its hinges," Donovan yelled. "One."

Clearly, Rusty wasn't going to make the long trek to Phoenix on twenty-five dollars. She did have Donovan's two hundred, plus his bankcard. Should she risk it?

"Two!"

Oh, dear God. He'd kill her for sure. At minimum, he'd yank her through the glass and beat her all the way back to the ranch house. Warily, Challie scooted across the seat. "Thanks anyway, Mr. Rusty. I won't ever forget your kindness." She raised the lock.

Was it possible to sever the handle from the door? Donovan tried. Glowering, he held out his hand, but she was too frightened to take it. As usual, he wrapped his fingers around her wrist and extricated her from the truck.

"Thank you again," Challie said to Rusty. "Will you pray for me?"

Looking bewildered, he nodded but averted his eyes when Donovan pinned him with a lethal glare. Challie started to look away when he turned his harsh gaze back on her. The ensuing stare down gave her pause, caused her heart to flip-flop, her stomach to cartwheel.

"I'll just get y'all's gear out. Where do you want it?"

She wished Donovan would help Rusty. Answer him. Instead, he spent the moments melting her eyeballs with his hot, unblinking laser beams.

A minute later, seemingly forever, Rusty said, "Got it all in back. Y'all take care now, hear?"

Where was Eduardo? Was he threatening his wife? Antonia had said he would never punish her physically. Lucky her.

Challie heard the engine rev. Left alone with a menace that seemed to grow larger by the seconds scared her to death. She wiggled her fingers, wondering if her circulation had stopped altogether. If he let her loose, she'd run. To anywhere. Across Horse Prairie and back to Phoenix. Maybe to the East Coast. Swim back to South Africa before this man beat her within an inch of her life. She'd seen the same kind of torture in her village. Defiant, a wife had resisted her husband's advances. But Challie hadn't opposed Donovan's sexual advances. Would he have beaten her bloody if she had? Challie shivered.

In any case, witnessing his glare now, the situation was much worse.

Run!

He must've recognized the intent on her face. With her in tow, she all but trotting to keep up, Donovan delivered Challie to the Jeep's passenger side. She started to use the running board, but he *put* her in the seat and slammed the door.

Behind her, Antonia whispered, "He's just a little bit upset, isn't he, *jíto*?"

"Undeniably pissed. Should've heard him at the house, in the car, when I saw you two riding with Rusty. You should've heard *me*, Antonia."

"But he won't hurt her, will he? I won't let him hurt her."

Antonia didn't sound fearful. She was fortunate to be with child. And well cared for by Eduardo. Challie wondered if claiming pregnancy would save her own life.

The driver's door opened and closed. The speeding ride to the Castillo home was in silence other than gravel clattering. As the Jeep halted, Challie considered taking the leap. She wrapped her fingers around the door handle. Except Donovan looked over his shoulder, glowering.

"Try it."

She wasn't that brave.

He went around the tank to help Eduardo get his wife out. Antonia's "sorry" shrug didn't make Challie feel any better. What could she do to stop Donovan during a killing anyway?

Then Eduardo said a few quiet words to him before he got behind the wheel again.

The continuing silence stretched Challie's nerves to snapping. What was going to happen once they arrived at the cabin, when they were alone? For the first time, she hoped Gunther was nearby. To stop the killing.

She played with her fingers for the last time. They'd never work again on a piano. On anything. He'd break them. Donovan's tone had been too controlled. Strained like the men who'd threatened her father so long ago.

When the Jeep halted, she bolted for the front door. Hot on her tail, Donovan caught her arm before she ran down the hall.

"Don't you ever run from me again. Woman, I will chase you down. Where the devil have you been?"

She swallowed. "We went, w-went to the salon and—"

"Did you have your nails worked on?"

"No," she replied quietly, fishing out his money and credit card. She held it all out in one hand, including her own twenty. He never looked at her hand. "Too expensive. Mrs. Ricki, the . . . the owner of the salon, wanted t-ten dollars for the m-manicure."

He puckered his lips then flattened them razor thin. "Did you buy lunch today?"

"Um, no. Mr. Ray paid for our lunch," she said brightly.

Donovan's scowl could peel paint off walls or the skin from her bones. A cold shiver raced through Challie's body.

"You, at least, bought groceries. You'd better give me the correct answer."

Huh? Was he expecting her to tell a fib? "Um, I tried to," Challie rushed out, "but Mr. Ray insisted we pay for groceries with the ranch credit card."

She thought he'd be happy.

She thought he'd burst open.

From the gleam in his eyes, the demon—a cavernous creature with arched wings, jagged teeth and yellow snake eyes—would soon surface. When Donovan stepped closer, she sucked in a breath and matched his approach in retreat.

"Did you spend any of the money I gave you?"

She shook her head, happy that she hadn't spent one dime. If he knew she'd saved all of his money, his anger might cool down. "It's all here." Hands trembling, she tried to give it back again.

"Keep it."

Why, when he was furious at her? But his calm tone frightened her more than the trampling moose.

"Did every cowboy on the prairie pay for you, take care of everything for you when I'd given you money for yourself and the frigging groceries?" When Donovan leaned down, she backed farther away. "Challie, you can't go around these parts letting every Tom, Dick and Butthead take you by the hand, leading you around."

Why not? He had!

"And you can*not* ride with strangers, especially cowboys. With or without a pregnant girlfriend."

"He—"

"Why were you sitting next to him?" His tone dipped lower than low, still echoing off the walls.

"Antonia—"

"Did he try to schmooze, talk trash?"

Huh? "He—"

"I'll kill him. I'll kill that son of a bitch before—"

"Stop cursing at me! Hate cursing. I'm really beginning to hate you. Rusty never cursed. He's a gentleman, unlike you." She dropped his money and plastic card on the chair, hiked her jumper above her knees and marched down the hall.

16

The bedroom door slammed shut with a bang.

Stunned, reining in his anger, Donnie knew he'd just put their relationship on the fragile thread of destruction. Plus, she'd called the cowboy by his first name without the "mister" attached.

Couldn't she recognize how much he cared? He and Eduardo were out of their minds with worry.

Eduardo had dropped by at two thirty. Donnie had already worn a new trail from the kitchen to the front door and down the driveway. Eduardo checked on his wife, but the walkie-talkie went unanswered. Anxious, they called everybody they knew across Beaverhead County. Then Donnie contacted the sheriff.

Eduardo had taken the phone from his hand before the man filed charges against him. He'd flipped out, had called the sheriff an incompetent, fat fucker when he'd never met the man. Luckily, Eduardo explained they were worried about their women, the reason for the outburst. The sheriff alerted his deputies, but Donnie hadn't cared. There weren't *that* many damn deputies in the county.

They hit the road, prepared to comb the area, ready to call the National Guard if necessary. By sheer luck, Eduardo spotted their missing women. If Donnie hadn't been so angry, he just might've dropped to his knees and thanked God they were safe, followed by snatching Challie into his arms, hugging her fiercely. Until she ignored him and locked the truck's damn door.

From the moment she'd climbed into the Camaro, he'd missed her. He'd missed her more than he thought possible. He'd stood over the stove, constantly stirring the meat sauce, except for wearing the rubber off his Nikes.

What the devil was wrong with him?

Now Challie was pissed, calling some fiancée-stealing cowboy a fucking gentleman, all but saying she hated her intended husband. To top that shit off, she'd just confined herself to the bedroom with her sole comforter. Tuxedo.

Somehow he had to make amends, explain his outburst. Maybe she hadn't understood his worry. He started down the hall when the telephone rang. Growling ominously, he backed up and picked up.

"Yeah," he said impatiently. Donnie straightened at the sound of the return voice.

"Tell me something good. The cops are harping. For you and for me. I don't need this shit, Donnie. They're dredging up ancient history."

"Wait a minute, Paul. What do you mean 'dredging up'?"

"Lana."

Hell's bells. Donnie had never heard the full story behind her death, but authorities thought they'd nail Paul for murdering his wife.

Lana Huntley had turned up pregnant. She and Paul married

young. She'd come from old and new money. Her family was loaded, owned more property than anyone in Martha's Vineyard. Lana's father was less than thrilled when his young, sensitive daughter had gotten involved with an Italian macho man. According to various sources, she'd had problems, mental ones resulting from her father's overbearing control. He'd run Lana's life, had told her what to do, when to do it and how since the day she was born.

Donnie hadn't learned much about the woman, except she'd given Paul a son. Ray was twelve years old when his mother was found crumpled on the floor.

"They can't use an old case against you, can they? You weren't charged or convicted."

"They're trying. The case was never closed. I need to find out who attacked Susannah if you didn't do it."

"What the hell does 'if' mean? I didn't."

Jesus Christ. How many times did he have to tell the man? He'd never abused a woman in his life! Never would. Challie would flip out.

Oh, Christ. She'd had a wild look in her eyes. Freaked. The same one he'd seen in the barn when he'd threatened to burn her ass. The same type when he'd nailed her in the alcove. But this one, this one was full of sheer terror. She was trembling, the vibrations transferring into his hand. Why hadn't he stopped the tirade then? He knew the signs, but he was so caught up in the moment he'd brushed it off. He'd terrorized her into thinking he'd hurt her.

No wonder she hated him. She probably believed he was the abuser who'd put Susannah in a coma. He was dead meat. He was going to prison for sure, unless . . .

". . . my new attorney."

Paul's voice filtered back into his stream of thinking. "What attorney?"

"The one representing me, idiot!"

"Look, I'm not your damn idiot, Paul. I've got my own problems."

The boss went silent.

"As for good news, none yet. So far, you and I are up the creek without a frigging canoe and paddles." Donnie hung up.

At Challie's bedroom door, he dragged in a fortifying breath, held it and rapped on the wood. He had one chance to prove he never would hurt her. The way his life was going, the U.S. Marshals might show up on Horse Prairie to lead him back to Phoenix in shackles. Losing Challie forever was not a happy thought, ground in his gut.

No answer as he exhaled noisily.

He tried the knob. "Please unlock the door, Challie. I won't hurt you. Promise." No reply came. "I've done some foolish things in my life, but I hope you realize I'd never bring harm to you. I'm sorry for acting stupid. I don't know what's wrong with me lately."

Sure he'd known, but he was too dumb to accept the realization, too chicken to admit it.

"Well, yeah, I do," he confessed. "But I need to talk to you face-to-face, not with this barrier between us."

Her silence continued. Damn. She was beyond pissed or much too frightened. He imagined she held Tuxedo in her arms, sitting on the bed, squeezed back into the room's tightest corner.

Losing confidence, Donnie balanced his forehead against the door. He tried the knob again. "Challie, please? I won't come within ten feet of you. Just give me a chance to explain. I'm hoping you'll understand."

He waited for too many seconds without a response. On the other hand, would she crawl out of the window? He didn't think so. He hoped not.

"Okay. I'll talk anyway." Feeling off-balance, he shifted from foot to foot. "Believe me when I say I'd never abuse you.

I've never, ever hit a woman. Never will. It's a . . ." Confessions were harder than shit, especially to a woman. If she would just listen. "It's a guy thing, you know, like Mr. Macho. Guys shoot their mouths off all the time. But when I make threats, kind of like bullying, it means nothing. Really. It's just a way to get your attention. I'd never follow through or hurt you."

He waited a few moments, hoping she would say something, even come out swinging.

On the verge of utter defeat, Donnie continued. "Does that make sense? Do you understand what I'm saying?" He braced both hands against the doorframe and sucked in a tortured breath. She had to have understood, but she didn't care to hear any BS.

"Okay. There's more. I'm gonna come clean." Licking his lips, he shifted his weight again. "I think from the first time I saw you, something changed. Then, when we got to Montana, something really changed. For me." He hoped for her too. "The big change was something I've never dealt with before, babe. And, like any Italian macho . . ."

The lock disengaged. Licking his lips again, Donnie held his breath. Was this an invitation to cross over the threshold or should he? The problem was he wanted to take her into his arms, show her how much he cared. But he also wanted Challie to make the next move—take the lead—at opening the door for him, allowing him back into her life without fear. He laid his hand against the wood.

Please. Just this once. "I am the macho—"

"Idiot?" Obviously, she'd heard his side of the conversation with Paul. The woman had an acute sense of hearing.

The door opened barely an inch. Challie peered out with one glorious gray eye. She held Tuxedo. The cat's furry face rested against her cheek.

"Yes. I'm an idiot, and I'm sorry." Holding her gaze, he asked, "Do you believe me?"

She stared at the floor then back into his eyes. "Maybe." The door inched open slightly farther, not enough for him to gain entrance into the room. "I don't like it when you curse at me."

"I'll never do it again, babe." Her eyes softened. "Never, but I've never cursed *at* you."

"I don't like cursing at all."

"Never another bad word in your presence."

She seemed to consider the declaration. The barrier widened slowly, surely. "All right, but what about when Mr. Gunther is nearby?"

He reached up to caress her cheek. "Not even when—"

The screen door slammed closed.

"If you lay one hand on her, I'll rip your damn head off!"

A split second later, the door banged again. "Hey, Ray, Challie's making a mean lasagna for dinner. You staying?"

"Oh, Lord," she said. "The groceries." Challie dropped Tuxedo and skirted around Donnie.

"Wait," he said, reaching to grab her. He missed. There were other things he had to tell her. Important things.

"Leave her alone." Ray barreled down the hallway.

"What the hell did he do this time?" Moretti shouted as Challie darted out the front door. "Let me at him."

Jesus Christ. Ray looked like a maddened bull with his sidekick-in-training behind him. Donnie was the red flag. "We were just talking!" he yelled when Ray drew a fist up. This was chaos.

"You had her running from you again. Eduardo was right. You are loco."

"The groceries! The groceries!" Donnie caught Ray's fist midswing. "We forgot about the groceries, man. They're in the back of the Jeep."

Moretti had reached him, joined in the melee.

"Stop it. Stop it," Challie screamed. She stood inside the screen door, both arms loaded with plastic sacks.

The bags hit the floor and she shot into maximum stride. The lady went ballistic on Moretti and Ray. Donnie had never seen a woman ruthlessly attack two men.

"Challie?"

She swung around and smiled, then looked away, went back to scrubbing the sink.

She heard Donovan's footsteps as he crossed the linoleum. Turning her around, he caught one wet hand in his, then took the dishtowel from her shoulder and tossed it toward the counter.

"I've done a lot of thinking. We have to talk."

Oh, no. This afternoon had blown out of proportion. She hadn't really meant to scream like a wild banshee. All right, maybe she'd gone too far. The patches of hair would grow back. She'd never intended to scalp Mr. Ray. And Mr. Roman's nose only bled a little bit. He wasn't permanently disfigured. Luckily, Donovan had gotten control of her and carried her into his bedroom. They were assaulting him. Two against one was so unfair. How many times had she suffered as the target of multiple abusers? Other children constantly tormented her for no reason. No one ever tried to stop them from throwing rocks or ganging up on her. She'd told her grandmother that she'd tripped and fallen, the reason for the bruises, cuts and an occasional black eye.

"I can't right now. The dessert I promised is almost ready. Mr. Roman has come in three times in the last fifteen minutes." She reclaimed her hand and wrapped her arms around his back, steadily glancing behind him. Moretti was also a very close friend to Mr. Tedesco.

"He can wait. I need to talk with you. Come outside with me."

"Fontana, are you trying to hold us up again?"

Donnie looked over his shoulder. "Live off the fat of the land for the next hour. For the next week."

"Mr. Fontana, please. Don't start an argument."

Donnie scowled.

"*Mister?*" Moretti and Gunther repeated loudly.

Gunther sat on the living room couch. He slapped the newspaper on the table. "Since when did women start addressing you so formally? His name is Donnie, Challie. You don't have to call him mister anything. Did he tell you to?"

"No—"

Donnie cut her off, staring straight into her eyes. "She *always* calls me Donovan. Why don't you both mind your own business for a change?"

"Go to hell, Fontana," Gunther said. "I'll kick your ass in a second."

"Deep in hell, you little shit," Moretti included. "You hit her, then you have—"

"Stop it!" Challie squeezed her eyes shut, pressed her hands to her ears and stomped her foot.

If these two idiots hadn't been here, none of this would've happened. Something in Challie's life had caused distress. Something devastating. Something Donnie knew nothing about. In time, he hoped she would confide in him.

He wrapped her in his arms, kissed the top of her head, swaying to a melody only he could hear. "I'm sorry. I'm sorry. No more arguing. No fighting." Twice in one day was too often for any sane person.

Her body was rigid, but she curled her fingers into his shirt and hung on while he soothed her, rubbing his hands up and down her back, squeezing gently. She felt good here. Fit perfectly. Like a wife should feel in his arms. She would be his wife soon.

"Take a walk, you two." He didn't bother turning around, just continued rocking Challie, hiding her from their view.

God, he hoped she wasn't crying. He wouldn't know what to do if she wept.

Donnie cupped her cheeks and lifted her face to see her eyes. They were clear as a brewing storm, long before the rain fell. She was a strong woman, not the type to resort to tears without good reason.

"I want to know everything about you," he said. "Everything."

She shook her head, stepped back from him. "No. Dessert. There's nothing to tell. Too busy. I-I can't. Dishes. There's no time."

Rambling, she wrung her hands. He'd never seen her so agitated.

"After dessert. I'll help with cleanup." He backed up. "Better yet, I'll tell Gunther and Moretti they'll have to clean if they want to eat."

"No! My job—"

"You're no longer employed."

He thought she'd faint on the spot and Donnie grabbed her arms to steady her. "Challie, I mean, you haven't lost your job. Think of it as a vacation. A paid one."

She seemed to regroup and gave her head a little shake. "I've never had a vacation."

"Never?" He couldn't believe it. Everybody enjoyed vacations, didn't they?

She shook her head again.

The hell if his wife would work her butt off and not get time off. In fact, his wife wouldn't work at all. She'd stay at home like Tedesco's old lady; do teas, go to lunch with the girls, play tennis or shoot pool if she wanted. Well, not in anybody's pool hall without him. But no wife of his would ever break a nail and not have it repaired by someone else.

He wanted her home when he came home.

In bed.

Naked.

Waiting for him to make love to her. Every single day.

Duke jumped bone-hard thinking about Challie in *their* bed. Best-laid plans ever.

First, he had to convince her to marry him—while he was sane and not under the power of her allure.

17

Moretti and Gunther balked at cleanup duty, but Donovan set them straight. When Challie advised them of kitchen detail, an argument started between the two over who had to do what. Donovan grabbed her hand and dragged her out of the house.

They crossed the road toward the fenced prairie. Montana evenings were beautiful—quietly beautiful—during sunset. But thundering around the hillside in the distance sped a big rambling truck.

Donovan unwrapped the chains holding the gate closed, then resecured them. They strolled for a bit, enjoying the peace, tranquility and the clean smell of sweet mountain air. He led her to a huge rock. The never-ending sky went on forever, it seemed. This was why people called Montana Big Sky Country.

When Donovan sat beside her, he pulled her close and wrapped his arm around her shoulders. Challie relaxed against him.

"First things first," he said. "I don't ever want you to call me mister anything. Understand?"

"Protocol, Donovan." The single word was ingrained in her mind, especially when addressing men and their guests.

"Forget protocol. We're beyond that."

"Only in private."

He tightened his arm around her. "All the time."

She sighed. He'd never understand.

"Ms. Smith, I want to know your real last name."

Challie flinched. Lies and little fibs were always found out. It never occurred to her that he'd want to know or even cared. "It's Baderleen."

"Spell it." When she did, he repeated it. "Is Challie your birth name or is it short for something else?"

"Only Challie."

"Middle name?"

"None."

"Challie None Baderleen. Different."

She leaned back laughing. "No, silly, I don't have a middle name."

He chucked her chin. "I like hearing you laugh. You should do it more often."

She would if she'd had reason to laugh. With the life she'd lived, laughter never came easily.

"How old are you?"

"Men aren't supposed to ask those sorts of questions."

"Maybe last century. This is a new millennium. Women are bolder now. Age is nothing."

"Twenty-nine."

"Yowza. You are old." She elbowed his ribs. "Just kidding. You said you were born in a hospital. In Arizona."

Huh?

"Were you?"

"Yes."

Her father had told her that she was born in a very small

hospital in an out of the way place. He'd never said exactly where, nor had he told her grandmother. He said it didn't matter because Challie automatically became a native of his country.

"What part of Arizona?"

"Look. Horses." She sat taller, pointing across the prairie.

"Tedesco owns quite a few. Do you ride?"

"I've never been close to a horse until we came here. They're not as big as camels." She'd weaseled out of his personal questions easily enough. If she could divert the conversation, she'd never have to lie.

"Camels?"

"Like at the zoo," she replied quickly. Good Lord. She was flustered again, but Hattie had taken her to Phoenix's zoo on her first day off work.

"Tomorrow morning, we'll go riding. Challie," he said, staring into her eyes, "in what part of Arizona were you born?"

How could she hold eye contact and tell another fib? Impossible. She looked away, but Donovan cupped her chin, forced her to meet his gaze.

"What part, Challie?"

"I-I," she stammered then swallowed. "I b-belong to another country far, far away."

He smoothed his hand over her hair. "I knew you weren't from the States with your accent. What country?"

She bit her bottom lip. "South Africa."

Shame washed over Challie and she tried to scoot off the boulder, but Donovan kept her from leaving, restraining her with one strong arm around her shoulders.

He could easily inform authorities, have her sent back to her ravaged village to endure a life of loneliness and despair. Was that the plan, the genuine reason the Tedescos sent her away from their home with Donovan? Had she disappointed them somehow? The chill of reality froze her heart. All of her dreams cracked in one pitiful second. She held her breath, waiting for the final devastating blow from a man she thought of as a caring friend. A secret lover in her own silly fantasies. He had the power to destroy her world, cause it to crumble around her.

"It makes no difference to me," Donovan said, leaning back, holding her with both hands. "I just want to know everything about you. Who you are, where you lived, your parents—"

Air rushed from her aching lungs. "My father is dead," Challie whispered.

He frowned. "And your mother? Is she living in your homeland?"

"I never knew her. N-never met her. She," and the word came out on a squeak. Trying to laugh to ease the tormenting heartache gathering now, a strangled sound left her throat instead. "She didn't want me."

"Ah, Jesus." He folded her into his embrace, lazily stroked his hands over her back.

Eight months ago, Grandmama had held and rocked her exactly like this for long minutes for the umpteenth time, the very last time she'd held Challie. On her deathbed, she'd given her granddaughter instructions: find the little wooden box and contact Hattie.

Hattie made it to her mother's bedside before she passed away. She'd tried desperately to get her niece to move to the United States. Challie had refused, even when Mrs. Tedesco had given Hattie the money for her travel. She gave most of it to the orphanage and to those who needed it more than she did. But, her life had not improved afterward. The villagers didn't accept her as an equal; adults shunned her and their children were afraid of her because of the horrible stories they'd heard—the demon witch with glowing eyes sent to steal their souls—had spread worse than grass fires.

Unable to endure loneliness any longer, Challie *gave* her grandmother's small home to the piano teacher, Miss Tamor, and her family. Without a passport and only having Hattie's phone number and a single piece of luggage, she sneaked aboard the cargo ship, stowing away instead of flying to America. She had enough money leftover to pay for the bus ride to Arizona as long as she ate sparingly. What would she have done otherwise, walk to Arizona? If it had been necessary, yes.

Leaving the only home she'd ever known had nearly broken her heart. Yet, her grandmother had never encouraged her to leave. She had high hopes for her only grandchild. Challie had promised to live up to expectations.

She rubbed her nose against Donovan's soft shirt. "I don't cry."

"Are you?" His voice sounded strained. Or pained.

Blinking rapidly to stop an overflow threatening to wash her cheeks, she said, "No."

"It's okay if you want to, um"—he swallowed—"weep."

Challie giggled at the sound of terror in his voice. For a man of his style and class, tears might fracture his macho attitude. "If I did weep, Donovan, what would *you* do?"

He huffed.

"Suffer with me? Become angry with me for putting you in a situation you don't know how to handle? Or walk away?" She looked up at him, straight into his eyes.

"I'd never walk away from you. Ever."

Ever, as in, until he met the next buxom woman who caught his interest or he became the object of her desire? His sexual prowess seemed to exceed most males who chased every woman willing to be chased. Lassoing wild horses might be easier for the lucky lady who snared any handsome man continuously on the prowl.

When she looked away, Donovan's hands tightened around her arms in a gentle but firm caress. "You believe me, don't you?"

Rather than return his gaze, Challie smiled and watched the

horses stampede across the prairie, dust clouding behind the herd like the fog clouding her brain. "Of course I do."

He kissed her. A sensuous meeting of the lips, and Challie gave in to the thrill again. She let Donovan begin taking her on another blissful journey, leaning back against the boulder, wrapping her arms around his broad shoulders. Until she realized where they were.

She shoved at his chest. "Someone might see us."

"So?"

"We were talking."

"Oh. Yeah." He readjusted his man-thing, sat up and pulled her with him.

No fight? No begging? No temptation? For the first time, Challie was shocked. "Are you all right?"

"I'm fine. Where were we?" he asked, frowning. "How long have you been in the States?"

Unbelievable. He made no other attempt to seduce her, simply went back to his inquiries. "One month yesterday."

He asked questions and she answered truthfully—as long as she stared into his eyes.

She learned a lot about Donovan and his family. Born and raised the youngest of seven in New York, he'd had a wild but wholesome childhood. He'd left the Big Apple's chill for the sweltering heat of the Southwest.

"Why didn't you marry, have a big family like your parents?" Challie asked. "It's the great American dream, isn't it?" She drew her knees up beneath the denim jumper and wrapped her arms around them.

"I had no desire to get jerked around by the old ball and chain action."

"What do you mean by old ball and chain?"

He looked perplexed, frowning. "Wildness."

Chuckling, she said, "You mean, too many available women,

even some who were not supposed to be available." She held her hand up when he opened his mouth, obviously to retort. "Like I said before, I don't have a problem with how you live your life, Donovan. You're a free man.

"When the right woman comes along, you'll marry her and make her a good husband, following your father's footsteps. Your wife will be the classic beauty like Mrs. Tedesco. She'll adore you. Together, you'll birth a dozen beautiful children with blond hair and blue eyes and live happily ever after in a lovely Scottsdale home."

Donnie wanted to strangle her. She'd said the words so matter-of-factly it struck him harder than a roundhouse slap. So what if he'd dated blondes? It didn't mean he intended to marry one. He hadn't planned to marry anyone until now. As for Tina Tedesco, yeah, he'd lusted after her, but never again. As for chasing women, those days were *finis*. As for the right woman, she sat within inches of him.

Why?

Because she didn't care about his background or condemn the lifestyle he'd led. She didn't give a damn about his money or his car or where he lived. Because she'd tragically lost her father as a child. Because her mother was an idiot for abandoning her daughter. Because she was beautiful and gentle, a passionate woman who played concert piano and refused to allow a man to witness her tears or pain. And she was afraid of mice.

All because of who she was, he'd fallen in love with her.

Ah, shit. I mean, shoot. Hell. Fucking A.

How the devil did this happen?

A simple trip to save his ass turned into a burning love affair with a woman who wanted neither him nor his name.

"You've just preplanned my life without my consent, Challie," he said. "Without, might I add, discussing it with me."

It scared the devil out of him to tell her the truth about their impending . . . well, once-impending marriage. He had to say something, be as truthful as she had been with him. Then maybe she'd change her mind. Once married, he could work on gaining her love. Sort of grow into loving him.

Damn, he wanted her to love him. Grow old with him. And if she wanted to bear his children, what a giant bonus. He could already picture their lives together, loving, caring, happy and lots of fucking.

No, no, wise up, idiot.

Making love to each other. Passionate love for years to come like the passion they shared now. Later, a dozen kids . . . maybe not so many . . . a half dozen gray-eyed baby girls to bounce on his knee. What great photographs that would make. Maybe one set of identical twins like his older sisters. He could flaunt pictures of his kids at the office. Taunt his coworking, single buddies. The first sniffing dog who thought they'd get their hands on his girls, he'd knock 'em out. Nobody would touch his daughters. Nobody would touch his wife, except him.

Satisfied with his decisions, Donnie said, "I have something I have to tell you."

"What? If you're going to talk about us getting married, forget it."

She could bruise his ego in one brutal second.

Shrugging off the sting of rejection, Donnie got to his feet and faced Challie. He took hold of her hands, planted a lingering kiss on her knuckles while staring into her eyes. He had no choice but to forge ahead, hoping for the best.

"I want you to keep an open mind, but please don't say anything until I've finished telling you everything. What I have to say will sound shitty—" He flinched at the crude word. "Sorry. I mean, ugly at first. It wasn't meant to hurt you. I never would hurt you. You know I wouldn't, don't you?"

He didn't give her a chance to answer. Ideally she realized he did have some integrity, if only a glimmer in most people's eyes.

His speech was straight to the point, but he did have to silence Challie's outrage twice, once with a sensuous kiss to calm her. She told him she had no idea Pearson's abuse lay squarely on his alleged shoulders. At least she believed he would never maliciously harm a woman. The reality added a mountain of pride to the love he already had for her.

One unsolved problem remained, hung heavily in the air. She hadn't agreed to marry him.

Donnie waited.

He finally climbed onto the boulder beside her, leaned forward, pressing his hands to his knees.

Long minutes went by as prairie birds chirped and sang. In the distance, cows lowed, moving through the field in a slow single-file gait. Horses whinnied, and gravel rattled under a vehicle passing behind them. Donnie waved impatiently when the driver honked.

But Challie sat in silence.

Why did Donovan have to dump this stuff on her shoulders? She had plans and they didn't include a husband!

He didn't love her. At least, he never said he loved her. How could she marry a man who didn't love her? How could two people wed not loving each other?

Oh, she was in love with him, but her love was only half the battle. The other half hadn't, and wouldn't, join the fray.

If she didn't marry Donovan, he might go to jail. Could she live with her decision? If she did give in, they'd both live a life of misery. Could she live with that, she loving him and Donovan wanting someone else? On a daily basis.

What about her destiny? What would become of all her dreams?

Granted, she would be legally in the country, not having to worry about immigration authorities chasing her. But a marriage of convenience? The phrase didn't sit well in Challie's somersaulting stomach.

From the corner of her eye, she could see Donovan staring at her, waiting patiently for her answer.

She looked down at his strong hands. They were free of jewelry, not even a tan line. Just like his body. Yet they were trembling.

It had to be from fear of going to jail.

Challie swallowed. "What if I agree—" A true smile spread across his face. "What if I agree *not* to say anything to the police? Tell them I don't know anything, didn't see anything." Any further inquiry from authorities was a huge risk she couldn't take, possibly drawing the attention of the INS.

All the color in Donovan's face drained, leaving his skin an unhealthy, pasty white.

"I mean, they couldn't put you in jail, could they?" she continued. "They'd soon realize you didn't commit this awful crime. I know you didn't do it, Donovan. I'm absolutely sure of it."

He simply sat there.

"Donovan, don't you understand? Someone else hurt her. I'll say whatever you want me to tell the police." *I would tell bald-faced lies to protect you.*

He looked away, staring off toward the setting sun.

Clouds had converged to form a dazzling twilight in brilliant reds and ambers and pinks. The sky's vivid, deep blue enhanced the rainbow of colors. Every sound, every noise seized.

A sudden chill in the air caused a shiver to race up Challie's spine. "Donovan?"

The change in his demeanor was almost tangible. His shoulders had gone stiff, his back aligned straighter than an ironing board. He didn't bother looking at her.

"It's time we went back to the cabin. It'll be dark soon."

Without wasting another moment, he slid off the boulder and extended his hand for hers.

She accepted his help, but he released her the second her feet touched the ground. His arm fell limply to his side.

Challie hated the ensuing silence.

18

Nightfall came quickly.

Donnie welcomed darkness as he lay in bed after showering under frigid water. Fully dressed now, fingers clasped behind his head, he stared at the ceiling. Shell-shocked by Challie's rejection, he'd lost all confidence in himself.

He'd spent little time this evening outside his bedroom, had skipped dinner. There was nothing for him to do. No one to talk to. No laughter. No harmony. Not even an argument.

Moretti and Gunther were occupied playing a game of checkers. He had no idea where Challie had gone. Probably into her own room. Probably curled up in bed sleeping. Probably curled up next to that stupid cat. All while he lay here agonizing over his own failed, damned fantasies like a lovesick puppy. Challie didn't care enough for him, didn't need him, and she sure as hell didn't love him even though he'd thought he'd seen some expressive look in her eyes.

How the hell did he let himself get into this emotional mess? Love was supposed to make a person happy, not make them feel like shit. He felt worse than cat crap warmed over. Did she care?

Oh, no. Hell, no. She doesn't give a shit about you.

"Well that's just dandy," Donnie muttered.

On the other hand, he couldn't let her perjure herself either. What if somebody found out she'd lied? The Feds would deport her. Nope. No way.

So he'd go back to Arizona, face the penalties the judge dished out and go to jail. And get fucked by some asshole—assholes—needing a girlfriend. Or die fighting them. Rolling to his stomach, he punched the pillow containing an image of an unknown jailbird. He sucker punched it again, seeing his own face magically appear.

Damn. Rejection hurt like a son of a bitch, more than he'd ever imagined. His body ached for Challie, his heart suffering a pain that threatened to split it down the center. He couldn't handle it. First time in love and . . . Wrong. He had been seriously in like once, almost in love, but when the chick mentioned matrimony, he'd dropped her flat, hightailed out of her life.

This was different. Challie was different. What they shared was different. Genuine.

Donnie rolled off the bed and staggered toward the open window. Bracing his hands against the frame, he drew in a ragged breath and stared out into the dark of night. A cool breeze ruffled his hair. He ran his fingers roughly through the thickness and looked up toward the heavens. Overhead, zillions of stars shined brightly, but the full moon hung as low as his spirits. From somewhere in the distance came the eerie serenade of Montana's prairie coyote, howling the pain Donnie carried inside his heart.

Jesus. God, help me. Help me keep from losing her. I need her. Please help me. I love her.

Swallowing a half dozen times to control an overwhelming

emotion he'd never suffered before now, throat closing, strangling . . .

"Donovan?"

He halted the torment in time. Every muscle in his body tensed at the sound of Challie's voice. So caught up in the anguished moments, he hadn't heard her enter his room.

"They're howling again."

He scrubbed his face with both hands then smoothed the hair off his forehead. He just needed a second to get a grip on himself and he cleared his throat.

"They'll stop soon," Donnie finally replied, turning to face her silhouette. She wore a white, floor-length nightgown, fitting of a virgin princess. Or a newlywed bride. "By the time you walk back to your room," he added.

He stuffed his hands into his jean pockets to keep them from vibrating. To keep from yanking her into his arms when she ventured closer.

"I can't sleep."

Neither could he, but the howling hadn't caused his insomnia.

"Can we sleep with you? Me and Tuxedo?"

He knew better than to climb into bed with her. He'd make love to her if she did. Make the pain worse than it already hurt when she, inevitably, would leave him. She was a passionate, giving woman and he knew she wouldn't turn him down once there. She never had before. Damn. He wanted to make love to her. Show how much he loved her with his body, his soul and all of his heart.

"If you'd rather we didn't," she whispered. Her voice sounded different, almost hurt.

"Stay." He had to touch her. Donnie moved closer to Challie, reached out and stroked her cheek. "Stay with me one more night."

He threaded his fingers through her hair, clenched a handful into his fist. Hesitant at first, Donnie bent his head, smoothed his lips over hers gently, then ran his tongue across her bottom lip and nipped.

She tasted so damn good. Unable to stop, he coaxed her lips apart with his tongue. The kiss went on a wild rampage.

Hauling her off the floor, he crushed her against him, which made the damn cat yowl.

He set her down and loosened his arms. Challie let Tuxedo drop, was back in his embrace before the cat hit the floor.

He wanted to get inside her badly, but not this way, not frenzied. He wanted to make tender, persuasive love to her, to prove how he felt about her.

She had his jeans unbuttoned, unzipped and his cock in her hands, stroking. "Pick me up."

"Wait," Donnie replied, swallowing. Just feeling her hands on his skin, he'd come in a second. "I want—"

"I don't know how to give head, Donovan. Next time you can teach me. I need you inside me. Hard. Fast. Now. Don't make me wait."

He didn't. He couldn't. He didn't want to wait. They'd make real love afterward.

Donnie yanked the gown over her head, lifted Challie off the floor, bent his knees and pressed her hips down while she guided him inside her. She was wet and wanting and needy. He forced her down his length until their bodies became one, joined at the flesh as he stifled her gasp, savaging her mouth with a bruising kiss. He tried to inhale her, to keep her protectively within him, to keep her from leaving him. To let her see the years of love he'd stored inside his heart. Waiting for her.

Lifting her again, he shoved her down harder, faster. Her body was hot. Inside and out. She burned, heat nearly searing the skin off his cock.

It was crazy. Frantic. Wonderful. Consuming.

Wrapping her arms around his shoulders, Challie hung on

and rode him hard, gripping his sides with strong legs, squeezing everything from his body, taking them both to the next rabid level.

Delirious now, Donnie swung her around, never breaking from the kiss. He cleared the tabletop with one swipe and settled her there. He wanted control of her, wanted all she would give him. Greedy. All she *had* to give him. She'd given him her body freely, but he wanted mind, heart, soul and all of her love.

Donnie shoved her legs over his shoulders and hammered on.

Challie ran her hands up his muscled arms, absorbed the sweat, the heat, the tension penetrating her skin. She welcomed his frenzied aggression, held suspended, unable to give back the wonderful sensations he was giving to her. He touched her core, opened her heart, not just the shell of her body. Could he see just how much she loved him, how she'd longed to be with him and why she'd come to his room? She'd give anything he asked for in life to make him happy.

Even if it meant sharing his body with another woman. Even if he said he loved her, the only words she wanted to hear from his lips. Even if he lied.

The first quiver attacked her nerves, but she wanted to wait for Donovan. He continued pounding, hard, in a wild, painless assault, taking her breath away. She dug her nails into his skin, flexed around him in frantic vibrations.

He let loose of her legs. He knew. As always.

"Donovan. Donovan."

"Reach for it, Challie." His breathing was labored against her neck, uneven. His voice strained. "Going together . . . to our love star."

Our love star.

"Now, Challie. Now!"

She burst on a shriek.

Blinded by the climax's intensity, she could say nothing more and let her heart explode with undiluted love, uninhibited feelings and an unlimited response to the lover holding her so tightly. Their bodies convulsed wildly while embracing their love star together.

"I love you. I love you. I love you," she chanted fiercely as Donovan's earsplitting roar charged the bedroom with high-energy voltage.

"Did you hear that?" Moretti asked Gunther. They'd finished the last game of checkers and were putting pieces back into the box.

"They're doing the nasty. Must be really good from the sound of Fontana's bellowing. Lucky him. Challie must have a tight-assed pussy to make a man holler. Or he's workin' the back door." He laughed obscenely.

"You're a sick son of a bitch, Gunther."

"Nothing wrong with different positions. Therapists recommend it. Makes life enjoyable, worthwhile."

"Sick son of a bitch."

"You're just a prude, an old fart." Gunther shoved the game into a slot on the shelf. "Got quiet in there. I'm gonna knock on the door, see what's happening."

"Leave 'em alone for Chrissake."

"Hey, if she don't marry Fontana, leaves the situation wide open for an orgy. I'm game. In fact, if Fontana doesn't marry her. I will."

Moretti shook his head. "She'd never marry you. You'd have to drug her first."

Gunther wiggled his eyebrows.

"You are sick. Sit your butt down or go to your own damn bed."

God help Challie, Moretti thought, *and Donnie.* She couldn't hide her feelings with a horse blanket.

He'd seen the look in Donnie's eyes when the pair returned to the cabin this evening. The boy was in love, written all over his face in bold script letters. Moretti smiled. But it faded as he pictured Donnie's rigid stance.

Something had happened while the couple spent some time together outside. Something weighed heavily on Donnie's shoulders. Something had changed him from the usual cocky, young bastard who Moretti treated like a son.

Had Challie turned him down? Or did she deny she was in love? Moretti shook his head.

The table wobbled unsteadily, but Donnie couldn't stop his body from quaking. Minutes passed before he was able to breathe easy. Longer minutes before he managed to speak coherently.

"Bed."

This was not what he'd planned, although every time they made love she sent him to heaven and beyond on a tempestuous ride. He'd wanted to make love to Challie in a slow, sensuous coming together, let her see the love he had bundled inside his body—all reserved for her. Not the frantic joining that turned him into an uncontrollable animal. She did that to him, though, as she'd made him fall in love with her.

Gathering his wits and what little strength he had left, he lifted Challie from the table and carried her to the bed, fully embedded in her heat, careful not to stumble over his jeans. He needed to get naked with her.

Start from the beginning as he'd planned. Start fresh. Start after he filled a basin with warm water and soap to bathe her then bathe his own body.

What he needed was a minute of rest. He sat on the edge of the bed with her on his lap, her knees on the bed. Kicking his jeans free, he wrestled his damp T-shirt over his head.

When he hugged her again, she moved. Lifted. Sank. Did it again.

"Challie," he croaked. He had to stop her, or they'd never . . .

"More."

She raised her hips again and Donnie's fingers flexed into her soft skin as she lowered her body, pleasure claiming his senses so soon.

He let her take the lead and helped her rise, let her sink, her hips in a perpetual circling motion. Over and over again. The scent of sex filled the air, taunted them, beckoning them toward their private love star.

"For the love of—They're doing it again," Gunther complained. "Son of a bitch. Here we sit, gettin' horny, listenin'."

"Stuff some cotton in your ears, dumbass."

Moretti tried reading the newspaper, had trouble concentrating on the small print. His bedroom was too close to Donnie's, so he'd decided to read in the living room. Gunther must've had the same problems and followed from his room a few seconds later.

"They got any sheep up here. They say sheep's about the same feel."

"Shut the fuck up. Take a walk or something. You're about to drive me outta my mind."

He dropped the sports section and looked over at Gunther. The man had a shit-eatin' grin on his face. A gleam in his eyes Moretti didn't like. "Touch me one time, hear? I'll splatter your brains all over this living room. Get the hell outta here."

When Gunther went outside, Moretti clamped his hand over his ears at the sound of Challie's hundred-decibel scream. A nanosecond later, Donnie's call of the stupidly wild joined hers.

God, they were loud. At one o'clock in the morning.

They *needed* to get married. Go some place with privacy. Some place with insulated walls.

He couldn't stand it any longer. Moretti stumbled outside.

She wore him out.

He had nothing left to give her. Donnie poured his life into Challie and she wrung out the last drop.

"We weren't," Donnie tried to say and swallowed. His throat was dry as parched earth. "It wasn't supposed to happen this way."

She shifted in his arms, lifted her head from his shoulder.

"I wanted to make love to you."

"You did, and both times were wonderful. You always make me feel so good."

"No, I mean, I wanted to make slow, passionate love to you."

"Oh." She sounded startled.

He couldn't see her eyes or the expression on her face in the darkness. Was it happiness or simple willingness?

Donnie lifted her off his lap, off his depleted cock, and set her on the bed beside him. He would make real love to her. After his energy level returned. "I wish we were alone," he said, grabbing her hand.

"We are."

"No, we're not. Moretti and Gunther." He heard her gasp. "Otherwise I'd give you a real bath, or we'd bathe together, make love there and in the shower afterward." Strange, he'd never bathed with a woman, but Challie wasn't any woman. She was the woman he wanted for his wife, his lover, his best friend, and he needed her to love him as much as he loved her.

"Did they hear us? Oh, God."

She was embarrassed. Her hand grew hot in his, and Donnie

squeezed it gently and smiled. He didn't give a damn if they'd heard their lovemaking. The walls were thin as paper.

"No, they couldn't possibly hear." He looked down at their joined hands and rubbed his thumb over her smooth skin. "Challie, I know I hurt you," he said, shaking his head. "But not intentionally. You make me crazy with want, with needing you." *With loving you.*

He couldn't risk declaring his love aloud, risk having her laugh in his face, denying she loved him, denying he loved her. At this moment, she could strip him of dignity so easily, leave him raw and bleeding. His heart bled now with excruciating pain.

"It's very late, Donovan. Maybe I'd better go back to my room before—"

Squeezing her hand tightly in his own as the pain intensified, carving a bigger slice from his heart, he grimaced.

The hours they'd be together grew short and, with what little time he had left, Donnie had to make every second count; touch her body to commit the feel of it to memory; kiss her sweet lips to savor the taste of this woman and drink from the fruits of her nectar to soothe him. If he could, he'd cut a lock of her hair to store away in a safe place and keep it near his heart to carry forever.

Only God knew he was no poet, but Donnie could think of a hundred poetic phrases he'd love to tell her now.

If he had the nerve.

She'd changed him, banished the senselessness in his life by being herself. How could he let her leave him? How could he live life happily without Challie beside him, loving her?

Lost in thought, he heard her whisper his name.

Donnie kissed the back of her hand. "I'll get a basin of warm water."

"But—"

He pulled on his jeans and was out the door.

* * *

Challie fell back on the bed, arms spread wide, feet dangling over the edge. She closed her eyes, smiling, remembering every moment he'd made delicious love to her.

Her smiled faded. He didn't love her. She'd made a bold declaration and he hadn't said those three special words in return.

The realization suddenly brought a rush of tears to her eyes. She swiped madly at them, but they continued streaming over her temples and into her hair. She knew better than to cry over a man. Hattie had warned her to keep her emotions under control. Always.

If you let your heart slip onto your sleeve, some man will claim it and, later, break it. They always do. Make sure you know they love you first.

Too late. She was the first and the last to fall head over heels. The only one in love.

Hearing the door, she dried her tears, drew in a shaky breath and let it out as quietly as possible. She would never let Donovan see her weakness, never let him see her weep. Besides, she should've known better than to dream, to fantasize beyond playing the piano. They had no future together from the beginning. Now or ever.

As he set the porcelain basin on the bedside table, Challie reached for him, needing to feel his arms around her. Needing comfort, wanting his tender embrace.

When his arms closed around her, she melted against him. His body was hot and big and strong. Comforting.

"Cold?" he whispered against her ear. He stroked her back down to her bottom in a sensuous rhythm.

"Not really. Just wanted to feel you against me."

She ran her hands up his muscled arms to his shoulders. Leaning back, she continued caressing his thick neck, then cupped his hair-roughened cheeks. He was more beautiful than any man she'd ever known. And she was here with him. Loving him. Breathing him.

One more night.

She had to face reality sometime.

"After I bathe you, I'm going to make love to you," Donovan said, kissing the palm of her hand. "My way." He leaned her back onto the bed, shifted her body with ease.

He did bathe her, starting with her feet, working his hands slowly up her limbs, following with his wet tongue.

Oh, my God. He was setting fire to her as slowly as coals ignited, one by one.

When his tongue touched ever so delicately to her most intimate possession, she squeaked out his name and tried to lace her fingers into his hair, but Donovan cuffed her wrists together, held them securely.

"My way," he said.

His way.

He delved into her body with his tongue and Challie lifted her hips to receive him. Gyrated. Urging him onward.

Mercy. Have mercy.

At the very moment her senses began to blur, he stopped. He stopped!

"My way."

He held her firmly in place, soothed her with teasing fingers, whispered softly and brought her back to earth in a gentle landing.

His way.

By the time Donovan finished his meticulous cleansing and torment, the basin water had cooled, but the heat in his hands sizzled against her skin, branded like a hot iron.

Restless and needy, Challie dragged in a shuddered breath. How much more could she take? He'd fractured every nerve, divided each molecule and scattered thousands of atoms within her being. She tipped unsteadily on the brink of shattering again. He refused to allow their bodies to join.

His way.

She was trembling now as Donovan hovered above her, exhaling his hot breath into her ear. He skimmed his teeth along her tender lobe, down the sensitive tendon along her neck, and Challie's breath caught in her throat. She started to come apart, piece by devastating piece and willed it to stop.

His way.

She knew his plan now. He'd never let her reach the stars.

Not yet. Not alone.

At last, he parted her legs, settled between them and lifted her arms above her head as she wrapped her legs around his waist. Donovan waited, pressing her body into the mattress with his own, the thick head of his man-thing against her sensitive flesh.

Pulsing. Teasing. Tormenting. Hot. So very hot. So very hard.

His way.

The words echoed in her brain, saturating her mind.

He eased forward, penetrated a mere inch, circling his hips. Withdrew in agonizing slowness. She tightened her legs, trying to bring him back, but he resisted. Instead, he kissed her lips—a long devouring kiss—a ceremonial joining that mimicked the lover's dance she craved. He released her wrists and she ran her hands delicately over his shoulders. The muscles tensed when she raked her nails down his wide, solid back.

Branded.

He growled against her lips, raised his head and pressed his hips forward by inches. Retreated leisurely.

"Ooh," Challie purred, her senses battered.

Again he moved. This time her breathing all but stopped, another low, mate's acceptance sound left her throat as he eased out of her slick passage.

Closing her eyes, she waited for the next divine entry, anticipation mounting as every single moment passed. He would give her more, give himself completely. He'd taken her so close to the edge, held her suspended precariously on the threshold of extraordinary rapture while she fought to keep balanced.

"Not yet," he whispered and her eyes flew open.

"Why?" Challie asked, frantic. He couldn't leave her like this! Not leave her soul hanging on the verge of insanity. He wouldn't. Would he?

"My way."

"Donovan." She was panting, unable to keep her senses under control.

"My way."

Oh my God. He meant to torture her. She couldn't stop her body from shivering, wanting to share the voyage with him now. Wanting to give her love with all she had to offer.

"Donovan, please don't do this," she whispered. Spontaneously, tears poured out of her eyes. She had to tell him while she had the courage, while her heart lay open and unprotected. She couldn't wait any longer. He had to know how much she loved him, how much she needed him.

But Donovan sealed her lips with a kiss, took siege of her body, gave her the setting moon, the planets and the coming of the sun, urging her toward their shining star.

Then . . .

They sat on the wooden fence under the moon's luminescence. Quiet filled the prairie night. Moretti sucked in the last hit from his cigarette. He flicked it across the yard while blowing out a stream of smoke between his teeth and huffed out a loud sigh.

"Whaddya think?" Gunther asked. "Is it safe? I don't want to go back in there with all that damn noise. I can't take it."

Moretti pushed the button on his watch and listened to the

chimes signaling the time. An hour had gone by already. "They gotta be asleep by now," he replied.

They hopped off the fence and went inside the cabin. As they started down the hall, they stopped in their tracks.

"Aw, shit," Gunther said.

"The son of a bitch." Moretti cursed more, his tone pervaded with fury. "Damn!"

Both men went back outside.

19

He never should've taken it this far.

He never should've been so selfish.

Donnie leaned back against the headboard, cradling Challie in his arms, squeezing her body tightly against his own, rocking. Her shoulders shook, her whole body trembled violently.

He had no idea it would come to this . . . The hell he didn't. Allowing greed to control his mind, anguish to rule his emotions and need to dominate his heart, he'd taken Challie beyond frustration, but short of fulfillment. He'd tortured her body and ransacked her nerves three times. He'd let her shatter. Three times! He broke her. A flood of tears drenched his chest, soaked the sheets.

Donnie kissed the wetness from her face, tried to comfort her with soothing words, gentle caresses. Nothing he tried stopped the downpour or stopped her from shaking.

What was he thinking? That he could force her into loving him, that she would change her mind about marriage?

He'd wanted her to admit what was in her heart, say the words he'd longed to hear from her own sweet lips. She had to love him. He could see it in her eyes, feel it in her body as she responded to him.

When she didn't admit the words, he'd punished Challie, left her suspended in a dimension worse than purgatory after telling her he'd never hurt her. She'd slapped at him, cursed him and kicked him with a violence he didn't expect. In the end, she fell limply into his arms, crying unashamedly, too late for him to undo the damage.

"Sshh," Donnie whispered. Her helpless sobs tore at his heart and would stay with him forever. "Please don't cry anymore, Challie. Please. I'm sorry. So sorry. Please don't cry anymore."

After long minutes, her tears finally ceased to fall. She seemed calmed except for an occasional hiccup.

At this stage, chances were she might never talk to him again. Never allow him to touch her. If she hated him before, she despised him now. Most likely, she never wanted to see him again. A punishment far short of the brutal one he deserved, but his day would come. Soon.

Donnie continued rocking, caressing her smooth skin while he had the chance. She relaxed as her breathing deepened. Challie dropped off to sleep, dead to the world. He shifted her body down the mattress. Donnie climbed off the bed, dragged the sheet over her, then the lightweight coverlet and tucked both around her shoulders. She'd drawn her legs up, folded her arms and curled into a protective position. All because of him.

Leaning down, he pressed a lingering kiss to her forehead, ran his knuckles over her cheek one final time, wiping away the single tear *he'd* left behind.

Swallowing a sizable lump lodged in his throat, Donnie grabbed his clothes off the floor and dressed quickly. With the guest rooms occupied, and unwilling to sleep in Challie's room, only the tattered, living room couch was available. He'd never sleep anyway. Couldn't.

He felt along the dresser top for his watch. At 5:05 AM the frail light of dawn would arrive soon.

By seven o'clock Montana time, Tedesco would rise for breakfast and spend the early morning hours with his wife and children. He would enjoy family time, enjoy the love they shared.

Donnie decided to have Paul send the jet promptly. No need for them to stay. No reason to have Challie deal with or tolerate his presence.

He'd have a few loose ends to tie up once they returned to Scottsdale. Paul would accept his resignation without discussion to keep his business problems at a minimum. Clearing out his office wouldn't take Donnie long. As for personal assets, a property management company could handle rental details for his condo until he was released from jail if he still owned it. One of his sisters had always wanted a sports car, and the bank would take care of his money if any finances were left after attorney fees, court costs and any other additions incurred by a lawsuit. Susannah Pearson's parents would undoubtedly sue him on her behalf.

His life had gone down the toilet. He'd flushed it down the latrine all by himself with stupid, selfish shit. Disgusted with himself, Donnie spun around and stared at the precious woman he'd fallen in love with and lost in a split second.

He reached for the doorknob and froze, paralyzed for several seconds as the full force hit him. He realized that after tomorrow, he'd never see her again. And the knife stabbing his chest wrenched deeply.

Sucking in air, he finally moved his lead-heavy limbs and turned around, blinking back the emotion he had all but lost control of now.

"I'll always love you, Challie. Always."

He closed the bedroom door.

It was over. *Finis.*

But not quite ended.

"I oughta break your damn neck."

Donnie grimaced. The walls were thinner than mountain air. On the other hand, he had to agree with the solution to the problems he'd created. Moretti should break his neck, put him out of his own damn misery, but he circled around the man and headed for the kitchen.

"Who the hell do you think you are? God's phony gift to women?"

He snagged a glass from the cupboard and filled it with water, wishing for a bottle of any kind of poison to burn him inside out. "Obviously the devil in disguise."

"Bastard. You really enjoy hurting women, don't you? Why hurt Challie, why make her cry? She's never done anything wrong to you!" Moretti stalked away. "You're the demon's scum kissing his filthy feet."

He was right. Donnie gulped down the lukewarm water, then slammed the glass on the counter and shattered it to pieces. A fragmented edge sliced a bloody gash across his palm.

A red river dripped to the white linoleum, formed a miniature pond. If he bled long and hard enough, maybe, just maybe, he'd suffer a slow sacrificial death, making everyone happy.

"Looks like you oughta do somethin' about that," Gunther said. He snatched the kitchen towel from the stove. "Here."

Turning, he walked away, marched out of the kitchen and left Donnie standing there. He didn't expect any more from a cold-hearted man like Gunther. Donnie was no less callous than the Scandinavian blond headed out the door.

20

At five forty, Challie forced her eyes open. Squinting into the glare of morning light, she pulled the covers over her head, still tired and weak, still hurt and, most of all, humiliated. She should've known better than to get involved with a whoring man like him—known! She refused to say his name.

Electric rage charged through her brain. So powerful, it brought her to a sitting position. Ready to lay into him with every foul word she knew, or thought she knew, Challie snapped her head around. The burning fury died a horrible death. He'd left the bedroom. Left her to suffer alone.

Challie closed her eyes and inhaled a fortifying breath, released it with gusto. She had pride. She would not cry, not shed another tear. Never, ever again.

Yanking the covers back, she climbed out of bed, stretched her arms overhead, lengthening her body, working out the kinks and knots, and cleared her brain of any lingering memories. She had work to do after showering. She snatched the crumpled nightgown off the floor, and slipped it over her head.

The hallway was empty in both directions. Quiet. Tiptoeing

to her room, there she found a pair of comfortable jeans. Hattie would have conniptions if she saw her prancing around the kitchen in skin-tight denim with a shirt tied at the waist. Well, she couldn't see her.

Twenty-five minutes later, Challie smoothed the loose strands of her hair after French-braiding it again. She started for the kitchen. Biscuits and gravy today. Turning the corner into the living room, she came to a dead stop.

Donovan.

He sat on the couch, elbows planted on his knees, pinching the bridge of his nose. His hair was mussed. He wore the same clothes he'd worn last night.

"Morning," she said flatly, continuing onward. He was lucky she'd given him that much of a greeting.

She washed her hands again. Mr. Moretti would surely be up early, looking for his morning feast.

After crumbling, frying, mixing and stirring, Challie heard Donovan's voice.

"Is she still in the hospital? . . . No change? . . . No new suspects either, huh? No big deal. Any chance you can send the jet today?"

We're leaving already? Challie wondered.

"Guess we don't have a choice . . . I've written out a few things for you, Paul. I'll have them on your desk as soon as we get back . . . You know, resignation . . . No reason to change my mind. It's inevitable."

What's inevitable? And, a resignation? Was he leaving his job?

"I'll keep in touch . . . No, it—it's not happening." A long pause followed. "Paul, don't . . ."

"Something smells mighty good, Miss Challie. How long before breakfast? I'm starved."

Why did this man have to interrupt? She so wanted to hear what Donovan finished saying. It just so happened his voice had dropped to a whisper. "Twenty minutes. Can you wait?" Challie snapped. She caught herself too late. Biting her lip, she faced Moretti. "I'm sorry."

"Don't be," he replied. He reached out and ran his hand down her arm in what felt like a fatherly caress. "How about a cup of coffee? I'll pour you some."

"No, thank you, but I'll make you a cup. Have a seat. I'm the maid here. It's my job."

"Job shmob," Moretti said icily. He spun around. "You don't work for anybody here."

Evidently his anger had escalated. By the gruffness of his tone, and without seeing his face, he had included the living room's sole occupant. Moretti went back to his room.

When Donovan looked up, feet braced against the iron table, legs arrogantly spread apart displaying his manliness—every thick inch he owned—she swallowed the next breath. Challie lifted her gaze to meet his. She couldn't make her body move, couldn't tear her eyes from Donovan's for several seconds. She finally managed to look down at the floor and turned her back on him.

My God. He looked awful. Red-rimmed eyes, sallow skin, hair-roughened cheeks and chin. He looked terrible. Hadn't he slept after leaving her?

Don't think about it. He hadn't worried whether she'd slept or not, hadn't worried about her frazzled condition last night.

She picked up an empty stainless-steel pot and slapped it on the stove. Marching, she crossed the linoleum to the refrigerator and snatched the door open. What did she need from this thing anyway? Standing there, frowning, hands on her hips, she finally slammed the door shut. Challie went back to the stove.

"Looks like you need to get away from here for a bit."

Gunther. She'd recognize his bass voice from a distance. And, yes, she did need to get away. From Donovan.

"Why don't I take you for a ride into town? Maybe have

lunch? Family restaurant with good sandwiches. Beer and drinks. Whaddya say?"

Sounded intriguing, even coming from this wolf. Challie contemplated the idea while stirring the aromatic gravy. "All right. Lunch sounds nice. We need dessert for tonight."

"Then it's a date, with shopping."

She jumped, hearing something heavy scrape the floor. Setting the spoon down, she turned the burner down to simmer and spun around. In the living room, the handmade iron table sat at an odd angle. Two magazines lay on the floor. Donovan was nowhere in sight.

The screen door slapped shut.

Motherfucker.

Growling under his breath, Donnie stormed toward the barn in long strides. He had to get out of the cabin. Get away from everything before he lost his cool. Before he jumped into Gunther's ass with all fours and beat the living shit out of him, beat him to a bloody, fucking pulp.

The son of a bitch. At the barn door, he tunneled his fingers through his hair. Hell.

She accepted. She's going with him. Donnie snorted. What right did he have to get pissed? None. Absolutely none.

You made your bed, now suffer in it. Damn but it hurt like hell. Rubbing his chest was little help against the sharp pain stabbing his heart. What the fuck was he supposed to do, sit back and watch Gunther make a move on Challie? Hell, he already *had* made his move!

"Lunch sounds goddamn nice," he mimicked badly, kicking dust with the toe of his Nike. He did it again. Pebbles flew against the barn like rapid machine-gun fire. "Nice my fucking ass."

Donnie started back for the cabin.

* * *

"Breakfast," Challie yelled. She set a plate stacked with homemade biscuits on the table beside the huge casserole bowl of sausage gravy.

Moretti came around the corner in a trot. "Lord, have mercy," he said, grinning. He pulled the chair out. "Here, have a seat. You gotta eat, too."

"Oh, no. Um. I'm not hungry. Would you like eggs? I scrambled some." Actually, she'd beat the devil out of a dozen to feed these hungry animals.

"Whatever you have to offer," Gunther replied, spinning a chair around on one leg so it faced away from the table. Straddling the seat, he wiggled his thick eyebrows.

She did not like this man. Maybe going into town alone with him was a mistake. She went back to the stove, bent over and pulled the platter of eggs from the oven.

"Gunther!"

Challie straightened at the sound of Donovan's scathing tone.

"What?" Gunther snapped.

"You're breaking your goddamn neck, that's what."

Challie frowned. Huh? Slowly, she turned around.

Murderous fury filled Donovan's face. Gunther . . . she couldn't see his, but she imagined anger and resentment colored it like his neck, which matched the shade of his red shirt.

"Get a grip, Fontana," Gunther retorted.

"All right, all right, you guys. Cut the bickering," Moretti said, wiping his mouth with a napkin, already starting in on the food. He smiled grimly at Challie. "No arguing. Pull up a chair, Donnie. Have some breakfast."

He did, directly opposite Gunther, seemingly an opponent of an impending shootout, sitting in the same spread-eagle fashion. Resting his elbows on the tabletop, he laced his fingers into one big fist, bright hazel eyes glaring at his adversary.

"Eggs anyone?" Challie asked.

Moretti raised his hand.

* * *

They devoured everything. Everything! She didn't get one biscuit. It seemed Donovan and Gunther had gathered for an eating competition. As for Moretti, his hands and mouth rivaled each other.

Challie sipped coffee to stave off hunger pains while two macho men cleaned the kitchen. Moretti insisted it was Donovan and Gunther's duty today. And what a sight. She'd have to re-tidy what these men thought they'd cleaned.

Gunther came into the living room. "How about we leave around eleven thirty. Doesn't take long to get into town. I know I'll be hungry by then."

"I-I guess so. We should get back by three. Dinner," Challie said. She wrung her hands then rubbed her jean-clad legs to stop from trembling. *It's just a trip into town. Just lunch.* Lunch with a glittery blue-eyed wolf.

She'd feel more comfortable if someone else rode with them. Staring at Donovan's back, remembering his stay-away-from-him words, she asked, "Will Mr. Moretti come—"

"No," Gunther cut in, brusque. "You and me."

As Donovan slapped a dishtowel onto the counter, Challie said, "Oh. All right. As long as we're back by three."

A two-hour turnaround time from the drive, lunch, grocery shopping, she figured. She could handle the time easily. If her stomach didn't somersault for the next few hours. Otherwise, she'd surely throw up before they climbed into the car, if she had anything in her belly.

"I'll be ready when you are," Challie confirmed.

She went into her room and fell onto the bed, not knowing whether to cry, scream or vomit.

Gunther damn well better have her back here by three.

Moretti had offered to help pick up equipment in Butte for a friendly neighbor. He'd asked for the Jeep's keys. Donnie had warned him to be back by two, no later than two thirty. He didn't trust the vampire even in daylight.

Meanwhile, he paced from room to room, unable to sit for more than a minute, worried, angry and boxed in like a caged grizzly.

Paul said he'd send the plane tomorrow. He needed it this afternoon and evening for a business trip, pretty much leaving them trapped in Montana for another day, giving shithead Gunther another stab at Challie tonight, damn him.

Paul had also said Pearson's condition had not been upgraded. According to him, Donnie was guilt-free so far, no real hard inquiry into his whereabouts. It didn't change a thing. To keep Paul's business out of this mess, Donnie had to resign. Nothing his boss said would change his mind.

However, Paul could cause Challie problems. He sounded pissed since they weren't marrying. He could easily threaten to have her deported.

Donnie hoped the boss's anger wouldn't boil over in that direction. What would deportation prove anyway? He'd still be a lovesick jailbird, although he didn't tell Paul about his feelings for Challie. Maybe he should have. Hell, what difference would it make now? After disappearing into the prison system, then reemerging, nobody wanted an ex-con. No woman with good sense wanted a broken-down, penniless mongrel. Especially Challie. She'd already lived, he believed, a tough life. Why would she want to continue living in as much misery?

She'll move forward. With her dreams, she'll move on to stardom within her own talented right.

Without him.

Donnie cursed, fell into the chair and scrubbed his face with both hands.

What the hell was he going to do?

* * *

Challie hung on to the seat belt harness with both hands. Gunther drove like a racecar driver, over bumps and dips, scraping the underside of the car. He didn't care.

Luck was with them when an antelope darted onto the two-lane road. At least, luck for the antelope. Gunther sped up and tried to hit the creature.

"Rental car," he'd said. "Piece of junk anyway."

Challie relaxed once they veered onto the interstate. Until Gunther broke the speed of light passing everything on the road. He accelerated around curves too. She glanced over once at the speedometer. Ninety. She closed her eyes and prayed, heart racing at the same speed. No wonder Moretti slept on the ride from the airstrip. He'd probably passed out cold.

Why did she come with this man? Why didn't she stay at the cabin with . . .

She tried to erase his name from her mind. They had no future together. Not after what he'd done. Lovers never humiliated each other. Okay, so they really weren't lovers at all. Temporary bed partners. A tramp and . . . Darn. No one saddled men with ugly names.

Challie squeaked out a groan when Gunther swerved around a tank hauling an oversized silver thing with windows. She caught sight of a big brown animal in back. Horse? She'd never find out. By the time she turned around, the vehicle would be miles back. They'd come close to hitting the vehicle when it edged out to pass the car in front. Crude as Gunther was, he leaned on the horn, cursed, then flashed his middle finger for some odd reason. She had no idea what that meant, but obviously something nasty since the other driver reciprocated the gesture and mouthed something, sneering. Challie sank down in the seat.

At this rate, they may not make it as far as town.

"Beautiful scenery," Gunther said. "Nice, huh?"

How could she tell? Mountains, trees and valleys flew by in a blur.

Finally. Finally, the road sign said Dillon. They took the first exit over a bridge.

Challie sighed with relief. She released the harness and looked down at her hands. Angry red lines crisscrossed over her palms. She rubbed them together, stretched her fingers to work out the kinks.

For a small town, Dillon had a lot of activity. Shade trees were all around. Old trees. Humongous trees. People roamed the streets. Cars showed consideration to pedestrians. Every male seemed to wear a cowboy hat and boots.

"Rodeo's coming to town come September," Gunther said. "Labor Day weekend is big stuff in this part of the county. They start partying early. Folks from all over, including Canada, come here for the fun. Ever been to a rodeo, Challie?"

She'd seen a few pictures. "No."

Gunther maneuvered the car into a parking space. "We're here."

Challie looked over at the clock. The ride only took twenty-nine minutes. Good. They'd start back to the cabin early.

Gunther led her inside a restaurant filled with tables, chairs and funny machines that children played. She'd never been to a place like this. Inside looked like a barn. Pictures of cowboys, horses, deer and bears hung on the walls. As well as lighted cans and bottles of beer.

They found an empty table along the wall near the bar. The only person wearing an apron sashayed over, set two glasses of ice water down and handed them each menus. She left just as quickly.

"They got great sandwiches," Gunther said. "Ice-cold beer to satisfy the thirst."

She never drank liquor, not a sip after seeing the drunken

fools at the Tedescos' last pool party. "I think I'll have iced tea instead."

"Whatever." He signaled the waitress.

He wasn't much of a conversationalist, Challie thought as she studied the menu. Luckily, the waitress came by to take their orders.

"So, Challie," Gunther said loudly over the growing racket. "You like Montana?"

How could she like a state she'd seen so little of in the last half hour? They'd zoomed past anything of interest. "It seems very pleasant."

"Good. Good. Would you like to stay in a town like this?"

Huh? "I'm very happy in Arizona. I have family there."

"Oh. Who?"

Was this man nosy or was this conversation leading somewhere? "Distant relatives, maybe," she said, staring at the table, unable to tell a fib while making eye contact. *And maybe my mother somewhere.*

She'd thought often of her birth mother, even wondered where the woman might live. Papa had refused to say her name and it had died with him.

The waitress came by with their drinks.

"I think you'd like staying here. Small town, quiet. Except during the big rodeo. Folks get a little wild. Lots of drinking and partying."

The noise in this place had reached a volume hardly tolerable. Kids screamed and laughed, country music blared and adults tried to talk over each other.

"This is the busiest place in town," Gunther said. He took a very long swill of beer then signaled the waitress for another. "By the time she gets here, I'll be finished with this one."

Lord, she hoped he wouldn't get drunk. How would they get back to the ranch? She certainly didn't know how to drive and wondered if a taxicab was available.

Lunch finally arrived. Challie picked at her food. Gunther inhaled his without another word.

"We're gonna take a tour of the town. Restroom is back there," he said, pointing. "Better hit it before we leave. I'm gonna order another beer and you a little more tea. Sure you don't want a beer?"

"No, thank you." She left the table.

Gunther signaled to his friend sitting at the bar. Slim slid off the stool and swaggered over. "Lean over the table. Block the view," Gunther said. He took out two small vials from his shirt pocket and dumped the contents into Challie's glass.

"Get the waitress over here. We need tea." She hurried over. "Only half," Gunther said. When she left, he said to Slim, "You got what I need?"

Slim, a tall, lanky dude, wearing a Garth Brooks black hat, nodded. He was a man of few words, chewing on a toothpick.

"Where's Lawson? He here yet?"

Slim nodded toward the poker machines. Lawson was a poker maniac. A loser.

"Call your old lady. Meet us at the right place in half an hour. She'll be fucked-up by then. Won't know her ass from a hole in the ground."

Slim nodded and swaggered away, boot heels scuffing the wooden floor.

When Challie came back to the table, Gunther said, "Drink up, sweetheart. We got places to go, people to see."

Sweetheart? Oh, he was a nasty man. And who did they have to see? He never mentioned meeting anyone. Challie drank most of the bitter tea. Must be the well water. Her home country's water was tainted with much worse. She licked her lips and set the glass aside.

Gunther grinned. Following his gaze, she expected to see a

woman grinning back. The man sitting at the bar flashed uneven teeth. She smiled.

"Ready?" Gunther asked.

Donnie had checked his watch every few minutes. Two fifteen. Where the hell was Roman? Where the devil were Gunther and Challie? An hour there, an hour back, an hour for lunch. Maximum ten minutes to buy dessert. The way Gunther drove, less time.

Hearing a vehicle outside, Donnie stomped toward the door and yanked it open.

The driver wasn't Roman.

Jennifer Ann. What the hell did she want?

She climbed down from the cab. How she managed wearing skin-tight, stonewashed jeans was beyond Donnie.

She tipped her hat back. "Afternoon, cowboy."

"Jennifer."

"Thought I'd stop by and check on y'all. Mind if I sit a spell? Mighty hot day for a Montana afternoon. Could use an ice-cold beer." She opened the screen door and stepped inside, boot heels clicking noisily across the linoleum.

This petite woman had bigger balls than Gunther.

Just then, Moretti drove up. Thank God.

"Sorry, Jennifer, we got no beer and we're sort of busy right now." Gunther had brought a case of Budweiser with him.

The woman's bottom lip seemed to drop to the floor and she lost her perkiness. "Sure you don't need some company? Got all afternoon."

Once upon a time, yeah. He would've jumped on her like stink on shit. Today, Jennifer was just another pathetic broad looking for a stud bang job. Well, not him. Those days were over.

"How'd do."

Donnie looked over his shoulder at Moretti, frowning. The

man was Brooklyn Italian. Since when did he start talking bumpkin? How'd do? "Where the hell have you been? It's after two," he bitched.

Moretti sighed. "Care to introduce me to our company first?"

"Jennifer. Roman," he snapped, thumbing each. "Where the hell have you been?"

"Butte, like I said. Jennifer, would you like—"

"No, she wouldn't. She's leaving. I'll walk you out."

Donnie put his hand under her elbow, forced the woman to her feet and guided her out the door.

"You sure are in a rush to get rid of me," Jennifer complained.

"Things to do."

She yanked her arm away and spun around to face him. "I can think of a lot of stuff to do, cowboy," she purred, running hands up his chest, locking her arms around his neck.

Pressing her pair of B52s against him like a jam sandwich, she gyrated her hips. Duke didn't rise. Donnie unwrapped her arms, disgusted.

"You'd best find yourself a real cowboy, Jennifer. I'm not on the auction block like the stud racehorse you're looking for. Git along, little doggie."

Lips peeled back in a sneer, she said, "You sure came out the gates pawing and whinnying last year. Twice."

Huge error delving into this cowgirl's drawers. "Good-bye, Jennifer. Tell your grandpa I said thanks for the cat. We'll get her back tomorrow." Donnie walked away.

In the kitchen, Moretti stuffed cheese into his mouth while he fixed his signature Dagwood sandwich.

"What do you think is taking them so long?" Donnie asked.

"Who?"

"You know exactly who I'm talking about," he replied, advancing on Moretti. "Challie and shithead Gunther."

For several seconds uneasy quiet spread through the kitchen then Moretti's head snapped around. "What do you mean? Where's Challie?"

"With Gunther. They went to town for lunch."

"What? Why the hell did you let her go anywhere with him?"

"Like I could stop her."

Moretti dropped the sandwich back on the counter. "Go get her, Donnie. Now. That son of a bitch. Check every restaurant. If you can't find them, check the . . . that son of a bitch. I warned Paul that the bastard would—"

"What?"

"Sneak off and try to marry her."

Donnie bunched Moretti's shirt in his fists, jerked him forward, nose to nose. "What did you say?"

"Back off! You don't have time for fisticuffs. Check the courthouse first. I got a call to make." Moretti dug into his pocket for the Jeep's keys. "Go!"

21

Challie blinked rapidly. Her vision stayed blurry. How many people lived in this town? Why did so many wear the same clothes, the same colors? Why were . . .

She couldn't keep her thoughts together.

She lifted her hand to her forehead and missed, bumping her eye instead. Her hand seemed to weigh a ton.

"How are you feeling?" Gunther asked.

"Funny. I feel strange." She licked her parched lips.

"Must be the heat and altitude. I'll pull over at that building up there. They got AC. Got a couple friends to meet," he said, waving his hand.

Something twinkled in the light. Challie squeezed her eyes shut, then opened them again. Something on his hand glittered. Couldn't be. She'd never met this man before coming to Montana. Must be the heat, as he said, and the altitude.

"You'll like them," Gunther continued. "You sit here with the air on. I'll make sure my friends are here."

It sparkled again. Trying to focus, Challie stared at the jeweled ring on his little finger. Or was it her fertile imagination? Fantasy?

Pretty, brilliant like one she'd seen before today. Where had she seen a pretty ring?

"I'll be right back. Sit tight."

She didn't care where he went. She tried to return the smile. What was wrong with her lips?

While Challie waited in the car, Gunther took the stairs two at a time. He swung back around, waved at Challie, chuckling. She could hardly lift her hand, but she smiled, sort of a crooked Cheshire cat grin.

Inside the courthouse, he found Slim standing near a closed door. "Same toothpick?"

The man nodded.

Gunther shook his head. "Everything set?" He received another barely perceptible nod. "We'll give her a few more minutes. By then she'll be putty in my hands. She's close now."

Slim shrugged. He might have a problem with Gunther's tactics, but he never said anything worth shit.

"Velma inside?" On the affirmative, he asked, "Justice of the peace?"

"Nelson's on the bench."

Probably the longest sentence Slim had ever spoken. "Good. What about Lawson?"

The door came open and a short, bulky woman with plain brown eyes and the same shade of thinning hair stepped out, leaning heavily on a cane. Slim's wife, Velma.

"Thought you was bringing the woman with ya. We ain't got all day," she said.

"She's in the car," Gunther advised.

"Problems?"

"None."

"Well, git her on in here." She ran her husband's life too.

"Hang tight, Velma, I want her agreeable to everything."

"She better be agreeable," Velma whispered fiercely. "I don't need no shit, Gunther. Bad 'nuff I drew up a marriage license, forged the names. Forged every damn thing. Got my butt on the line here."

"It's not a problem, Velma. Quit bitchin'."

She reared back. "Damn right, I'm bitchin'. This no-account man lost his hayin' job. I'm the one bringin' home the bacon. Got five other mouths to feed. And two of 'em ain't mine," she said, glaring at her husband.

Velma was an ugly woman. With half of her front teeth missing, she could pass for a worn-out bull rider whose last ride ended on her face.

"You bring me some money?"

"I got it, Velma." Damn, she was pushy as hell.

"Well, hand it over. Don't want you tryin' to sneak out without payin'."

For Chrissakes. Gunther reached into his hip pocket and dragged out his wallet. He thumbed through twelve one-hundred-dollar bills. "Here. Now, shut your mouth."

"The license, the fees, the—"

"Here," Gunther snapped. He handed her another C-note. "Not another cryin' dime."

Velma stuffed the bundle of bills down a pair of waist-low boobs. "Go get her. Nelson's waitin' on us. Where's Lawson? He s'posed to witness too. Damn men are worse than kids. Can't ever find 'em when you need 'em."

"I'm here. Quit your bitchin', Velma." He limped down the hallway. Gunther had no reason to ask why.

"Quit your howlin', Lawson," Velma snapped. "Judge Nelson don't like a whole lot of noise in his building."

"You got your damn nerve. She *is* the loudest wicked witch from the east," he replied to no one in particular.

Gunther walked out of the building. He couldn't wait to get out of this place. He found Challie laughing and singing. She'd turned on the radio. It blared loud enough for him to hear outside the car. "Achy Breaky Heart." Gunther rolled his eyes.

People moseyed down the street staring.

Gunther cut the ignition.

"Why'd you do that?" Challie asked, laughing, leaning back against the door. She had her bare feet propped up on the dashboard, wiggling her toes, her skirt hiked up to her hips. Another inch or two and he'd catch a teasing glimpse of pussy. "I like song. I wanna sing more."

Shaking his head, Gunther went around the car and opened the passenger door. And lunged to catch her when Challie nearly back-flipped out. She giggled like a class full of kindergartners.

Hell's bells. "Get ahold of yourself, woman. We gotta get inside." Thank God she wore sandals. He shoved them on her feet.

"I wanna stay here and sing." Her eyes crossed. She reached out to grab the door. Missed.

Gunther dragged her from the seat, but holding her upright was a feat in itself when bones straightened like melting rubber. He leaned her back against the car. Jesus. He must've put too much in her drink. "Stand up, Challie. Take a couple deep breaths. Damn."

She did, then threw her arms out wide and roared, "God bless 'Merica! Land I love!"

Oh, shit. An elderly couple stopped in their tracks, frowning. Other pedestrians whispered to each other, nodding toward this loud woman. Gunther had to admit, she did have a decent voice, but he covered her mouth with his hand in midroar.

"Shut up, Challie. Stand up straight."

She seemed to understand him this time. She stood tall, saluted, then put her hand over her heart and went on another singing tirade. This time, the National Anthem. A round of applause erupted after the first line, but Challie sobbed.

Wrapping his arm around her waist, Gunther half carried, half dragged her up the stairs into the building and led her to an empty alcove. "Why are you crying?"

"I can't 'member words. I-I learned when I come here. I wanna be 'Merican."

"You will be. In a few minutes. Stop crying."

"Will?" she asked, sniffling, wiping her eyes dry.

"Yep. All you have to say is yes every time the nice man asks you a question. Got it?"

"And . . . and I be 'Merican?"

Her knees buckled. Gunther hauled her up, but her eyes crossed again. Christ. "Yep. But you have to stand tall, proud like one."

Challie inhaled through her nose, drew her shoulders back and lifted her chin. " 'Kay. Be 'Merican."

"Hold on to my arm and we'll go see the judge together. You'll meet my friends. They'll witness to make it legal. Can you do that?"

She nodded, took hold of his waiting arm and took a tentative step. " 'Merican. Yes?"

"Yep. Just say the same thing on every question. Don't even think about what he's asking."

" 'Kay. Yes. Yes. Yes. Say yes?"

"Right."

" 'Kay. Right. Right. Right."

Jesus. "No, no. Yes."

"Oh. Yes."

They moved slowly toward the judge's chambers as Challie chanted the affirmative on each step. At this rate, they wouldn't get hitched until tomorrow.

At the door, Gunther reached out to turn the knob and Challie grabbed his arm, pulled his hand closer to her face.

"Pretty ring. Sparkle. Jewel. Jewel ring." She frowned.

"Diamonds," he replied.

She looked up into his eyes. "Yours?"

Something crossed her face he didn't like. Recognition? Tension began seeping through every muscle. He hadn't worn it at the ranch. He did have it on at the party.

Gunther twisted the ring off his finger and shoved it into his pocket. "Was a friend's. I won it in a poker game the night before we came to Montana. I plan to give it back when he gives me the money he lost."

"Oh," Challie replied, blinking rapidly. " 'Kay."

Gunther relaxed and opened the door.

Velma and Slim were talking to the judge sitting behind his desk. The man stood. He was tall, slender, with thinning white hair. He had a weathered face and pasty skin, but he wore a good-looking black bolero around his neck.

"Judge Nelson," Velma said. "The happy couple."

Gunther scowled. "How long is this gonna take?" In Challie's current condition, they needed to hurry. Simplemindedness wasn't the only effects of the drugs. He'd have to get a motel room before she mutated into a humpin' bitch in heat.

Nelson scowled back. "Just a few minutes. Are you ready?"

"Yes," Challie said.

Gunther chuckled. Good girl.

"Take her hand," Velma whispered.

Nelson asked for all necessary paperwork and Velma handed them over. "Let's see," he said, hesitating. "You're Vernon Gunther. And you're Challie Bader—"

"Yes," she said.

Gunther squeezed her hand and smiled when Nelson looked up, frowning. "Baderleen. She's just excited, Judge. Nervous. First time."

"He got pretty ring," Challie said, grinning.

"For you?" Nelson asked.

"Yes." She looked up at Gunther and he winked.

"So you've already seen it?" Nelson said.

"Yes. Saw before. Pretty. Sparkle."

Gunther's jaw went slack.

"Well, now, you're a very lucky woman, aren't you?"

"Yes." She started sliding toward the floor. Gunther held her up.

"Ms. Baderleen, are you all right?"

"Yes."

"Let's get on with it, Judge," Gunther said. *Shit. Does she remember seeing it at the party?* Sure sounded like it.

Nelson began the ceremony. As long as he didn't direct questions to Challie, she was okay. Fidgety, but okay.

"Do you, Miss Challie Baderleen, take this man, Vernon Gunther—"

The door burst open, hit the wall with hurricane force.

"Here, here," Nelson said. "What's the meaning of this?"

"You dirty motherfucker." Donnie stormed into the room, wasted no time and plowed his fist into Gunther's jaw, knocked him out cold.

"Deputy! Grab Charlie Lawson and get the security guard," Nelson ordered. "Young man, one move and I'll have you booked and jailed."

Big deal, Donnie thought. Jail here was much better than prison in Arizona. "Whatever." He turned to Challie. Tears streamed down her face. "What's wrong, babe?"

"Wooined."

"Ruined?" Oh, hell, she wanted to marry Gunther? "Why?"

"I never be 'Merican."

"What?" Nelson snapped. "You were marrying that man just to get citizenship? Not in my courthouse, you won't!" He snatched the license from his desk, ripped it to shreds.

"Marriage?" Challie repeated.

Donnie watched her eyes cross. What the hell?

"Gunt say you make me 'Merican. I sing for you, yes? I know words." She put her hand over her heart, belted out the first line to the National Anthem. Sort of. She'd mixed another language with English.

"That son of a bitch drugged her," Donnie said. He burst out laughing as Challie continued singing.

From the corner of his eye, Donnie saw the lanky bastard, who once stood beside Gunther and Lawson, and the woman slinking toward the door.

"Come back here, Slim, Velma," Nelson hollered. "Benton, put them in cuffs." The security guard handcuffed them together.

Nearly an hour went by before Judge Nelson permitted Donnie to take Challie out of the building . . . rather . . . carry her to the Jeep. After Donnie explained his behavior and that Gunther had drugged her for nefarious reasons—brainwashing, which sold the judge—he lied about Challie's citizenship. He presented his identification and told the man she'd left her purse, ID, everything at the ranch. They were free to go.

As for Gunther, Lawson and Slim, Judge Nelson ordered the sheriff to jail them on a number of charges. With bail set at twenty-five thousand apiece, they weren't going anywhere soon. The woman named Velma got off easy. She had kids to care for.

Donnie shifted Challie from his arms to the passenger seat. She was tore up and jabbering. As he buckled her in, she wrapped her arms around his neck.

"Donnie?"

She'd used the nickname once before in the heat of passion. It sounded sweet coming from her. "Hmm?" He straightened the harness and lap belt, made certain they were snug.

"Take me bed."

He'd love to take her to bed, but not in this condition. "Close your eyes and sleep."

"Make love. I want feel you inside." She ran her fingers over his cheeks, then leaned up and kissed him. A long, sensuous kiss, devouring, tongues clashing.

Donnie cupped her chin and leaned farther inside the car, pressing her back against the seat, giving more than he knew he should.

He hated pulling away, but this may be the last kiss he'd ever share with her once the drugs wore off. She'd hate him for taking advantage of her. Hell, she already despised him. She just didn't remember.

"Challie—"

"Please?"

He hesitated, then said, "Not now, babe." And Duke was iron hard. Just like that. After one kiss from the woman of his dreams.

They left the city limits and started down the highway. If he drove back as fast to the ranch as he did coming in, they'd be relaxing at the cabin in twenty-six minutes.

Challie was quiet but awake, fidgeting. "I need love with you."

Oh, shit. Duke had gone to sleep, but Challie woke him with one simple statement. How much more could he take? God, he really wanted to make love to her. Bad.

He left the highway and took the ranch's exit. To keep his mind on something other than making love, Donnie gripped the steering wheel with both hands and sped up, trying to think of something—anything—conversational.

"How do you feel?"

"Horny."

Fuck. "I mean, do you have a headache or anything, feeling sick?"

"No. Horny. Ache. For you."

Too afraid to look over at her, he concentrated on the road ahead, flexing his fingers. But from the corner of his eye, he saw her move.

Challie unbuckled her seat belt. She scooted toward him, sitting on the edge of her seat. "Can't wait." She ran her fingers up and down his hardness with such a gentle touch, he nearly came right then.

He grabbed her hand, squeezed it around his cock. *Shit.*

"You want head?"

Fucking A. He'd wreck the damn car in the process.

She unzipped his pants and Donnie lifted his hips while Challie finagled Duke out into the open. Thank God he wore baggy jeans today. She stroked him with loving care. For a woman who'd never given head, she knew foreplay well.

Leaning into him, she kissed his cheek, the corner of his mouth and, when he turned his head to receive her, her tongue darted inside in a sensuous dance.

Christ Jesus.

Donnie about lost control of the Cherokee and jerked the wheel.

He pulled her hand away, at the same time easing the vehicle back onto the road, and said, "Challie, don't. Not now, babe. I can't drive and—"

Her head went down. Her sweet mouth engulfed Duke's bulging head. Donnie lost his breath. She worked him in a manner that he'd never known before now. Inexperienced, awkward, teeth grazing the taut skin. He had to force his eyes open, feeling her tongue caress the length of him, circling his girth, sucking.

"Good?" she asked.

Oh, hell, yes. His throat dry, he had little power over his own voice. "Yes. Yes." Then he began to shake. "Enough. Enough." He tangled his fingers in her hair, but instead of pulling Challie away, he forced her head down again.

She came up gasping for air. "Too big. Need inside me."

What in the hell was he doing? She'd strangle on his cock. Jesus.

He wheeled the Cherokee onto the next dirt road they encountered. Gravel spewed in every direction and clattered noisily against the undercarriage. Up ahead, a thick grove of trees would allow privacy. Donnie floored the gas pedal.

But she was all over him, straddling him, tongue in his ear, hands roaming over his body, hips moving in a smooth, timeless motion. He felt her fingers wrap around his cock, teasing, tormenting, guiding.

Donnie veered off the road, down a small embankment. He jammed his foot on the brakes and came to a sliding stop beneath the shade tree.

"Wait," he said as her hips raised and sank. "Let me . . . Jesus."

And he was already inside her, fully embedded in liquid heat, slick as oil, tight as hell.

He finally set the break and powered the seat back after fumbling through a mess of switches. Every window went partially down, mirrors moved. Donnie swore under his breath.

"Ooh," Challie purred, closing her eyes. "Yes."

When she lifted again, he raised her blouse and latched onto her breast, pressed her down his full length in slow, excruciating pleasure.

Oh, yeah.

This is where he belonged—with Challie, buried to the hilt, loving her.

Donnie dragged his feet back, gained stability and raised his hips, spreading her legs wider, sliding in farther and pulsing to their own music. Lowering, she came down harder, tightened around him and purred again. The sound was soothing to his ears, the feeling extraordinary, and he caressed her thighs up to her waist. Nipping at her breast, he teased her nipple with his tongue. When she arched toward him, he took full advantage of her body.

"Mmm," Challie cooed.

He licked a path up her chest to her throat, bit the tendon gently along the side of her neck and sank his teeth into her chin before claiming her lips. She was his. All his.

For now.

They moved in tandem, helping each other, lifting, pressing down, enjoying the feel.

"Donnie?"

"What, babe?"

"I think—" She sucked in air and clamped around his cock viciously. "Donnie." Challie gasped and wrapped her arms around his shoulders.

He held her tight against him, fighting the pressure building inside. Jesus God. She wrung the shit out of him, but he hung on, kept his juices from flowing and squeezed his eyes shut. Otherwise, she would surely know they'd had sex.

"I love you . . . love you . . ." she chanted against his cheek.

He came undone. "Challie." Donnie lifted to join her, delirious with pleasure, consumed with her at what she'd willingly confessed. He emptied.

When the last drop of loving left his body and he was able to control his breathing, Donnie rocked her.

She loved him. She'd said the words aloud in the heat of passion. With her face buried against his neck, Donnie stroked her hair and smoothed his hand down her backside. He was wasted. She was as limp as a ragdoll, his doll, but she loved him, the only thing that mattered.

"I love you too, Challie. I love you more than anyone. Marry me. We can drive back to town and get a license, be married in three days. I don't want to wait until we get back to Arizona. I want you as my wife now. Forever."

She didn't move, didn't say anything.

"Challie?" Ah, hell, if she turned him down now, after admitting his love, he'd never live another day.

Donnie waited for an answer. And waited longer.

"Answer me."

Son of a bitch. She was snoring. Snoring! Dead to the world. He'd spilled more than juice. He'd spilled his guts and she'd slept through it all.

"Hell."

At the ranch, Donnie carried Challie from the Jeep to the cabin. The snores had stopped, but she was knocked out cold.

Moretti met them at the door and swung it open. "What the hell did you do to her this time? Jesus Christ, Fontana. I'm gonna find a whip and—"

"Gunther drugged her," Donnie replied, marching toward his bedroom.

He shifted her in his arms when Moretti hurried in and pulled the covers back. "Careful," he said. "Be gentle."

Donnie slipped her sandals off and looked over at Moretti. "You know something."

"Donnie—"

"You're as much a bastard as Gunther!"

Challie groaned.

Moretti clenched his fists at his sides. "Stop shouting. You know how sensitive she is to arguing. If you'd married her . . . If you hadn't hurt her . . . If I wasn't so damned old and didn't have my mind wrapped around someone else, I would've married Challie my damn self."

"What good would it do? Why is everybody willing to marry Challie? What does Paul have against her?"

"Out of the room. I don't want her flustered since you can't keep your voice down." Moretti marched toward the door, and Donnie followed him into the living room. "He's trying to save your butt."

"And marrying Gunther, or you, will save my butt? Bullshit."

"Not Gunther, damn it! I would've taken her out of the state for a while, far away from any inquest until you were cleared. Marriage was the only way, Donnie. She wouldn't go otherwise. Her aunt means too much to her, and Hattie's the only family Challie has in the country. Family means everything to her."

"Hattie's her aunt? She never told me. But Challie would've said anything to protect me."

"Maybe so, before you made her cry."

Flustered, Donnie fell into a chair.

"What *did* you do to her?"

He refused to answer, despising himself.

"Well?" Moretti's voice rose to an explosive level.

"That's between me and Challie, but things have changed. I know she cares for me as much as I love her." But did she really love him? Drugs made people say and do stupid stuff.

"And?"

"I don't know if she'll remember admitting that she does." When Moretti frowned, he said, "The drugs. We were making . . . she was under the influence at the time."

"Hell and damnation." He sat beside Donnie. "Where's Gunther?"

"In jail. He and his lousy partner in crime, including fuckface Lawson. Judge Nelson ought to throw the book at them. I should've put my foot in the Scandinavian's ass."

Moretti relaxed. "Doesn't solve your problems."

"I'll be damned if I'll let you marry her."

"Then you'd better think of something good, sonny, before we get back to Arizona."

"Wish I had more time."

"Got the week."

"Plane comes tomorrow morning," Donnie replied.

"Shit. You need a plan. And I think I know exactly what you can do. Years ago, it worked on my wife."

Moretti must've lost his mind, Donnie thought.

How the hell could he believe sitting beside Challie while she slept, persuading her that she loved him, would help? What'd he call it?

The power of suggestion. Get real.

He'd gathered a few supplies for the duration. A pitcher of ice water and a glass, snacks and a couple romance novels, then dragged a chair to her bedside.

Moretti had said to look through the books, find a few parts to help him along. Donnie thumbed through them, found some passages of love thoughts by the hero and heroine, and folded each page's edge.

Challie had slept like the dead. He doubted she'd heard a word he read.

Finally, Donnie used his own methods of persuasion, stroking her soft skin, kissing her sweet lips. She slept through the night, through all his tender ministrations.

At six thirty the next morning, he staggered out of the room and ran into Moretti.

"Did it work?"

"Only if comatose people can hear. She's still knocked out," Donnie confirmed. "I need coffee. Stayed awake all night. I read more than I've read in my entire life."

"What time's the plane due in?"

"Ten. Liftoff at eleven. We'll see what happens when she wakes. I won't push her, Moretti. She'll either respond as I hope or . . ." He let the sentence hang.

22

Challie ignored him. She didn't know what to say to Donovan while they drove to the airstrip outside Dillon.

During the flight back to Scottsdale, he sat across the aisle staring out the window while Misters Ray and Roman engaged in quiet conversation at the back of the plane. She couldn't hear them over the engine's noisy roar.

What had happened yesterday after she and Gunther left the restaurant? Only a few images came to mind, but she couldn't clear the haze. Except the ring. She'd recognized the jeweled piece. Its image had stuck in her brain.

Donovan hadn't hurt the Pearson woman. Gunther had. He was the last person with her.

I'll tell Mr. Tedesco and the police what I know. I'll tell them everything. He'll be happy. So will Donovan. He'll be a free man, free to go back to his carousing, free of me. Long gone with the key to my broken heart when the INS send me back to Africa. I can deal with suffering again, alone and utterly despised. I'm strong, will always be strong.

The Immigration and Naturalization Service wouldn't have

any choice. They would never let her stay in this country. Soon she'd say good-bye to the one person living in Arizona who cared. Aunt Hattie.

Eduardo and Antonia had stopped by earlier this somber morning. They'd exchanged phone numbers and addresses, but Challie had realized their short-term friendship was long lost now. She'd treasure Antonia's sisterly company forever. As for baby Miguel, Hattie would gladly mail the welcome-into-the world card and gifts Challie planned to buy with her final wages. Something as blue as her current mood.

Tupa, the limousine driver, had met them at the airport. As the car stopped, Challie looked up. This was not the mansion at all.

While the driver waited for the gates to open, she glanced in Donovan's direction. Unshaven, hair unkempt, pale skin and dark shadows under his eyes, he looked worse today.

He'd look better after she told Mr. Tedesco about the true woman beater. All of his worries would dissolve.

Say something. Tell him he has nothing to worry about anymore. Her lips moved, but getting the words out was a problem when tears burned the backs of her eyes. She looked away, blinking rapidly. Donovan loathed seeing a woman's tears.

When Challie found the courage to open her mouth, the driver opened the passenger door. Donovan climbed out without a second glance, without saying good-bye, shattering her heart into tiny pieces.

"Donnie, aren't you forgetting something?" Ray asked.

Back turned, he hesitated. "Thanks for everything."

Challie knew she'd never shed tears again. She'd never fall in love again, either. She stared blankly at Ray's sad-looking gaze and at Moretti's, then at the floor again.

"Rotten little bastard," Moretti mumbled.

She wanted to go home to Hattie's apartment. Obviously, the Tedescos had other plans for her. At the mansion, she grabbed her suitcase from Tupa's hand and ran to the door. After the melodious chimes ended, Hattie opened the door and held her arms out.

"We have a surprise waiting for you."

Challie broke down, crying unashamedly.

"What's the matter? Did someone hurt you?" She took the luggage from Challie's hand and set it on the floor.

"Yes."

Hattie held her at arm's length. "One of those men? Come in here. We'll go to Mr. Tedesco right now." She wrapped her arm around Challie's shoulders, guided her through the foyer.

"No," she said. "It's not like that. It's not like that at all."

Just then, Tina hurried toward them. "What happened?"

"She started crying the minute I opened the door, Tina. Something went on at that cabin and I intend to find out. I'll not have my niece abused by crazy men. Where's your husband?"

Tina? Since when did Hattie start using her first name? Protocol, she'd always instilled protocol in Challie's brain. "No, please, don't say anything to anyone. Please," she begged. "It's not like that."

"Challie, what is it, sweetheart?" Tina asked. She slipped her arm around her waist. Why did it feel so good to have her here comforting too?

But, sweetheart? Lord. Have they all gone stark raving mad?

Drying her eyes, she said, "I do need to talk with Mr. Tedesco about something important."

"Paul's in the library. Are you sure you don't want to talk with us first?"

"What I have to say will clear Donovan's . . . er . . . Mr. Fontana's name. He won't go to jail."

Hattie and Tina looked at each other, eyebrows raised in tandem. They led her to the library.

Instead of knocking, Tina pushed the double doors open.

"Paul, Challie needs to talk with you. Something about Donnie."

Without looking up, he said, "I don't have time." He sounded angry and continued writing.

"Now, you listen to me, Tedesco," Tina snapped.

Challie jumped, and Tedesco's head came up.

"It's about Donnie. You will listen to what she has to say." She turned toward Challie. "Go ahead, honey, tell him."

Challie stared in disbelief. Mrs. Tedesco demanded attention and she got it. Her husband rose slowly to his feet, his face tinged with color.

"I know who hurt that woman, Mr. Tedesco. It wasn't Donovan, I mean, Mr. Fontana. It was Mr. Gunther. I remember seeing the ring on his finger, a diamond ring. She was with him after Dono . . . Mr. Fontana left her. I'll tell the police the same thing. I'll tell the judge. I'll do anything necessary." Oh, God, the INS would come after her the first minute the police start probing into her life. But she'd saved Donovan. That's all that mattered.

"Don't go any further," Tedesco said.

The faucet automatically turned on. Tears flowed, a raging river down Challie's face. She knew it was coming, knew it the moment she saw his death mask. He despised her with an unbelievable hatred. Tedesco picked up the telephone receiver.

"Tina, you'd better do something," Hattie said fiercely. "You can't let him do something outrageous."

"We n-need more time," she stammered.

"Tina! We've been friends for thirty-two years. If you don't straighten this mess out, by God, I will."

Her shoulders sagged as she wrung her hands. She stared out of the window then looked back at her husband. "Paul, hang up. Hang it up now. There's something I must tell you."

Hesitant, he replaced the handset to its cradle.

"Challie," Tina said and swallowed, "is my daughter."

For the first time, Challie couldn't breathe, couldn't move. The air around her seemed to vanish into a vacuum. Daughter? She moved away from the woman claiming to be her mother and crowded up to her aunt.

"This isn't news to me, Tina," Tedesco said calmly. "I've known for years."

"What?" she said in a tiny voice. "Why didn't you say something?"

Challie couldn't breathe yet. Her mother? She looked at Hattie, who nodded, smiled. As her strength began to desert her, her body shaking like a windblown tree, she clutched her aunt's hand.

Tedesco shook his head, his eyes softening as he stared at his wife. "One day, I was looking for a certain book in our old house. You were visiting your mother at the time. I'd missed you the second you walked out the door. Then I happened upon the first book of poetry I'd bought you; the frayed, well-used one you wanted on our first anniversary instead of the diamond necklace. I thought it only right for you to tell me."

What did a poetry book have to do with these startling revelations?

"When Challie came here," he continued, "I thought for sure she'd found out or she'd already known. Either way, I assumed blackmail—"

"Blackmail," Challie said loudly. Why would she consider blackmailing anyone?

"Until she got here. She was such a diligent worker," Tedesco finished. "Actually, I was perturbed because she was employed with us, and *you* had employed your child as a maid. Then I understood why. How else could you keep her close while getting to know each other?"

This time, Mrs. Tedesco . . . er . . . Tina . . . er . . . the woman claiming to be . . . anyway, her face flooded shocking pink.

How could this be? Tina, her mother, a blue-eyed blonde?

Impossible. *We look nothing alike,* Challie thought while glaring at the woman.

"Challie, honey," Hattie started to say.

"All these years, you knew, and you didn't tell me!"

"I hinted in the letters. Didn't you read them?"

"What letters?"

"Oh, good Lord. Your grandmother again. I bet she read them, burned them."

Surely not. Grandmama would never do such a thing, would she? Or maybe they never reached them. They moved often from village to village.

"Darling," Tina said, her voice sounding strange, distant. "You are my daughter." When she reached to cup Challie's chin and Challie backed away, her hand fell limply to her side. She trudged over to the bookcase and pulled out a brown tattered volume, plucked a folded paper from the binder. "This is your birth certificate, the original. I've kept it here, kept it safe."

"Safe?" Shuddering, Challie staggered backward, refusing to lift her hand or read the paper offered. Safe from what? Or whom?

"Yes, in case—"

"In case I just *happened* to find you? Do you realize that every child needs a loving mother, especially when in pain? What about when they hurt physically? What about when they just need someone who cares enough to chase the pain away?" Her voice rising, she'd let her anger boil over.

"No, no. In . . . in case my baby was ever returned to me."

A sickening laugh left Challie's throat. "You expect me to believe you, after all these years? After twenty-nine years? I was lucky to have my grandmother. She cared for me. She'd hold me when I needed holding, soothe me when I needed soothing. She loved me without reservation. *She* was my mother all those years!"

"Now, just a minute young lady," Hattie snapped, shaking

her finger in Challie's face. "Let me tell you what really happened. Let me tell all to clear the air.

"Your sneaking father—my brother—kidnapped you from the hospital! Yes," she confirmed when Challie shook her head. "God forgive me, I'd promised not to tell anyone where he'd taken you. Well, I couldn't keep that promise for long. Tina had a right to know, but it was too late by then."

She walked away, then came back to stand directly in front of Challie. "While Tina recuperated from surgery, your father left the country with a woman who masqueraded as his wife, carrying a small baby in her arms. That woman was your teacher, the same witch who gave you piano lessons."

What? How could this be? She'd given Miss Tamor her grandmother's house—lock, stock and candles. Free! By now, Grandmama was clawing her way out of the grave, ready to scratch the gray from her granddaughter's soul-stealing eyes.

"Oh, but it gets better. Or worse," Hattie went on, "depending on how you see things or whether you keep an open mind. Life isn't always a bed of roses, honey." She must've witnessed the horror on Challie's face. "I had to make a sacred promise to my mother—your grandmother—that I'd never mention a word to anyone. She knew all along. *She* encouraged your father to take you back to South Africa, and she flat out refused to return you to America after his death. Tina tried everything, *every*thing, Challie. Lawyers, the State Department, the INS . . . our government could do nothing. Mother made damn sure no one would take you away from her."

"Grandmama would never do those things. I don't believe it. She'd never—"

This was too much to comprehend, and the room spun. No one had truly loved her after all, not one person. Nothing but lies all of her dreadful life? What had she done to deserve this web of deceit?

"She's telling the truth, Challie. Even with my contacts, I

was powerless." Tedesco went around the desk to his bewildered wife's side. He lifted her hand, kissed her knuckles. "I'd secretly tried to help to no avail. Incidentally, darling, now that we've exposed our naked truths. I bought back every piece of jewelry you sold over the years. They're in a safe place." He turned to Challie. "You see, my wife pawned her jewelry to pay for legal expertise, private detectives, even went as far as hiring a sleazy bounty hunter who I warned once about . . . She also contributes to a fund to help the poor in Africa and the underprivileged right here in America. The jewelry kept in this house is fake. Reproductions."

"You knew about that too?" Tina asked.

"Nothing gets by me, love, when it has to do with my family, especially your happiness." He enfolded his wife into his arms.

Funny, Challie thought as her anger simmered down by one hundred degrees, the hard lines of his face had eased.

"Is her room finished?" she heard Tedesco whisper.

Tina blushed again. "Not quite. I wanted her opinion before we began the final touches."

What room? Did she expect an estranged daughter to move into this house without so much as asking first?

"Hey, Dad."

"Ray, what are you doing here?" His wife eased out of his embrace. "I told Roman not to—"

The telephone rang. Tedesco marched over to the desk and answered before the second ring ended. He didn't look happy as he lowered his voice. He spoke quietly. Everyone looked at each other, but Challie heard part of his hushed words. Thompson, the man Donovan had mentioned. And another name she'd never heard before. Wheeler.

Evidently, whomever he spoke to had failed to agree with him. He snapped the phone shut and hurled it at the stone fireplace. It screamed, splintering on impact.

"Paul, calm down," Tina said. "What's happened?"

"One of my men. It's no concern of yours." His wife didn't look satisfied.

"What's up, Dad? Roman said there might be a problem, few details. I want details."

Tedesco's eyes glinted lethally. "Roman talked to you?"

"Yeah. He was concerned."

"That's right, Paul." For his size, Moretti slinked into the room quiet as a mouse. "He had a right to know. You can't keep everything under your strict control. There are other folks who care, always will be."

"I want you out of here ASAP, Ray," Tedesco said. "Don't ask any questions."

"What? Why?" His son moved closer to the mahogany desk. "What's going on?"

Puckering his lips, Tedesco eyed everyone in the room, particularly his eldest son. "A certain person has dragged some old stink from the past to the present. I don't want any of the family around when he comes around sniffing."

Huh? Stink? What does that mean? Challie wondered, sniffing the air.

"Tina, I want you and the children packed. Tupa will transport you all to the airport within the hour. The jet will be fueled and ready. Roman, you're going to the ranch as well."

"What old stink are you talking about?" Ray braced his hands against the desk, leaning forward. "Mother?"

Tedesco flinched.

"Maybe it's because somebody finally realized that he did kill his first wife, that now they realize he's the guy who put Susannah Pearson in the hospital."

Hearing Donovan's voice, Challie swung around. He stood in the doorway. How long had he been listening?

"I've done no such thing, Donnie."

He'd made a cruel and unforgiving accusation. Tedesco had

the power to scare bark off any hardwood tree with a single penetrating glare, but Challie hardly believed he would kill. And he was not wearing a diamond ring like the one she'd seen on Gunther's hand the night Pearson was attacked. In fact, she'd never seen him wearing a single piece of jewelry other than his wedding band. Besides, Tedesco was fastened to his wife's side all evening.

"Guess writing out my resignation had purpose after all. I can't work for a man like you any longer."

"Donovan," Challie whispered. "You don't have to resign. You're not going to jail."

"Neither is my father."

"The fucking hell he won't!" Donovan said, explosive, shaking his fist toward his boss.

Tupa came into the room, but Tedesco waved him off.

"Mr. Fontana, please. You promised not to swear."

He glanced at Challie, frowned.

"The hell he will," Ray countered quietly.

Donovan stepped up to the ranch owner, face-to-face. "Your father wanted me to go to Montana with Challie, with a pistol. He wanted me to eliminate the problem. Challie was his problem. He thought she would identify him. End of story."

"You're wrong again, Donnie. I said no such thing. I said, 'Do whatever's necessary to take care of the problem.' "

Donovan tsked. "Your play on words, Tedesco. Only it didn't happen, did it? The big boss didn't get his way. You lost."

"Let me get this straight," Ray said, folding his arms over his chest. "You're saying that Dad sent you to Montana with Challie to take her out? You must be nuts. Loco. Don't you see? He sent you out of the state to protect you, and the gun was meant for your *and* Challie's protection. The same way he sent me away when my mother was found dead. Dad deliberately made himself a target to keep the cops away from me."

"That's enough, Ray."

"No, Dad, it's not enough!" His voice ricocheted off the walls. "It's about time, don't you think, for people to hear the truth?"

Challie backed away with Hattie, crowding behind one of two wingchairs, trembling. These outbursts were a grim reminder of years gone by, ones she'd sooner forget. She resisted clamping her hands over her ears or diving for cover. All sorts of truths had been revealed today. Loud or not, what harm would come from another discovery stirred into the pot?

"Keep quiet, son. This is not the time."

For an instant, Challie saw pain etch Tedesco's face. His wife had also noticed the change. She went to his side, looped her arm around his. Together, they were a beautiful, loving and supportive couple. Challie imagined their children had lived the perfect life, unlike her tormented childhood.

"She died," Ray whispered, "because of—"

"Don't," Tedesco commanded.

Emotion charged the room with a powerful energy. Captivated, everyone waited for an imaginary wire to buzz and snap, sparks flying.

"Me," Ray continued. His eyes filled with unshed tears.

Stunned, Challie—like all other listeners within earshot—sucked in the last bit of oxygen, held it, unable to exhale, unable to move. Time froze for the next few seconds while the antique clock, tucked away on the bookshelf, tolled the afternoon's fourth hour.

"You see, Dad loved my mother no matter what problems she had. She knew he did, but Mom had trouble controlling the demons in her head leftover from my grandfather's numbing influence. And he hated my father for taking his little girl away, really for losing the death grip he had on her." Dragging in a shuddered breath, Ray clenched his fists, relaxed, then clenched them again into sizable mitts, skin stretched taut.

"You don't have to do this, son. Buried forever. Let's keep it that way."

"Buried too long. For years, my grandfather did his best to bury you after Mother's death. I would've told the police, the judge, the world, about that horrible night. Instead, you sent me away with Moretti and Thompson." He looked in the family friend's direction, received a nod. Turning his gaze back to his father's, Ray said, "You suffered alone through two years of hell. I knew, but there was nothing I could do to stop Grandfather or the police from hounding you, accusing you, torturing you. They tried their damndest to break you."

Tedesco blinked several times and swallowed. He wrapped his arm around his wife, squeezing her tighter to his body. It was obvious he knew the undiluted tale was on the verge of sprouting wings. "Please, don't say another word. Everything came out all right. I was unscathed. They had no proof, had nothing to go on."

"I'll not let anyone—*anyone*—blame you again for my despicable behavior." The words tumbled out bit by uneasy bit.

Good Lord. Who would've thought that beneath the soft tissue of this kind gentleman was a . . .

"You killed your own mother?"

As if a tennis match final were in progress, all heads swung around toward Donovan. Only he had nerve to ask the question aloud. Then on cue, anticipating an answer, every head shifted back toward Ray.

He huffed. "I was a spoiled-rotten, little shit. I played my mother. I played my grandmother against her husband, the same man who hated me as much as he hated his son-in-law because I was of his flesh. I played anybody who would fall for the game, but there were two people I couldn't roll: Dad and Roman. They, eventually, taught me how to be a man."

"You didn't answer the question." That sarcastic statement came from the brash one.

"If you're asking if I pushed her, the answer is . . ." Speculatively, he eyed each person, finally settling his gaze on his father's stricken face. "In a sense, yes."

"What the devil are you talking about, 'in a sense'? Either you shoved her or you didn't shove her over the balcony!" Donovan's tone raised an octave on each accusing word. "Which is it, Ray?"

"We were arguing. I don't remember what it was about or whether it was worth it. Probably something I foolishly wanted again. A worthless toy. For once, Mother became the brave soul Dad had always said was imprisoned by her father's cruelty. She decided to take control of the situation. She threatened to lock me in my room, to take my toys and give them away."

He wandered toward the tall window. Pulling back a length of drapery, he stared up at the sky, or the heavens, silhouetted by sunlight.

"I was big for my age. There was a struggle."

23

Clamping a hand over her mouth, Challie managed to stifle a gasp, unlike Hattie, whose sharp intake of breath sounded worse than a vacuum cleaner through an auditorium's loudspeaker.

This man had murdered his mother over toys!

"She got the best of me." Ray spun around to face the father who'd taken the blame for his son's reckless behavior. "Naturally, I was enraged. I said terrible things, things no mother should ever hear from her child."

"What was that, son?"

Huh? Didn't he know? Wasn't he there? Didn't he see what had happened, the reason for sending his son away?

"Bare minimum, I told her how much everyone hated her. I told her that no one wanted a crazy woman around. I told Mother the only reason you stayed married to her was because of me."

For a man of his broad size and status, his eyes misted, and his father started toward him.

Ray held up both hands. "No, that's not all. Let me finish," he said in an odd voice.

Never having seen a grown man on the threshold of weeping, Challie wasn't sure she could bear hearing specifics. She swallowed back the pain rising in her throat as her heart went out to him. He was but a child at the time.

One or two minutes passed before Ray was able to continue.

"All these years, everyone thought you'd caused her death. Even you."

He scrubbed both hands over his face. "It wasn't you at all. You didn't drive her over the edge. She jumped, Dad. She took the plunge because of me, not you, and that kept you from loving another woman for so damn long. Until Tina."

Tedesco yanked his son into a fierce embrace. "It's okay. It's okay. You're not to blame."

Unease settled into somberness. No one seemed to know what to do or say while father and son embraced.

"Finally clearing the last of the muddied waters."

Wide-eyed, Challie peeked around Hattie at the newcomer.

"What are you doing here, Detective Wheeler?" Tedesco snapped, stepping in front of his son. "Who let you in my home?"

"A singing canary," Wheeler replied. "You should be happy I dropped by early or I might've missed something."

Challie started from the top and worked her gaze downward on this striking man. His face was clean shaven other than the thin mustache. And his dark complexion appeared smooth, flawless over chiseled features. His well-barbered hair was short-cropped with a thin part on the left side. Graying at the temples. Impeccably groomed in a navy suit, maroon shirt, shoes buffed to high gloss, he wasn't as tall as Donovan's height, nor was he as broad-shouldered, but he was as handsome. Extremely handsome and mature.

"Had I missed hearing your son's story, I would've resorted to staying on your ass for the rest of *our* natural lives. The cat-and-mouse pursuit has finally come to an end. The case is officially closed."

"Thank you, Wheeler."

He turned, saw Challie, and smiled. His hawklike dark eyes would certainly pin a nervous person to the wall. She sensed her shoulder blades pulling together. Embarrassed, she looked away and witnessed Donovan's glare. Daggers were less frightening. Did Wheeler feel a piercing in his back?

"Ladies," Wheeler said. He nodded.

Leaning backward slightly, peering around her aunt, Challie couldn't help but watch the detective as he walked out of the room. He commanded attention in any arena. Down the hall, he shook hands with Moretti and said a few words. She heard a faint ringing sound. Wheeler answered the phone as he opened the front door.

"He's married," Hattie whispered.

Caught blatantly staring, Challie stood upright, wondering how his wife might keep her husband from carousing, the norm for good-looking men. One woman was rarely enough for them.

"She's a divorce attorney."

That should keep the man in his place.

"You had Moretti pay off Wheeler, didn't you?" Donovan said loudly.

Huh? What was he saying?

"When I didn't accomplish exactly what you wanted, you used your running buddy for clean-up duty. How convenient. Well, I won't let you hurt Challie, damn you."

Had he gone completely crazy? The nerve of him anyway, when he'd hurt her without thought or care. He'd reserved the right all for himself.

"Mr. Fontana, Mr. Gunther is the guilty party. I saw him go into the room with Ms. Pearson." Challie raised her hands, palms up. "After you left her."

His face instantly brightened with red coloring. "You didn't see Gunther attack her. You have no proof."

Someone would believe her. Gunther was an evil man. "But—" Challie began.

"I forgot to mention Pearson." When had Wheeler sneaked back into the room?

Seeing him again . . . wow.

"She woke this morning. Where's Gunther?"

"Dillon, Montana," four men said simultaneously.

"In jail," Donovan added.

"Perfect. Makes my job easier," Wheeler said. "I need to talk with you for a moment, Tedesco."

When they left the room and closed the door, no one moved, no one said a word. Challie tried to listen in on their conversation like everyone else. Her sense of hearing was exceptional, but not through heavy wood and solid walls.

Minutes later, Tedesco came back. "The doctors expect Susannah to recover completely. I might as well let you all know that another tragedy has surfaced. The phone call earlier," he said, eyeing his wife. "Wheeler said someone found a body yesterday. No ID."

"Oh, no," Tina murmured.

"They've identified him. Thompson's wife had reported him missing. Initially, Wheeler thought I had something to do with his death."

"Sweet Jesus! Because he was with me and Roman after Mother's death? He thought you were getting rid of people, one by one?" Ray asked, incredulous.

What a complicated nightmare, Challie thought as Tedesco nodded.

"Preliminary report says he died from an overdose."

"Thompson wasn't a user," Moretti said. "Gunther drugged Challie. I bet he drugged him too."

She was drugged? No wonder she barely remembered anything.

"Good possibility," Tedesco replied. He looked dead into Challie's eyes. "Thompson's wife also wanted to know what happened to his diamond ring."

"Well, now. It's all coming together, isn't it?" Ray said, staring at his father then at Donovan. "Remember when I said that Dad's funny about people. He gives them a fair shot first. When they screw up, he hands over a length of rope and watches if they knot the noose around their neck. I'd wondered how long it would take him to provide Gunther with a sturdy lasso. This isn't the first time for that jackass. Hopefully, it'll be the last."

"Fine," Donovan said to his boss. "But you used Challie for bait, knowing something hellish might happen."

Pinching the bridge of his nose, Tedesco said, "Let me explain something, Donnie, since you're unable to process what's happened or explain your cocky self!" His voice chilled the library. "I'd watched you when Challie was in your presence. You were different, not the same dick-leading shit—"

"Paul," his wife reprimanded, and his blush started beneath the collar of his starched white shirt.

He licked his lips. "Not the egotistical, macho idiot you've always flaunted. There was something arcing between you and her, something I recognized." When he looked at his wife, she smiled.

She had a dimple too! Challie felt heat burning beneath the surface of her skin. She stared at Donovan, embarrassed. What if the Tedescos knew what had happened in Montana?

"What's that got to do with anything?" Donovan shot back. "You sent her—"

"You don't get it, do you?" Ray shook his head. "WNB. Get in touch with your—"

"I don't have a feminine side!"

Propping his hip on the desk, Tedesco sighed long and hard. "Do you remember how often you stared at Challie, looked for her when you stopped by, pretending you needed a drink or something to eat, anything to get her into the same room as you? Do you remember volunteering to drop by here for papers when Tupa could've easily retrieved them?"

He did? Of course! He'd found another tramp to take to bed, to free her mind, leave her body stuttering for more of his passion. He'd made her believe that together they'd found something poignant, something special to keep for memory's sake. Obviously, he'd had a plan and, during the short stay away from home, it had worked. Her mood quickly soured.

Hattie nudged her and whispered, "Is there something you haven't told me?"

"Nothing worth our time or conversation," Challie replied shortly.

Tedesco caught her in the act of glowering at Donovan. Who cared?

"I have something to talk over with Donnie. And others," he added, glaring at Moretti. "But I believe it should not be discussed in the company of women. I'm sure the three of you have quite a bit to talk about."

They were prepared for a cursing war. Challie was sure of it. As for "quite a bit to talk about," the impending ladies' chat was long overdue. And welcomed. Sort of. Challie could hardly believe it. Her own mother, this beautiful woman, had wanted her ugly-duckling daughter in her life after all. Where should they begin? Where would the beginning lead to later? What did the future have in store?

"Well," Hattie said. "We have a surprise for Challie anyway."

"Actually," Ray said, "I've got one for Dad." He winked at Challie. And all this time she'd thought he was plotting against her with his father.

Tedesco came around the desk. He cupped his wife's cheek and pressed a kiss to her forehead before the trio of ladies filed out.

"Hattie," Moretti said, holding on to the knob of the ten-foot door. "Can you put together one of your specialty sandwiches? I'm starved."

She smiled. "Of course."

"Thanks, doll." He swatted her bottom.

Challie's mouth fell open. "Aunt Hattie?"

"Two years, darling," Tina said, "is how long they've been an item. Hell of a crazy family you're finally joining, isn't it?"

She'd cursed! She never cursed. Come to think of it, Hattie had dressed particularly well today, wearing heels, a see-through blouse, and flowing skirt. And those nights when she'd disappeared for hours, was she with Moretti? Was everyone losing their minds?

Gliding gracefully back across the marbled floor, Tina hummed the melody to "Love Is in the Air." She looped her arm around her newly found daughter's, and Challie didn't resist. "Close your mouth, honey. There are things you absolutely must do something about."

Fine. Except moving into this mansion was not on her priority list. On her list at all. Not yet. Maybe never. However, the greatest piano also lived in this house, whispering her name. Challie couldn't care less about decorating a room or selecting drapery fabrics.

"First, let's get you freshened up," Tina said.

She'd love to soak in one of the guest room's swimming pools, bathe and shower to forget today's heartaches and . . .

"And out of this . . . garment."

Paid for with hard-earned wages, Challie thought haughtily. "I need my suitcase."

"If you insist. Tupa, bring my daughter's luggage to the new room." She smiled at Challie. "We women must always be on our toes, prepared for the best of times. Isn't that right, Hattie?"

"And sometimes the worst."

Huh?

"Close the damn doors, Big Bird." Tedesco's voice filtered through the mansion.

"I believe he was talking to Roman," Hattie remarked.

No one but Challie knew how to bust Donnie's chops without throwing a punch. Except Paul Tedesco.

On the flip side, Moretti had picked up a thing or two over the years. He'd thrown a few jabs, especially when the boss had already cut him off at the knees for summoning an outsider—Detective Wheeler, his nemesis—to take part in Tedesco business. Luckily, the mansion was made of sturdy construction. The shouting match had contained enough volume to shatter windows and blow out walls, sending pieces flying all the way to Montana.

In the end, their friendship bursting at the seams, Moretti mumbled, "Yeah, well, I should've refused to let the cops in the office, given them a set of fake employee names and SSNs and let the DA put a grand jury together to indict your sorry ass."

That barb had obviously stung deep. Paul's face blanked out faster than a dead computer screen. But Donnie *had* thought PT Industries employed illegal immigrants for its sweatshop.

"They raided the office and you didn't tell me?" Paul asked.

"Two weeks ago, but not a raid in any sense of the word. You had other things on your mind."

Staring at his father, Ray's eyebrows arched. "Well, now. Don't you have something to say, Dad?"

Ray had gotten in touch with his feminine side way too many times. Paul would never—

"Sorry, Roman."

Son of a bitch.

"Skip it. We've been friends for too long. Like I've said many times before, there're other people who do give a damn about what happens to your sorry butt."

Since his grudge had time to marinate, Donnie snickered. And that stupid mistake brought around the heads of all three men.

Thick fingers glued to a thicker waist, Moretti asked, "You got something to say, Fontana?"

"I've said my peace," he replied, watching Ray shove his sleeves to his elbows. *What is this, a lynch mob? Bring it on.*

"Are you sure?" the ranch owner asked, folding Popeye-thick forearms over his chest.

"I'm good."

"Good, huh? Sit." Ray had learned to intimidate under the king's dominant tutelage.

Donnie was not daunted or in awe. "I don't work for you. I don't work for—"

"*Sit,*" Paul blasted, "down." *Boom.*

"Yes, sir." Donnie's butt smacked the wingchair.

"Let me get one thing off my chest first." Paul moseyed around his desk. He lowered himself into his favorite business chair, leaning his chin against his thumb, fingertips balanced against his temple. Glaring at Donnie, he said, "Have you lost your damned mind?"

He shifted in the wingchair. He hadn't thought so, until he'd met Challie Baderleen. She'd done something to him—a hex, magic, something. No way he'd put his business or his private thoughts on the table.

"No answer? All right. Let's start from the beginning, then.

Roman, why don't you do a rundown and give me a chance to cool off."

"If it'll keep your bellows to a squeak, gladly." On that sour note, Moretti launched into a speech beginning with Gunther's hiring.

Yeah, the man was an idiot. Too bad Paul hadn't listened to Moretti. Designating the boss as "macho idiot" didn't sit well with Paul as he glued a fist to his cheek, glowering at his best friend. Sure, Donnie knew Susannah was Paul's lead secretary, but, no, he didn't realize Gunther was boinkin' her. Okay, so jealousy had gotten the best of the Scandinavian. Happened to all males when a dame shot her mouth off and belittled a proud man. Donnie chuckled to himself. Gunther's wares must be out of Duke's dominating league.

He rethought that. If Duke's raiding ability was so great, why was Challie checking out Wheeler? The detective was already attached. She had no business tempting a married man.

"What the hell are you scowling about?" Ray asked. "If Roman hadn't guessed what was up, Challie would be married to that jackass right now, no thanks to you."

"What?"

"That's your whole problem, Fontana. You don't listen," Moretti said, "or learn. Cocky little bastard."

"That's enough, Roman." Paul's intervention had Moretti flipping him off. "You see, Donnie, Gunther is a natural-born, conniving liar who—"

"Which I saw right away and you didn't," Moretti snapped.

Paul ignored him. "Anyway, I'd put a little too much trust in the man."

"Against my suggestions," Moretti put in. "He never listens to me."

"Are you finished?" Paul asked, rounding on him. "I've had just about enough for one day."

"Yeah, I'm done."

Paul waited a beat then continued. "Anyway—"

" 'Til tomorrow," Moretti muttered.

"For God's sake, Roman. Put a sock in it," Ray ordered. Moretti's middle finger was the only reply.

"According to Susannah, per Wheeler, Gunther had a plan, stupid as it was," Paul said. "He thought with Susannah's help he'd move up the corporate ladder since she worked directly with me. Granted, I wasn't as careful as I should've been, and don't you say one word, Roman."

He was ready to spout something sinister. His mouth was wide open, even while Paul's back was to him. Moretti clamped it shut.

"Gunther came into my office while I was on the phone with one of the lawyers. He overheard me talking about Tina and Challie."

"So? What about them?" Donnie asked.

Paul frowned at first. "Ah, that's right. You weren't here. Tina is Challie's mother."

"What?" Donnie slowly got to his feet.

"We'll get back to—"

"I've got a few things to say about your wife." Boy, he had a ton to unload about Tina Tedesco and the child she'd tossed away.

Paul jammed his hands into his suit pants, jingled something there. Couldn't be coins. Keys? Shoulders hunched forward, eyes narrowed, he said quietly, "In due time. But think very carefully about what you plan to say *and* how."

Donnie's butt found the wingchair again.

"Now, where were we?" Paul asked.

"Gunther," Moretti provided. "Snooping. Susannah."

"Ah, yes. When Susannah was no longer a help in getting him promoted, she thought Gunther put together an alternate plan. Marry Challie, marry into money and get a healthy slice of my family pie. Fortunately, eight years of loyalty to me won out. Susannah likes her job. And, for whatever reason, she dumped him for you, Donnie. Except, I'm guessing you managed the short-term relationship as always. The hit-and-run technique."

Yeah, well, that was his motto, but not now. A gray-eyed doll had changed him. *Problem is she doesn't care if I live or die.*

"She said Gunther saw you two together the night of the party. That's when it got ugly. In theory, he assumed you'd be nailed for assaulting her. When I sent you to Montana—*as a protector* of my stepdaughter until Susannah's attacker was apprehended—it must've put a kink in his plans."

No doubt Paul pulled out all the stops when guarding his family.

"He silenced Thompson to get to Challie. Whether he intended to kill, who knows?" Paul said. "And, whatever you did encouraging her to leave with Gunther, his kink magically unknotted."

Giving Donnie time to digest the implications, Paul removed his suit jacket and hung it in the small closet. He crossed the room to the elaborate bar—mirrors, lots of glass. The single ice cube rattled inside crystal. He poured a double shot of some high-dollar bourbon, the only liquor he drank besides wine at dinner or champagne on special occasions. His tasting cellar contained the finest drinkables available, seating a dozen people comfortably.

Donnie needed a drink, but he knew Paul tended bar to no one, and no one poured without invitation. Moretti was a recovered alcoholic. Ray never drank before six o'clock. Donnie remained attached to the wingchair, contemplating, while his boss sipped on his cocktail.

He'd done it this time, thanks to Duke and his own stupidity. Not only had an innocent woman suffered an unconscionable act of brutality because of him, he'd put the woman he'd fallen in love with in danger and lost her in the end. Jesus, what a jackass.

"Now," Paul said, cutting into his thoughts. He set the glass down. "Let's deal with you."

Oh, hell. All eyes zeroed in on him.

"And focus on the love I have for every single person in my family."

Donnie had no idea how much time had passed. Tedesco and his entourage had beaten him to the ground. Stomped his ego, shamed him relentlessly, and all but reduced him to Eduardo's characterization. A sniveling idiot.

But Ray's cell phone saved him from parading the dreaded feminine side.

"Antonia's in labor," Ray said, smiling broadly. "She's asking for Challie."

As Ray went out the door, Donnie wished he were the chosen one to give Challie the news. She hadn't smiled at him in so long. He missed her smile, her sass, everything about her.

"Roman, we have some papers to go over," Paul said.

Automatically dismissed without a word, Donnie got to his feet. Whether the three stompers believed it or not, he'd listened and listened closely. Challie still had feelings for him, even when he'd reduced *her* to tears, an emotion she'd valiantly kept hidden from him except on one terrible night.

As he passed through the doorway, he thought one way or another . . . Then he saw her, flanked by her mother and aunt, gliding down the wide staircase.

She'd done something different with her hair. It hung around her shoulders the way he loved most, free and waiting for his fingers, with a glittering clasp or wide barrette holding a thick mass at the top of her head like a miniature tiara. She'd changed clothes, wore purple better than anyone he'd ever seen, showcasing perfect legs beneath the slinky dress cut several inches above her knees. High heels.

Donnie sucked in air and Duke twitched, ready for a gamely raid.

She was all smiles until she spied him. Challie made a one-eighty, taming Duke's unruliness.

"If you run from me again, I will paddle your—"

"Fontana!"

Donnie flinched, but the biggest threat hadn't come from Paul's scathing tone or from the library. Three pairs of eyes—blue, gray and brown—glared hotter than flamethrowers.

"You go ahead and try," Challie countered.

Rubbing his forehead, thinking the three dominant females had burnt a hole that had penetrated brain matter, Donnie said, "We need to talk, Challie."

"He can't force you, honey," Hattie said. "Not with your family protecting you."

"Darling," Tina cooed. "Remember, there are many people anxiously waiting to hear you perform."

Damn it. Once she showed her talents, he'd lose her forever. "Can I talk to you?" Looking from Tina to Hattie, he said, "Alone?"

"Make him beg." That lousy comment came from bigmouth Moretti.

"I agree," Ray said from the balcony. "He deserves to get down on his knees and plead for your forgiveness."

Donnie shot a fuck-you glare in both men's direction. No way would he beg, but his knees were already weak. "Please, Challie, I just want some alone time with you."

She didn't answer right away, which put a knot in his gut. "Patio. Ten minutes." Chin up, shoulders square, she turned her back simultaneously with her mother and aunt. The sass had returned, but not her smile.

Donnie watched her climb the staircase, hips swaying seductively, until she disappeared from sight. Sighing, his shoulders slumped.

"Cocky little bastard's lost his spit."

"I'd say rightfully so."

The object of their taunts followed orders. Defeated, Donnie wearily shoved the patio doors open.

Ten minutes to get his act together. Ten minutes to stew. Only ten minutes of praying, and if that didn't work, he'd drop to his knees for sure.

Challie was on the verge of coming apart at the seams by the time Hattie closed the bedroom doors.

"Bravo, darling," Tina said. "You performed beautifully. Brilliant smile. Abrupt change to your demeanor upon seeing him. Walking away. You gave us a few extra minutes of preparation to bring the arrogant devil to his knees."

She wasn't so sure she had enough courage. She'd kept her gaze squarely on Donovan's chest. Alone with him, staring into his eyes, she was subject to blowing the charade. And a performance? Too many days had passed without so much as a minute of piano practice.

"Am I really supposed to audition?"

Tina smiled. "Not yet. You see, I called Ray."

"Oh. *Is* Antonia in labor?"

Hattie sat on the elaborate sleigh bed beside her. "Not that we know of for now."

Challie huffed. Caught in a deceitful travesty: no baby, no debut, denying her feelings for Donovan.

"Chin up, darling," Tina said. She touched her fingertips to Challie's quivering chin. "There will be plenty of time to explain later, but I guarantee you'll make a smashing debut. And Paul will be the one presenting you, whether he knows it or not. Right now, you absolutely must change your clothes."

"But—"

"Hattie, remove the barrette and braid her hair while I give her a few pointers and get her redressed in her old garment."

While she'd bathed in the sunken bathtub, they had a nice girlfriend-type talk, mostly about Donovan. In the shower, she'd never had so much water spraying from all directions. Afterward, Tina tried to apply makeup to her face. Challie begged off, except she opted for shimmering lipstick because it smelled and tasted delicious. How did the company manage to put real strawberries in their product?

The walk-in closet was full of clothes in every imaginable style and color. Same with shoes, matching purses, satin lingerie, even bras, which she'd never worn. Hattie said she and Tina had a ball shopping for Challie at her mother's favorite boutiques. Saks and Neiman's. She'd never heard of either. They must've depleted the stores' merchandise, spent much too much money. One or two outfits would've been sufficient. Why didn't they shop at Target or Walmart? Their clothes fit her fine, probably a few dollars cheaper as well.

Working every day, how long would it take to pay back the Tedescos? One month or two? She'd have to draw up a payment schedule, take a little bit out each week. On her good salary, she could afford to dole out twenty-five dollars weekly and *still* send money to the orphanage.

After a fast makeover and last-minute instructions, Challie drew in a cleansing breath and descended the staircase. The scheming women had insisted she keep the "arrogant man" waiting an extra five minutes. How was she supposed to manage this alone?

Reaching the landing, uncertain, she peeked out onto the patio. There he was, pacing back and forth. Her heart skipped two beats. She squeezed her eyes shut and swallowed hard around the lump rising in her throat.

What if they're wrong about the situation? How do they know Donovan cares for me? If he calls my bluff, what am I supposed to say?

Rather than suffer complete and utter humiliation, Challie

lifted the jumper's hem and started hightailing back up the stairs.

"Challie!"

She stopped, held her breath. Clutching the jumper's fabric, she gauged the distance to the balcony and the bedroom, wondering if she could outrun him. Donovan had long legs, though. She'd sprinted many times, knew she was fast on her feet. And she was already halfway to the top. Challie bolted.

Three steps on the run he caught her, stopped her dead.

Drawing her back against him, Donovan said, "Didn't I tell you I'd chase you down? You can't keep running from me, babe. I can't take it."

Babe. She remembered the first time he'd used the endearment, instantly melting her heart. At the time, she'd witnessed sadness in his eyes. Today, the sadness was much worse, more than she could bear.

Wrapped in his arms again, the heat from his body penetrated hers. Challie inhaled his manly scent—pure male—and the memories of their time together flooded her brain, washing away her mother's coached words. She shuddered.

"You make me crazy," Donovan whispered and brushed his lips across her cheek. "So crazy, I've said and done some terrible things. Challie, I want to marry you. For no other reason than being in love with you. Have been since the first time I saw your shy, big gray eyes."

As the words seeped into her brain, the tension in her body subsided. Challie turned in his arms, stepped back and said, "Patio. Ten minutes." She needed time and someone's expertise.

He already had her jumper bunched in his hands. "Damn it, Challie—"

"You curse too much. Hate cursing."

"I won't ever say another bad word as long you never run from me again."

On occasion, she just might like the results following his